FED UP

"*Fed Up* is the wonderful fourth entry in the Gourmet Girl series, and this reviewer's favorite so far—and I've loved them all. Highly recommended to the discriminating connoisseur of cozy mysteries!" —*The Romance Readers Connection*

"A pleasant cozy so packed with food tips and appended recipes that it could cause a food frenzy." —*Kirkus Reviews*

"Recipes, some by pro chefs, round out this delectable chick-lit cozy, which ends on an emotional cliff-hanger for Chloe." —*Publishers Weekly*

"Jessica Conant-Park and Susan Conant turn up the heat... and cook up another winner! Take a pinch of poison, a heaping spoonful of intrigue, and a dash of romance. Then toss them all into a pressure cooker of a reality cooking show, and the result is another delicious read. You won't want to miss a bite of this delectable mystery!"

—Karen MacInerney, author of the Agatha-nominated
Gray Whale Inn Mysteries

"Reading *Fed Up* is like having a four-course meal at a gourmet restaurant. This scrumptious read offers up a mélange of humor and intrigue, including a culinary-based reality TV show gone horribly wrong and a zany wedding scene that will have readers bubbling over with laughter. Prepare to be treated to a cliff-hanger ending and recipes that will leave you hungry for more of Gourmet Girl's antics."

—J. B. Stanley, author of
The Battered Body

continued . . .

Turn Up the Heat

"This mother-daughter writing team combines a nicely detailed Back Bay setting with plenty of insights into the restaurant business, its kitchen characters, table-service staff, purveyors, and guests...Recommend this one to fans of foodie crime."
—*Booklist*

"A delicious murder complete with a sprinkle of betrayal, a generous dash of suspicion, and more than a pinch of danger."
—Leann Sweeney, author of
the Yellow Rose Mysteries

"Murder's on the menu at Simmer, a popular Boston restaurant, in the third saucy cozy to feature 'Gourmet Girl' Chloe Parker from daughter-and-mother writing team Conant-Park and Conant. The authors serve up another delectable dish of detection."
—*Publishers Weekly*

"Chloe's third outing, spiced with mystery, romance, and recipes, is an insider's look at life in a restaurant kitchen."
—*Kirkus Reviews*

Simmer Down

"Deliciously delightful...A heaping helping of simmering suspense and just plain fun."
—Alesia Holliday, author of
Seven Ways to Lose Your Lover

"The writing is breezy yet polished, the plotting adept, the overall tone funny without trying too hard...The Josh-Chloe pairing is perfect—he loves to cook and she loves to eat."
—*Cozy Library*

"A delicious new series with engaging characters, a unique pet, a fascinating milieu, the right touch of romance, and lots of fantastic food and recipes—what more could any mystery reader want?!"
—*The Romance Readers Connection*

"The talented authors Jessica Conant-Park and Susan Conant have created a pleasant blend of romance, food, and mystery. Any fan of romance or mystery will find it an enjoyable read with lots of recipes included. Enjoy."   —*New Mystery Reader*

"This is a fun Gourmet Girl Mystery . . . Readers will enjoy the heroine's escapades as she risks her life to uncover the identity of a killer. The mother-daughter team provides the audience with a delicious chick-lit cozy filled with lists, recipes, and asides as Chloe takes on Beantown."   —*The Best Reviews*

"Packed with delicious recipes . . . the Gourmet Girl Mysteries have quickly become one of my favorite culinary mystery series."   —*Roundtable Reviews*

STEAMED

"All the right ingredients—fresh characters, a dash of humor, and a sizzling romance. *Steamed* is hot."
—Elaine Viets, national bestselling author of
The Fashion Hound Murders

"This delectable collaboration between Jessica Conant-Park and her mother, Susan Conant, author of the Cat Lover's and the Dog Lover's mystery series, introduces an appealing heroine . . . This scrumptious cozy, the first of a new series, has it all—charming characters, snappy dialogue, and mouthwatering recipes."   —*Publishers Weekly*

"Famous writer of mysteries involving cats and dogs Susan Conant teams up with her daughter to write a refreshingly charming chick-lit mystery."   —*Midwest Book Review*

"*Steamed* is a gem. It grabs you from the start, as the heroine is witty, down-to-earth, and rolls with the punches. Great competition to anything Diane Mott Davidson has ever offered. I am thoroughly hooked. Top this already winning combination off with some decadent-sounding recipes, and I can guarantee *Steamed* will be topping the bestseller list in no time."   —*Roundtable Reviews*

FED UP

Jessica Conant-Park
& Susan Conant

BERKLEY PRIME CRIME, NEW YORK

THE BERKLEY PUBLISHING GROUP
Published by the Penguin Group
Penguin Group (USA) Inc.
375 Hudson Street, New York, New York 10014, USA
Penguin Group (Canada), 90 Eglinton Avenue East, Suite 700, Toronto, Ontario M4P 2Y3, Canada
(a division of Pearson Penguin Canada Inc.)
Penguin Books Ltd., 80 Strand, London WC2R 0RL, England
Penguin Group Ireland, 25 St. Stephen's Green, Dublin 2, Ireland (a division of Penguin Books Ltd.)
Penguin Group (Australia), 250 Camberwell Road, Camberwell, Victoria 3124, Australia
(a division of Pearson Australia Group Pty. Ltd.)
Penguin Books India Pvt. Ltd., 11 Community Centre, Panchsheel Park, New Delhi—110 017, India
Penguin Group (NZ), 67 Apollo Drive, Rosedale, North Shore 0632, New Zealand
(a division of Pearson New Zealand Ltd.)
Penguin Books (South Africa) (Pty.) Ltd., 24 Sturdee Avenue, Rosebank, Johannesburg 2196,
South Africa

Penguin Books Ltd., Registered Offices: 80 Strand, London WC2R 0RL, England

This is a work of fiction. Names, characters, places, and incidents either are the product of the author's
imagination or are used fictitiously, and any resemblance to actual persons, living or dead, business
establishments, events, or locales is entirely coincidental. The publisher does not have any control
over and does not assume any responsibility for author or third-party websites or their content.

PUBLISHER'S NOTE: The recipes contained in this book are to be followed exactly as written. The
publisher is not responsible for your specific health or allergy needs that may require medical supervision.
The publisher is not responsible for any adverse reactions to the recipes contained in this book.

FED UP

A Berkley Prime Crime Book / published by arrangement with the author

PRINTING HISTORY
Berkley Prime Crime hardcover edition / February 2009
Berkley Prime Crime mass-market edition / January 2010

Copyright © 2009 by Jessica Conant-Park and Susan Conant.
Cover illustration by Brandon Dorman.
Cover design by Diana Kolsky.
Series logo by axb group.
Interior text design by Kristin del Rosario.

ISBN: 978-0-425-23206-4

BERKLEY® PRIME CRIME
Berkley Prime Crime Books are published by The Berkley Publishing Group,
a division of Penguin Group (USA) Inc.,
375 Hudson Street, New York, New York 10014.
BERKLEY® PRIME CRIME and the PRIME CRIME logo are trademarks of Penguin Group (USA) Inc.

PRINTED IN THE UNITED STATES OF AMERICA

10 9 8 7 6 5 4 3 2 1

For Melissa, a friend for life

ACKNOWLEDGMENTS

For contributing mouthwatering recipes, we thank Angela McKeller, Ann and Michel Devrient, Meg Driscoll, Josh and Jen Ziskin, Nancy R. Landman, Barbara Seagle, Raymond Ost, Bill Park, and Dwayne Minier.

And for testing some of those recipes, we thank Mary Fairchild, Gina Micale, and Rita Schiavone.

For detailing icky restaurant health code violations, we thank Deborah M. Rosati, R.S., food safety consultant.

Many thanks to Natalee Rosenstein and Michelle Vega from Berkley Prime Crime and to our agent, Deborah Schneider.

And for rescuing the real Inga, Jessica thanks her husband, Bill, who knew that the starving, neglected Persian would be the perfect addition to our home.

ONE

I peeked in the rearview mirror of my car, touched up my lip gloss, and ran my hands through my hair. I was, after all, going to be on television, so I had every excuse in the world to double-check my appearance. Okay, well, it was actually my boyfriend, Josh, who was going to be on television. Still, I was going to be in the vicinity of the taping of a television show, and if the camera just so happened to find its way to me, I had to be prepared. My hair disagreed; far from behaving itself, it was doing everything it could to fight the anti-frizz and straightening products that I had slathered on this morning. I got out of the car, slammed the door, and cursed Boston's triple-*H* weather: hazy, hot, humid. I should've taken my friend Adrianna's advice about wearing my hair curly. I had taken her advice, however, about wearing a cute, if uncomfortable, outfit. I tugged at the hem of my lime green and sky blue retro-print dress and tried to smooth out the wrinkles that had developed during the drive. And these darn toeless pumps that matched the green in the dress were going to be hell; I could already feel my big toe whining about being squashed. *You have to suffer to be beautiful, you have to suffer to be beautiful,* I repeated to myself.

The parking lot of the upscale grocery store, Natural High, was moderately full for four o'clock on a Monday afternoon in late August. I was there—on location, as I liked to think of it—because Josh had been invited to participate in a local cable reality TV show called *Chefly Yours.* I was tagging along, but Josh was one of three local chefs competing to win the prize of starring in a new eight-part cooking show. The other two contestants were Josh's friend Digger and a woman named Marlee. *Chefly Yours* was scheduled to have nine episodes, three for each chef, with the contestants competing in rotation. Josh, Digger, and Marlee had each filmed one episode. Today was Josh's second turn. When all nine episodes had aired, viewers were going to call in to vote for the winner. Each episode followed the chef contestant into a grocery store, where the chef approached a shopper and persuaded the surprised stranger to participate in the show. The chef then selected and bought food and accompanied the shopper home to cook a gourmet meal. The hope was that the chosen shopper would have a spouse or partner at home, an unsuspecting person who'd provide moments of drama by expressing astonished delight—or filmworthy rage, maybe—when the TV crew burst in. *Crew:* considering that the cable station, Boston 17, provided one producer-director, Robin, and one cameraman, Nelson, the term struck me as a bit generous. Also, the premise of *Chefly Yours* hit me as disconcertingly similar to the premise of a big-time national program hosted by a hot Australian chef, but when I'd told Josh that Robin was copycatting, he'd brushed me off.

Still, my boyfriend's first episode had gone well in spite of an unexpected challenge. Because the "lucky shopper," as Robin called her, turned out to have numerous food allergies, Josh had been forced to cook an incredibly simple seared fish fillet with practically no seasoning. To his credit, instead of throwing up his hands in frustration, he had used the episode to showcase his technical culinary skills, and he'd taught his shopper and the audience how to break down a whole fish and cook it perfectly. Nonetheless, I was hoping that today he'd find a truly adventurous eater. I hadn't been present for the taping of Josh's first show. When Robin had given me permission to watch today's taping, she'd made me swear that I wouldn't make Josh nervous. I'd given her my promise.

The location, Natural High, was an elite market in the Boston suburb of Fairfield, which our local papers always described as the wealthiest community in Massachusetts. As the store's name suggested, its specialty was organic produce, but it also sold fresh meat and seafood. As the automatic doors opened and I stepped in, I felt a surge of irritation at the show for what was obviously a search for wealthy guest shoppers. It seemed to me that the people for whom it would be a big treat to take a chef home were middle-income and low-income shoppers at ordinary supermarkets. The station, however, evidently preferred to have a good chance of shooting in a lavish-looking house with a luxurious, well-equipped kitchen. I consoled myself with the thought that Natural High did have a few advantages. The butcher at the meat counter, a guy named Willie, was the brother of my friend Owen, so at least Willie would get some airtime, and Josh was hoping to stop at a nearby cheese and wine shop run by Owen and Willie's brother Evan.

I found Josh huddled close to Robin in the produce section of the market, where both were scanning for a desirable shopper.

"Found any victims yet?" I placed my hand on Josh's lower back.

"Hey, babe." He grinned and then gave me a quick kiss. Clearly fired up for today's filming, Josh was wearing his white chef's coat from the restaurant where he worked, Simmer, and his gorgeous blue eyes twinkled with energy. Josh usually left his dirty blond hair to its own devices—a look I found adorable—but today he had obviously spent a little time in the mirror styling his waves. As delicious as he looked in person, Josh had managed to look even yummier on TV, as if his enthusiasm for the competition had seeped into the camera. Although he wrapped his arm around me and pulled me in tightly, he continued looking at Robin's clipboard.

"Hi, Robin," I said to the producer.

Robin whipped her long brown ponytail to the side without dislodging her headset. She gave me a curt smile. "Chloe. I didn't know you'd be here today. Nice to see you."

She did so know I was going to be here! "Nice to see you, too."

Robin looked back down at her clipboard and began frantically writing as she talked. "Okay, Josh, so I'd prefer to find a male shopper this time. We've already had three women. And he has to be camera friendly. Since we don't have hair and makeup people, it's got to be someone attractive. And find out about his kitchen. We don't want to end up in some hellhole with cockroaches and no cooking equipment." Robin's sharp voice matched her appearance: a small, pinched nose; perpetually squinty eyes; and pursed lips. She had a very thin, dainty frame, and her no-nonsense clothes fell shapelessly on her body.

Josh and Robin started peering around the store again. When I stepped aside to let them work, I bumped into Nelson, the cameraman, and nearly toppled over.

"Um, hi, Nelson." I stared into the big black lens of his camera, which was pointed directly at me. The light shining from the camera made me squint.

Nelson briefly leaned out from behind the camera to beam at me. "Hi, Chloe."

Nelson, who was in his early thirties, had a prematurely bald head so shiny that I longed to pat his scalp with blotting paper or dust it with talc. His eyes formed two perfect circles, as though they'd been drawn on his face by a first-grader. He was close to six feet tall, and his bulky build must have made it easy for him to carry the heavy camera.

After tucking himself back behind the safety of the camera, he asked, "How are you today? Has school started back up yet?"

"No, I have a few more weeks." My second and final year of graduate school was looming, but I was nowhere near ready to give up on summer. "Oh, I see Digger and Marlee are here. I'm going to say hello."

Josh and his chef friend Digger had enjoyed a friendly rivalry during the past month of taping. The other two chefs were along not just to watch how their competition performed but to serve as sous-chefs if Josh needed them.

"Hey, Chloe!" Digger called out in his husky voice. "What's up, kid?" His curly brown hair was pulled back in an elastic, and his dark skin was even more deeply tanned than the last time I'd seen him. Digger had strong, angular facial features that I found somewhat intoxicating; although he wasn't traditionally handsome, he was masculine and striking. "Has Josh got anyone, yet? We've been here for twenty minutes, and Robin has already rejected four people Josh picked out." Digger cupped his hands to his mouth and called across a bin of red peppers, "Seriously, come on Robin!"

Robin ignored Digger, but I saw that Josh was trying not to smile.

"You know Marlee, right?" Digger gestured to the woman next to him.

"Yes, we met at one of the planning meetings." I held out my hand to the slightly plump woman. "Good to see you."

Marlee let my hand sit in the air. "You, too," she said distractedly. "I wonder who Josh'll end up with this time."

For reasons I didn't understand, Marlee seemed oddly nervous. Today was Josh's show and not hers. Since the last time I'd seen her, Marlee had cut her thin hair into an ear-length bob that did nothing to flatter her round face. Actually, Marlee had a distinct roundness to her entire being; without actually being overweight, she was blah and shapeless, not to mention pasty and bland. She wasn't particularly feminine, but since she worked in a male-dominated industry, maybe she deliberately downplayed her feminine side? I stared at her and prayed that she'd put on makeup before the taping began. She seriously needed color in her cheeks, and I had to peer rather rudely at her to see whether she had any eyelashes at all. Oh, yes! There they were. Would she mind, or even notice, if I pulled out a mascara wand and started coating her lashes?

"Oh, look. He's pointing at someone now." She and Digger craned their heads to get a look, and then Marlee sighed. "Nope. Robin nixed that guy, too. They really better get moving."

Even though it was only a little after four in the afternoon, Marlee was right. Shooting an entire episode would take until at least seven tonight. According to Josh, Robin was particular about nearly everything and liked to reshoot some scenes three or four times, maybe for good reason. After all, she had only one cameraman, and the lighting available in markets and home kitchens had to be less than ideal.

Marlee, I suspected, was hoping that Josh would get another dud shopper, thus improving her own chances of winning the show. Even though *Chefly Yours* was relatively small and underfunded, not to mention imitative, it was still television, and I knew that all three chefs were dying to win the chance to star in the solo series. Marlee was the chef at a small South End restaurant called Alloy, but aside from that, I knew little about her. Josh and Digger had both been reviewed a few times in newspapers, in local magazines, and online, but I'd never read anything about Marlee's restaurant, and I had no reason to think she needed or wanted to win more than the male chefs did.

"Maybe we could help them find a candidate," I suggested to Digger and Marlee.

We headed toward Robin, Josh, and Nelson just as Josh was approaching a well-groomed man in his early sixties. "Excuse me, sir. I'm chef Josh Driscoll, and I was wondering if you—"

Robin practically body-slammed the poor man out of the way. Out of his hearing, I hoped, she hissed, "God, not him, Josh! He's totally wrong! Did you or did you not see his plaid shirt?" She rolled her eyes. "Plaid shirt equals hippie equals crappy TV, okay? And for God's sake, Nelson, why are you filming this?"

"It's reality TV, Robin." He smiled. "This is good stuff

here. This is how you capture moments that create a damn fine film."

Robin's only response was to write yet more notes on her clipboard. Was she grading Nelson as we went along?

"What about him?" I pointed unobtrusively at a college-age guy who was examining a bunch of beet greens. "He looks interested in his food."

Robin shook her head at what she all too obviously regarded as a stupid suggestion.

"Oh, well," I said, "you're the dictator." Oops. "Director! You're the director!"

Robin eyed me suspiciously and crinkled her already crinkled nose.

Just then, a young mother with an infant strapped to her body approached us. "Hey, I recognize you! Are you all from that show—"

Instead of responding to the eager fan, Robin stepped away. Sulking, she said to us, "No, she won't do at all! A man! We need a man. And she certainly doesn't look like a man to me."

The enthusiastic mother was atypical; most people scampered away from us and especially, I thought, from Nelson's bulky camera. I was starting to think that we'd be lucky to find anyone even willing to talk to us; Robin was in no position to drive away interested shoppers. The mother would've been fine, I thought. She and her baby were both attractive, and she had a look of prosperity that suggested the possibility of a snazzy, photogenic kitchen. I gave the mother an apologetic look as she walked away. It was already four thirty, and I thought that by this point Robin would've found any shopper acceptable.

After Robin had rejected four more perfectly normal—and male, I might add—shoppers, her eyes suddenly lit up. "Oh, look, that's the one!" She pointed eagerly at a man entering the store. I couldn't see what made him so special. To me, he looked ordinary: short hair, average height, lean build, brown suede jacket, and delicate round glasses. But Robin, I reminded myself, was the expert; she must know who'd look good on camera and who wouldn't, and she was probably better than I was at guessing the value of the suede jacket and the glasses, which, for all I knew, had cost thousands.

Robin marched confidently over to her selected shopper and pulled down her headset. The rest of us followed. By then, I was convinced that this headset was connected to nothing more than an empty box that she wore attached to her belt. I mean, whom could she possibly be communicating with? Nelson, who was right next to her? The headset, I decided, was a prop intended to make her look official.

"Good afternoon, sir," said Robin, extending her hand to the mystery man, who cautiously took her hand and shook it. "My name is Robin, and I am the producer of a televison show called *Chefly Yours*. We're here today to film an episode of the show, and we'd like to offer you the talents of our chef, Josh Driscoll." Robin shoved Josh in front of her as proof of her statement. "If you'll allow us, we'd like to film you and Josh as he helps prepare a meal for you. Perhaps you have a loved one at home who could use a special dinner tonight? We'll come to your house and give our viewers a lesson in how to prepare high-quality meals in their very own homes." Robin beamed.

"Oh! Uh, I guess that would be okay." He adjusted his small glasses and looked at all of us as we stood expectantly before him.

"Wonderful!" Robin whipped her head around and inadvertently, I assumed, smacked Josh in the face with her long hair. "Nelson? Are you getting this?"

"Yes, ma'am." The cameraman sounded annoyed. "I do know how to use this thing. I am a professional, you know." Nelson turned the camera away from me. I'd been too focused on Josh's potential shopper to realize that I was being filmed. Clearly irritated, Robin reached out and shoved the camera so that it was aimed at Josh. Nelson protested, "This is all part of the reality of the show, Robin. The process, you know? And Chloe's part of this."

I glanced sideways at Nelson, who increasingly felt like a weirdo. "Um, you really don't need to film me, Nelson." I couldn't help feeling flattered that Nelson thought I was camera-ready, but I still found him a bit creepy. I do have to admit, though, that I checked my reflection in one of the store mirrors. Hmm, my red hair could use a hint of styling serum . . .

"And your name is?" Robin prompted the man.

"Um, I'm Leo." Evidently unnerved by the presence of the camera, Leo tucked his head down to glance into his empty cart.

"Wonderful!" Robin practically shouted. "This is Nelson, our cameraman."

"Field operator," he corrected her. "And filmmaker. We've got great color temperature in here, so it's going to be a good shoot today."

Robin sighed at Nelson, introduced the rest of us, and then gave Leo a brief rundown on how the show worked. She explained that for the three chefs, the show was a competition. "Okay, then, Leo. We'll have Josh walk you through the market, and the two of you will select ingredients for your dinner. Then we'll all drive to your house and capture every tiny little detail of the culinary process. Isn't this exciting? Who will we be cooking for this evening?"

"My wife, Francie. She'll be home pretty soon." Leo glanced nervously in Nelson's direction.

Uh-oh. If Leo's wife, Francie, was on her way home, she was presumably dressed and groomed in a presentable fashion. I had the impression that the station preferred to film an episode in which the shopper's stunned spouse or partner looked entirely unprepared to be on television. Ideally, the wife, Francie, would've had a mud mask on her face and rollers in her hair when she discovered that she was appearing in a reality show. I looked at Robin to see whether she was going to nix this shopper, too.

"Well, whether your wife is home yet or not when we get there, won't she be surprised!" For once, Robin was doing her best to be charming. I was relieved that she hadn't tossed Leo into his cart and sent him careening down the aisle before resuming the tedious search for the perfect victim.

Josh stepped in to take over for Robin, who was, I thought, on the verge of frightening Leo into refusing to participate. "Just ignore the camera, okay?" Josh put a hand on Leo's shoulder and guided him over to a display of fresh corn. "So tell me about you and Francie. What do you two like to eat?"

Leo seemed to relax a bit. "Well, you may have a challenge on your hands, Josh. My wife eats meat, but I'm a pesco-ovo-lacto-vegetarian. I eat fish and dairy but not meat. Are you sure you still want me to be on your show? I'm not sure if I'm going to help you win," he said apologetically.

"This is actually going to be great, Leo. I'll get to show the audience how to work around dietary needs," Josh assured him as he examined a perfectly ripe mango.

"I'd like you to make some meat, though, for Francie.

11

Since I don't usually cook outside my diet, it'd be a treat to have someone cook with her in mind, huh?"

"Excellent. We'll make something for both of you then." I could see Josh's eyes light up as he shifted into his chef mode.

Two

"WE could do a beautiful pesto that we toss with fresh gnocchi. And serve that with seared scallops for you and some kind of roasted meat with vegetables for Francie. We're almost getting into fall now, so maybe some root vegetables? And how about a gorgeous mixed tomato salad and cheese course? This is a great time of year for fresh tomatoes, so I'd love to use some of those. Check out these yellow pear tomatoes here." Josh reached into a wooden wagon that served as a display for a variety of tomatoes. He proceeded to give Leo and the television audience a short discourse on the joys of tomato season.

"Lucky bastard," Digger said under his breath.

Marlee clicked her tongue. "Yeah, seriously."

"Why is Josh lucky?" I asked the two chefs.

"Josh gets to show off even more now. He's going to

make something awesome even with that pesco-veggie-whatever guy. This is going to make him look good. I'm going to have to find an even better one on my next turn. Maybe someone who only eats flatbread. I can do wonders with flatbread," Digger teased with a smile.

"This blows." Marlee sighed, blew her bangs out of her eyes, and examined her fingernails. For a chef, Marlee certainly had dirty fingernails. I didn't like to think about her handling food in a restaurant kitchen!

"For dessert, what about a peach and raspberry cobbler?" Josh suggested. Leo nodded enthusiastically and helped Josh gather the fruits and vegetables for the meal.

We kept out of the way as we followed Josh, Leo, Robin, and Nelson. From what I could tell, Josh was doing a beautiful job. He chose a variety of ingredients, held foods up to the camera, kept his body from blocking shots, and dealt with Robin's intrusive style better than I would have.

"What about some beet greens, Josh?" asked Robin, reaching for a large bunch. "These look gorgeous."

"Um, maybe—"

"Or arugula? They've got a beautiful selection today." Robin invaded the camera space and handed Josh a plastic bag.

"Actually, we could make a delicious arugula pesto for the gnocchi. Maybe with some Calamata olives in it? And we'll find a good cut of meat for Francie and some seafood for you both. We'll get some nice wine and cheese next door, too."

Leo nodded in recognition. "Sure. I know the place. Um, the only thing is . . . I sort of hate arugula. But Francie will love it, so I think we should make it anyway. I can just have butter on my gnocchi, right?"

"Sure, of course. If that's okay with you, that's what we'll do."

As Leo and Josh worked their way through the produce department, they filled Leo's basket with potatoes, Vidalia onions, heads of garlic, fresh oregano, basil, and parsley, and other items that met Josh's high standards. Nelson followed the pair and managed to keep the camera on his subjects.

So far as I could tell, Robin did nothing except interject unhelpful commands. "Get some radishes!" she ordered. "Those will look great on camera. Remember to look up at the camera, both of you!"

Josh cleared his throat. Then, trying to look simultaneously at Leo and the camera, he said, "Let's head over to the meat counter. When deciding on your pick and cut of meat—"

"Josh," Robin said, "turn your body a bit to the left so Nelson can get the shot. There! Good!" Although Josh must've been ticked off at the interruption, his face showed nothing, but Leo looked like a deer caught in headlights. When Robin had positioned the pair to her satisfaction, she said, "Now, say that again, Josh. About the meat."

Josh uttered three words before Nelson stopped him. "Wait. Sorry. My mike isn't working right." The microphone that protruded from Nelson's camera was covered in a fuzzy sheath. After jiggling the mike with what struck me as unnecessary vigor, he said, "All set. One more time."

Instead of launching into his third attempt to explain how to select meat, Josh said, "Okay, let's talk to Willie, the meat guy here." Josh faced the counter and waved to Owen's brother. "Willie! How are you, my friend?"

Willie looked up from the counter, where he was cutting and breaking down an enormous piece of beef. "My man, Josh! How's it going? And, hey, Leo. How are you? And how's Francie?"

Leo turned to Josh. "My wife and I come here a lot.

We've gotten to know Willie. Well, Francie more than I, since she's the meat eater in the family. But Willie always takes care of her."

"So what's with the entourage today, fellas?" Willie winked at me, wiped his hands on a dish towel, and leaned against the counter.

Josh explained the show and asked Willie for suggestions.

"Well," Willie said, "I know Francie's been eyeing these lamb chops, but I think she didn't know what to do with them. How to cook them exactly. And they're pretty pricey. Worth it, though."

I'd promised myself that I'd keep quiet, but keeping the promise took a lot of effort. How could anyone have absolutely no idea how to cook lamb chops? In terms of culinary challenge, they weren't exactly shad roe or calf brains.

"Dude, those look nice," Digger commented from behind Josh. "Really fresh."

"You're right," Josh agreed. With what I felt sure was no intention of insulting Francie, he said to Leo, "It's hard to ruin a good lamb chop. The worst thing you can do is overcook it, but I'll show you how to avoid that. Okay, Willie, give us a couple of chops for Francie."

Willie selected two from the depths of the refrigerated counter and placed them on plastic wrap on the scale. "So, I'm going to be famous from this show, I assume. If I'd known you were coming, I would've spent a few extra minutes at the mirror this morning." Willie scratched his chin. "Might have even shaved for you."

"You're as pretty as always, dude," Josh said with a laugh. "But we're going to see Evan in a bit to pick up some cheese and a bottle or two of wine. We'll see who's prettier then."

"Tell my brother I'll always win that contest. Hey,

Chloe," Willie called over the counter to me. "How's my soon-to-be sister-in-law doing? She ready to pop yet?"

Willie meant my best friend, Adrianna, who was going to marry his brother Owen in a couple of weeks. Adrianna was eight months pregnant and looked as if she were carrying triplets. As far as anyone knew, there was only one baby inside her, but I was beginning to worry that the one baby weighed forty pounds.

"Well, she's okay. Aside from comparing herself daily to a variety of large mammals and insisting that Owen take over for her and incubate the kid himself. So, you know, she's doing great," I said sarcastically.

"Aw, poor thing. I'll have to give her a call and check in." Willie wrapped the lamb chops in white butcher's paper and passed them to Josh. "Good luck. And tell Francie I send my love, okay?"

"Will do," Josh said with a nod. "Now let's get your fish."

Josh got enough halibut to make a first course for Leo. Then we cruised down an aisle lined with shelves of fancy oils, vinegars, and prepared sauces in imaginatively shaped bottles and jars.

"I've used some of these sauces before." Leo pointed to a series of bottles that bore the pretty green label of an imported brand. "That tends to be how I cook, I guess. With jarred sauces."

As Josh nodded in understanding, Robin nudged Nelson. The signal was unnecessary. Nelson already had the camera on Josh's face, which expressed his passion for helping people to make wonderful food in their own kitchens. "That's true for a lot of people," Josh said. "And it's great that there are high-quality products for when people want to get a meal out quickly. But the downside is that the at-home cook can really miss out on simple, delicious sauces, salsas, chutneys, and marinades, all kinds of things that can be put together with minimal work. As good as some of these products can be, nothing beats the taste and aroma of freshly chopped herbs blended with a fantastic Spanish olive oil. Or a sauce that you've slowly simmered on your stove so you've brought out all the flavors of your ingredients."

Josh and Leo continued making their way through the market, adding products to the shopping cart until Josh was sure he'd have everything he'd need. "I assume you'll have some basic seasonings at your house, Leo?"

Leo nodded. "I think I've got everything you need." He grinned shyly at Robin. Was Leo trying to flirt with Robin? If so, Robin completely ignored him and returned to checking her notes.

All of us finally ended up at a register, where Robin paid. A benefit of being selected for the show was that the station covered the cost of all the food in the cart, including whatever had been in there before Robin and the chef had even approached the shopper. Today, of course, Robin had picked out Leo as he'd been entering the store, so the policy didn't matter, and in any case, most of Natural High's clientele needed no help with food bills. Still, the generous practice spoke well for the station.

"The cheese shop is next," Robin instructed us while simultaneously scribbling on her clipboard. I was beginning to suspect that she followed the David Letterman approach to note taking, which was to say that her notes were nothing more than random scribbles with no bearing on what was happening. "Since it's basically next door, we can just walk over there. Digger and Marlee, you can put the bags in the van for us."

While Robin's back was turned, Digger saluted her and

started pushing the shopping cart. Marlee stayed with him as Robin marched impatiently through the exit door, with Josh, Leo, Nelson, and me hurrying to keep up with her. Everything about her manner and her posture suggested that all of us had been hanging around and wasting time, whereas, in fact, Robin herself had been the sole cause of the delay. Looking back over her shoulder, she had the nerve to call out, "Let's go, people! We're on a timetable here!"

The cheese and wine shop where Evan worked was unimaginatively called the Cheese and Wine Shop. Its setting was no more intriguing than its name. It occupied one of the storefronts in a little strip mall across the parking lot from Natural High. Flanked by a knitting store on one side and a handmade crafts boutique on the other, the Cheese and Wine Shop distinguished itself by displaying a cheerful striped awning that welcomed visitors.

"Welcome! Welcome!" Evan's greeting sounded more affected than genuinely affable. Posed next to a display table that showcased the wine of the month, he had one hand on the table and the other at his waist. I could practically smell calculation in the air. As if to confirm my hunch that Willie had called to give Evan a heads-up, Evan exclaimed, "What a surprise!" After pausing to bestow a toothy smile on everyone, he continued. "And what are you all doing here? Could this be a *Chefly Yours* episode?"

Still trying to keep my vow of silence, I waved to Evan, who, like everyone else in Owen's family, was extraordinarily good-looking—reason to feel confident about the genes that Owen was passing on to his baby. Evan and Willie were a year apart but could almost have been mistaken for identical twins. Evan, however, was a bit bulkier than Willie, probably because Evan was fond of overindulging in the delicious triple-crème cheeses available here.

"And is my friend Leo here the target of all your shenanigans?" Evan's theatrical effort to project made him speak so loudly that Josh and Leo stepped back.

"I am, I am," Leo answered. "I had no idea when I walked into the store today that I would wind up with the services of a talented chef. It's wild." Leo turned to Josh. "I'm a bit of a regular here, as you might have figured out."

Evan shook Josh's and Leo's hands, and then Josh introduced Robin and Nelson.

"Okay, start shooting, Nelson," Robin ordered.

Nelson flicked on the camera's light and moved his eye behind the camera while muttering, "I think I know what I'm doin' here . . ."

Josh nodded and moved to Evan's side. "So, Evan, we're looking for some cheeses to serve after dinner and some nice wines to go with everything. What can you recommend?"

The bright light seemed to have panicked Evan, who began to sweat profusely. "Well, Josh," said Evan, while beaming maniacally into the camera lens, "there are several wonderful choices that I happen to have here." He moved to the counter by the register and pulled out a tray on which eight or nine cheeses, each with a label, were attractively and all-too-conveniently arranged. "Ahem, this is a lovely Tomme de Savoie. And here we have a Serena, which comes from the mountainous Extremadura region of Spain. Oh, and a rich Gorgonzola, which I think should be on every cheese tray— very smooth and creamy. Would you like a sample?" Evan seemed to be loosening up as he eased into his cheese comfort zone, but when he wiped his forehead with his sleeve, I saw Robin wince.

Evan's anxiety made me long to alert Leo's wife, Francie, to the imminent arrival of her husband and his newfound group of television friends. It was five thirty, and I guessed that Leo's wife might be home any minute. I couldn't believe that most people would welcome strangers with a camera into their homes with absolutely no notice. It was easy for me to imagine times when even I, who would drop almost anything for a gourmet meal, wouldn't want *Chefly Yours* descending on my condo. Of course, I didn't have Francie's number and had no way to find it. I didn't even know her last name. The poor woman! And what if she freaked out when we all showed up at her house? What if she ruined Josh's chances of winning? For all I knew, the unknown Francie might toss us out like yesterday's fondue!

Evan cut samples of the powerfully flavored cheese for us all and moved on to a mouthwatering Explorateur. "Decadent and luxurious is how this cheese is best described." Evan cut through the rind to reveal a creamy center. "This is a triple-crème at its finest." He really was nervous! He knew as well as I did that cheeses should be eaten in order from mild to strong. He spread the cheese onto four crackers, and in spite of the competition from the lingering taste of the Gorgonzola, all of us, even Robin, groaned and murmured approval.

Decadent and luxurious indeed! I closed my eyes to savor the rich flavor. The thin, crispy, free-form crackers were perfect. Others might not appreciate the need for a good cracker, but I hated ruining an extraordinary cheese by smearing it on the equivalent of cardboard and then having the whole mess break apart in my hands. Just as bad were the kinds of crackers loaded with seeds, nuts, or spices, textures and tastes that bonked you over the head, obliterating the taste of the cheese. Ick!

Evan gestured around the store at the walls filled with bottles. "Tell me about your meal, and we'll match you up with the right wines. I have a few open bottles that have been breathing for a while, so we can start by trying those."

Josh described the menu, and Evan helped with the choice of wines. My mind wandered. I was more interested in the food than I was in what we'd drink with it. In particular, the little samples of cheese had whetted my appetite for more, and I had no idea how I'd resist absconding with Josh's cheese tray and leaving none for anyone else.

When we'd left the shop, Robin again started giving orders. "I'll ride with Leo so I can fill him in on the release papers he'll have to sign. And you'll follow us. Don't lose me! And we'll meet you outside Leo's house, okay? This is it, people! Are we ready to roll?"

"You bet." Josh clapped his hands together. "This is going to be a fantastic meal, Leo. You're going to be in great hands tonight."

THREE

FOLLOWING Robin turned out to be easy. Leo's house was only a few blocks away. Its appearance surprised me. Fairfield was so uniformly upscale that I'd expected to find Leo and Francie living in a large, beautifully maintained place. As it turned out, their house was a brown-shingled Victorian in decent condition, but the yard, which must once have been attractive, was a neglected mess. My parents run a landscaping business, Carter Landscapes, and I had the strong urge to sic both of them on Leo and Francie. On the upside, the house, much older than the others in the neighborhood, had the charm notably missing from the new construction that dominated the street. I'd waited in the parking lot to make sure that mine was the last car to leave; I hadn't wanted to get there until the rest of the group had arrived. Lingering, I again primped in my rearview mirror, and then locked my purse in my Saturn, took my keys with me, and made my way past overgrown shrubs and weeds to the back door, which stood open. Through the screen door, I saw Josh standing at the kitchen sink.

"There you are," he called to me.

"Sorry." Smoothing my hair and reapplying makeup must have taken longer than I'd calculated.

My first thought on entering Leo's kitchen was that Robin must be having a fit. So much for the theory that Leo's appearance meant that he'd have a fancy, photogenic kitchen. At a guess, it had been updated thirty or forty years earlier, and renovations done since then had been partial. The cabinets were made of a pale synthetic material intended to simulate birch, and the floor was covered in brick-patterned linoleum. The walls were white, as was the refrigerator, but the dishwasher was black, the sink was stainless steel, and the stove a hideous avocado green. Although the room itself was large, there was little free counter space, and the layout had evidently been planned by someone who didn't cook. The refrigerator was far from the sink and stove, and I wasn't sure that it would be possible to open the refrigerator door without smacking the new-looking but awkwardly placed granite island in front of it. I sighed softly. Well, if anyone could work in this space, it was Josh. And at least the range was gas, and at least Josh had a cooperative subject, Leo.

In contrast, Francie, as I assumed her to be, looked less than cooperative. She was a slim, almost scrawny, woman with frizzy waves of dark hair. She stood with her arms crossed while addressing Robin in a high-pitched voice. "It's just that we don't seem to have the best setup here, and . . . well, I just don't know about all this." She uncrossed her arms and waved her hands around almost in the manner of a startled infant. "I'm not, uh, someone who belongs on TV." Then, as if having hit on an effective argument that stood a chance of driving her unwanted guests from her house, she said with confidence, "I really think you could do better." She ruined the effect, however, by throwing a pleading glance at Leo.

"Hey, it'll be fun, Francie! Lighten up. I was a little nervous at first, too, but wait until you see what this chef here, Josh, is going to make for us. Actually, what he's going to teach us to make. There's lamb for you. Lamb chops. You love lamb chops. Come on!" Leo whispered something into wife's ear.

She shrugged and forced a smile. "Well, I guess so. Why not? I am starving." Francie took off a navy linen blazer and tossed it on the back of a chair by a small breakfast table. When she turned to face us, she had a hint of a smile. Although she was not even close to beautiful, she was striking, with high cheekbones and a strong jaw. With the right makeup—she wore none that I could see—she'd have looked distinguished. Now that she'd taken off her blazer, her white linen shell revealed a surprisingly curvaceous build. "So, what do I do?" she asked.

Josh already had the cheese selections unwrapped and coming to room temperature on a plate, and the rest of the ingredients were spread out across every available space. Within minutes, Josh, who was used to running a restaurant kitchen, had finished assigning all of us to separate work areas. Digger, Marlee, and I were given the humble task of peeling potatoes for the gnocchi. Josh was showing Leo and Francie how to make the arugula pesto. We potato peelers were stationed at a small table, and although we kept bumping elbows, our spirits were good. Josh had had the foresight to bring a lot of his own kitchen equipment, including some pots and pans, but Leo and Francie did have an adequate supply of the basics, including a Cuisinart food processor.

At the counter near the sink, Josh was teaching Leo to make pesto in the Cuisinart. Standing next to Leo, he was supervising as Leo put the ingredients in the bowl of the machine. "So, we have arugula, pine nuts, garlic, Parmesan cheese, Calamata olives, lemon juice, a little salt, and olive oil. We'll blend this all up and have a fantastic, spicy pesto for the homemade gnocchi."

The loud noise from the food processor almost drowned out Nelson's voice. "Sorry. Sorry. Hey, Josh? Excuse me. Can we do that again, Josh? Something is going on with the camera."

I gritted my teeth. What was Josh supposed to do? Cast some magic spell that would make the pesto ingredients fly apart and reconstitute themselves? Josh was a great chef, but he was a chef. He wasn't Harry Potter.

"Seriously?" Josh glared at Nelson but kept his cool. "Okay, we have enough here to make another batch." Josh emptied the Cuisinart bowl, had Leo repeat the process of making the pesto, removed the container from the food processor, dipped a spoon in, took a taste, and nodded to himself. "A touch more salt, and that's good to go." He handed spoons to Francie and Leo and let them try. Both responded with smiles.

Robin squeezed between Josh and Leo, grabbed the Cuisinart bowl, and angled the pesto toward Nelson. "You have to hold it like this so we get a good view. Here, let's put it in something more attractive." Reaching across the counter, she wrangled a spatula out of a ceramic vase that held cooking utensils and knocked over the vase and its contents. Ignoring the mess she'd made, she grabbed a little hand-painted bowl that sat on a windowsill. "There, here's a nice bowl for the pesto." Nelson lowered his camera and waited until Robin had finished meddling in Josh's business.

When Josh had dutifully transferred the pesto into the pretty bowl, I reluctantly realized that Robin had been

too small for the generously proportioned room and too chunky for the chairs. The piece of furniture that dominated the dining room was a gigantic sideboard with little mirrors and elaborate carving. It seemed to me that the dining room, like the kitchen, had been assembled bit by bit, without any sort of overall plan or theme to guide the selection of elements, none of which had anything in common with any of the others. While I'd been busy in the kitchen, someone had tried to impose eye appeal on the unfortunate dining room by creating an attractive table setting. The matching runner, place mats, and napkins were made of a Victorian-looking fabric with stylized flowers and vines on a black background. The stainless flatware was heavy and oversized—at a guess, the pattern had the word *Hotel* in its name—and each of the two places had two stemmed wineglasses, one large and one small. Someone, maybe Marlee, had opened two bottles of wine, one red and one white, and had placed them on the table. Although I knew very little about wine, I knew that red wine, or at least some red wine, was supposed to be opened ahead of time so that it could breathe. But white wine? And wasn't white wine supposed to be cold? Or at least cool? I didn't ask. Fortunately, as I reminded myself, the show was more about food than about wine; it certainly wasn't supposed to be about interior decorating.

As Josh served Francie and Leo, I noted that he deserved a lot of credit for seamlessly putting together separate dishes for a couple with radically different food preferences. Leo's plate of halibut and buttered gnocchi, Francie's plate of lamb chops and pesto gnocchi, and a platter of roasted vegetables all looked divine. Probably because of the shared vegetables, I had the sense of one coordinated meal, not just a collection of separate items. Leo's willingness to eat the vegetables had surprised me, since they'd been cooked in the same roasting pan as the lamb, as Leo knew. Leo had participated in the cooking, he'd seen the vegetables in the roasting pan, and Josh had even pointed out that they'd been cooked with the meat, but Leo had said that they were fine for him. I'd heard him myself. In any case, now that the main course had been served, the table looked beautiful.

Nelson's camera light shone on the pair of diners. Looking jovial and pleased with himself, Leo poured white wine into his own glass and red into Francie's. Then, just as Leo raised his glass, presumably to make a toast, Robin stopped him. "Wait!" she cried. "We need to get some good footage of the dishes before anyone eats them. Marlee and Digger? Why don't you carry everything back to the kitchen, to the breakfast table, and Nelson can shoot the plates there, where the light's better."

"Sure thing," Marlee said as she handed the vegetable platter to Digger and then removed Francie's and Leo's plates. "While we're at it, we'll sneak a little taste for ourselves from the leftovers in the bowls."

Josh, I knew, would take it as a compliment that another chef wanted to sample his food. My private thought was that Marlee was hungry. I certainly was, and I suspected that everyone else was, too.

Digger sighed as he carried away the platter. "At this rate, the food is going to be dead cold by the time they get to eat it."

He wasn't kidding. It must've taken Nelson ten minutes to film the food that had been taken away, and when it was finally returned and Leo and Francie finally got to take their first bites, Nelson stopped them and announced that they'd have to reenact their first tasting. Poor Josh looked ready to wring someone's neck, and Francie and Leo were exchanging glances of exasperation. Marlee and Digger both looked uncomfortable in some way that I couldn't interpret. Was Josh's competition sympathizing with him? I doubted it. And when Digger suddenly started to beckon Josh, as if he wanted to call him aside to have a word with him, I was furious. This was no the time to chat it up with Josh! This was his big moment! The thought crossed my mind that when Digger and Marlee had carried the food back to the kitchen, they'd concocted some nasty plot to spoil Josh's chances of winning, a scheme that began with getting him away from the table. Fortunately, Josh ignored Digger and, with Robin's unwanted help, rearranged the food on the plates. My heart went out to Josh. He took tremendous pride in everything he prepared. Although the plates now looked appetizing, Josh's hot food must now be lukewarm, if not outright cold.

Even so, once Leo and Francie were at last permitted to eat, Leo raved about his halibut. "This is just spectacular. The fish is cooked perfectly, and I love the sweet crust on it. That's just from the sugar you sprinkled on it?" He took a bite of the gnocchi. "These are heavenly. And the roasted vegetables smell incredible!"

Francie, on the other hand, looked anything but enthusiastic. After she'd tasted her lamb, she grabbed a water glass and took a large gulp. My stomach dropped as I watched her force herself to swallow a few more bites. I looked nervously at Josh, who was staring so intently at Francie that he looked frozen in place. What could possibly be wrong? Even the best chef makes a mediocre dish now and then, but Josh had never cooked anything inedible. Of course, the lamb chops should have been served hot. Maybe the fat had congealed, I told myself. Still, even if the lamb wasn't at its best, it just couldn't be as repugnant as Francie seemed to find it. Francie, I told myself, must be a picky eater, someone who whined and complained about everything she tasted.

"And how's your dish, Francie?" prompted Robin, who had been so focused on Leo that she'd obviously failed to notice Francie's grimacing.

Francie dropped her fork and made eye contact with the camera. "The truth is," she said emphatically, "it's just awful."

FOUR

"FRANCIE!" Leo admonished. "There's no need to be rude."

With a vigorous shake of her head that made her dark, wavy hair fan out, she declared boldly, "It's vile, it's positively disgusting, it's revolting, and I simply can't eat any more. It is by far the worst thing that has ever been my misfortune to taste in my entire life." After a brief pause, she said, looking at Josh, "I'm not trying to hurt anyone's feelings, really I'm not, but something has gone horribly, hideously, dreadfully wrong with this dish."

Nelson lowered the camera.

Leo was seething. "Francie, this no time for your damned theatrics. Do you know how lucky we were to be chosen? We've got a talented chef in our house preparing a gourmet meal for us. Everything I've tasted is better than what we've had at most restaurants, so just chew and swallow. And for once in your life, smile!"

Belatedly, Robin turned her attention to Nelson. What she saw made her blow up. "Nelson, what the hell are you doing?" she demanded. "What we have going on here is action! Emotion! Conflict! What we have here is reality! And where are you? In outer space!"

"Sorry," Nelson said weakly. Clearly, even Nelson's heart went out to Josh.

"Oh, for God's sake, now we have to do everything all over again," Robin complained.

This time, Marlee and Digger took a turn at fussing over the food in what was now a futile effort to make it look freshly plated. Josh stood silent and watched as other chefs tended to his plated dishes.

Meanwhile, Robin chastised Nelson for his incompetence. "Could we possibly get through the rest of the meal without further interruption from you? Hit the On button! Hit it once! Hit it now! And don't touch it again. Is that something you are capable of doing?"

Nelson practically snarled at Robin. "Well, of course—"

"Rhetorical question, Nelson! I was asking a rhetorical question!" Tendrils were beginning to come loose from Robin's once-tight ponytail, as if her fury at her inept cameraman had somehow electrified her brain and escaped through her hair. "And now, for the last time"—she waved at the dinner plates—"let's roll!"

Nelson's light went on.

Francie leaned back in her chair. "I really think I've had enough of this dish."

Leo took a bite of the roasted vegetables and spoke with his mouth full. "Francie, there cannot possibly be anything wrong with your food. Have you even tasted anything? I don't think you have, because if you had, you'd know that it's spectacular." He smiled at Josh and gave him a thumbs-up. Miraculously, Nelson caught the gesture on tape.

Francie, however, was adamant about not tasting another bite of her food. Having watched her more closely than her husband had done, I knew that she had, in fact, eaten some of what she'd been served, but I had no idea whether she was whining about nothing or whether there was actually something wrong with her lamb.

"Absolutely not," she told Leo. "For your information, I have tasted it, and not for anything on earth am I choking it down again."

Josh had had enough. He stepped between the bickering couple and removed Francie's plate. Fumbling for words, he finally said, "I can't apologize enough. I'd be happy to make you something else, something . . . uh . . . if you can you tell me what's wrong with this?"

I seriously thought that Josh might cry. This experience was positively humiliating for him. If he'd been cooking for a private party, he'd have been mortified to serve food that made one of the hosts nearly gag. But this occasion was anything but private! And how many viewers would vote for Josh after watching and listening to Francie? None, I thought. Not one viewer. His chance of winning the competition had just dropped to zero.

"Yes," said Francie, "I can tell you exactly what's wrong. It's bitter beyond bitter." As if she'd failed to make her point, she added, "Horribly bitter! Really very foul tasting."

"The arugula," Josh said hopefully. "The arugula has a sharp bitterness to it."

"No." Francie shook her head and again sent her wavy hair flying. "I'm very sorry, Josh, but that's not it. It's not right. I can't eat this."

Following Robin's orders, Nelson had the camera going. Digger and Marlee both stood rigidly still with their eyes nearly popping out of their heads. The two chefs obviously knew that Josh had completely blown this meal. Neither one looked terribly happy, but they didn't look torn up over Josh's failure, either. I thought I would be sick; Josh looked absolutely crushed.

"There's no time to have Josh make something else. I don't know what to do." Robin bit her lip and seemed momentarily lost. "Well, we'll have to move on. It'll just have to be part of the episode. What happens, happens, I'm afraid." I saw a slight but unmistakable glint in Robin's eye as she savored the prospect of airing this episode of *Chefly Yours*. From Robin's viewpoint, Francie's dramatic condemnation of Josh's food was far better than pleasant murmuring about how delicious everything was. Josh's pain was Robin's idea of great TV.

"Why don't we move on to the tomato salad and cheese course," I suggested. "And dessert, too." I took Francie's plate from Josh's hands, carried it to the kitchen, and braced myself against the counter. *Oh, Josh! What happened?* Maybe he was so nervous that he accidentally added something weird to the food? Or the old oven didn't cook the lamb at the proper temperature and . . . ? No. Francie had complained about bitterness. Overcooked or undercooked lamb chops would be tough or raw or flavorless, but they wouldn't be bitter. Like Josh, I thought of the arugula. At this time of year, it was all too easy to buy lettuce and other greens, including arugula, that had gone to seed and turned bitter. Maybe most of the arugula had been fine, and Francie had somehow ended up tasting a tiny bit that had been ruined by summer heat.

A second later, my dejected boyfriend followed me into

the kitchen but avoided looking at me. "Leo's finishing up his fish," Josh said, "and I'm going to serve the rest of the meal." He swore under his breath and then slammed a pair of tongs into the bowl that held the remains of the gnocchi. "There is nothing wrong with that lamb," he growled.

"Well, why don't we taste it?" I whispered.

Josh looked at me. "Yeah, good idea." He cut a bit for both of us from Francie's plate. "Now, don't think I normally go eating off customers' plates at the restaurant, okay?" He managed a little smile.

Until he tasted the lamb.

"Oh, my God." He wrinkled his face and quickly spat out the offending meat.

"Oh, stop! It can't be that bad." Curious, I sampled a tiny slice. *Bitter,* I realized, was a gross understatement. Gagging, I turned and spat the meat out into the sink, which was, thank goodness, equipped with a garbage disposal, exactly where the vile piece of lamb belonged. I filled glasses of water for us both and did my best to wash out the taste. Francie was, after all, right. The taste was worse than awful. It was hideously and inexplicably dreadful.

"I didn't do that," Josh said softly. "I did not do anything that would make the lamb taste like that. Did I?" He tasted the vegetables from the roasting pan. "These are pretty good. Although it's hard to tell right now with that flavor still in my mouth. How the hell did this happen?"

Here's proof of my love for Josh: in a noble act of self-sacrifice, I risked having that revolting bitterness invade my mouth again. In other words, I tasted the gnocchi with pesto. And again, ahem, used the sink. When I was done, I said, "Oh, hon! The gnocchi with the arugula pesto has the same problem the lamb does. Francie was right. It's that same bitterness." I shook my head. "Not from the arugula or the olives, either. At least, I don't think so. I've had arugula that's turned bitter, but it's not like this. And olives can be bitter, but this is something different, something much, much worse. Josh, what can do this?"

Before he answered, Robin called to him from the dining room. "Josh, we're ready for the next course."

Josh took a deep breath and carried the tomato salad and cheese plate to Francie and Leo. Francie looked hesitant to eat anything that Josh put in front of her, but she did help herself to tomatoes, tasted them, smiled, and offered unmistakably genuine praise. "The flavor and seasoning of the dressing is perfect."

One piece of good footage.

Nelson kept filming as a morose Josh presented the dessert cobbler. Leo again dug in with pleasure and oohed and aahed, but Francie did nothing more than move her spoon toward her dessert plate. The hot peach and raspberry concoction smelled fantastic. Wasn't she tempted to try it? And couldn't she see how miserable Josh looked? Didn't she want to make amends to him for her harsh criticism of the lamb and gnocchi? Not that I could really blame her—the bitterness lingered on my own tongue—but out of love for Josh, I sent telepathic messages to encourage her to speak kind words and help Josh to save face.

"I have to go to the bathroom," Francie announced curtly. So much for my telepathic abilities.

"Please, can you just finish dessert? And then we'll wrap this up." Robin looked desperate to bolt, but she was probably no more desperate than the rest of us were. Every single one of us, I thought, had had more than enough of this episode of *Chefly Yours*.

"We're almost done. I promise," Josh pleaded. He looked ready to sprint out of the house in shame.

"I feel sick." Francie rose from her seat and walked unsteadily from the table.

Join the club! After the whole fiasco, I wasn't feeling too well myself.

Francie staggered out of the dining room into a large front hallway. From where I was standing, I could see her head toward a staircase. Gripping the handrail, she slowly began to make her way up the steps.

"Christ, we're never going to get through this." Digger looked at his watch. "This is like a never-ending day. This blows for Josh, man."

"Yup, but at least it's been interesting," Marlee added.

Robin drew Josh aside and was gracious enough to put her hand on his arm as she spoke softly to him. I hoped she was saying something reassuring. Maybe that the TV station would never in a million years air this horrible episode?

Appalled by everyone's seeming lack of compassion for Francie, who clearly was not just feigning illness, I decided to check on her. I made my way to the front hall and up the stairs. By the time I reached the landing at the top, I could hear gagging and groaning. Following the sounds, I rounded a corner and on the floor ahead of me saw Francie's feet projecting from what was clearly a bathroom. Bright yellow towels hung on towel racks fastened inside the open door. Even before I entered the bathroom, I realized that Francie was horribly sick. She'd obviously been too ill even to close the bathroom door. Besides, the air in the dark hallway reeked. For a second, the taboo against barging into an occupied bathroom made me hesitate, but the dreadful sounds had now stopped, and the silence frightened me.

I stepped into the bathroom and knelt just inside the door. "Francie? Can I help you?" I put my hand on her shoulder. Francie didn't respond. She lay curled up on her side on a yellow bath mat, her hair in her face and her arms wrapped around her stomach. Bodily fluids were spattered on the old white ceramic bathroom fixtures and lay in pools on the cracked tile of the floor. The stench was overwhelming. Holding my breath and fighting nausea, I grabbed one of the thick yellow towels that hung from the door and made a senseless, panic-driven effort to rid Francie of the wet filth that clung to her dark curls and stained her white linen shell. Covering my hand with the towel, I brushed her hair away from her face, and as I leaned in to clean her mouth and cheeks, I realized she was having a terrible time breathing. Before that moment, my efforts had been directed at restoring Francie's dignity, I suppose. The sight of her sprawled on the floor, splattered with her own bodily wastes, had triggered a powerful impulse to clean her up and make her presentable, to spare her the humiliation being seen in this godawful condition. Now, all at once, the gravity of the situation hit me. At a minimum, she was dangerously dehydrated. Without question, she needed immediate help that I couldn't provide. My experience in hands-on first aid consisted of having treated small children with scraped knees. Now, I was facing a life-threatening emergency.

I'd left my cell phone in my purse in the car, and even if I'd been willing to leave Francie alone, I'd have had no idea where to find a phone upstairs in the house. "Josh!" I screamed. "Robin!"

I looked down at Francie, whose jagged breathing frightened me. "Francie?" I whispered. Then with near ferocity, I demanded, "Francie! Francie, can you hear me?" I uselessly dabbed the towel on her face.

Francie made a small, throaty noise and groaned softly. Almost inaudibly, she said, "Oh, shit." Her eyes were barely open, and her skin had a gray tinge.

I heard footsteps and then Josh's voice. "Chloe, is there another bathroom up here? I'm not feeling so great."

"Josh! You need to call nine-one-one! Get an ambulance! Now!" Panic had set in. My own voice sounded distant and unfamiliar. "Get an ambulance!" I screamed.

Looking up, I saw Josh grab one of the yellow towels. Then he retreated to the hallway, where I could hear him being violently sick.

"Oh, God," I whispered to myself. Then, in spite of the nauseating stench, I took a deep breath and bellowed, "Robin! Leo! Help! Call an ambulance! *Help! Help me!*"

Footsteps heralded the arrival of Robin and Leo, and I heard Robin say, "God, it smells awful here," and then, "Josh, what are you doing?"

I was still kneeling on the floor next to Francie. Rising a little, I again pleaded for help. "Call an ambulance! Francie is . . . For God's sake, call an ambulance!"

Instead of responding to the emergency, Leo stepped into the bathroom. "Francie?" he asked. "Francie, get up! You don't want people to see you like . . . We'd better get you to bed. The smell in here is . . . what a mess!" He held his hand to his nose and mouth.

Robin poked her head in and quickly withdrew.

"Chloe," Leo said, "can't you open the window? And help get Francie—"

When I'd first seen Francie, I'd also failed to grasp the reality of her situation. Still, I was furious at Leo. "Never mind the damned window!" I snapped. "Call an ambulance! Now!" I reached and almost punched Leo on the leg. "Go! Call nine-one-one!"

"Chloe, shut up!" Robin called out. "Cut the hysterics!"

"This is an emergency!" I insisted. "Call an ambulance!"

Robin, apparently addressing Leo, said, "Well, now we

know why Francie thought the food tasted bad. She was obviously coming down with a stomach bug. That norovirus thing. Is that what you call it? And she was starting to feel sick."

"Josh?" I called out. "Josh, are you okay? Can you get to a phone? Please! Please call for help!"

Josh cleared his throat. "Yeah, I'm all right now, I think."

I looked down at Francie, whose eyes were now shut. "Francie? Francie?" I rolled her onto her back and shook her. At first she appeared to be unconscious, but when I leaned my ear against her chest, I didn't hear the ragged breathing anymore. "Francie?" I was yelling now, repeatedly saying her name in the vain hope of rousing her. There was no response from her. Nothing. Nothing at all.

FIVE

I practically had to leap over Josh to get out of the bathroom. Then I flew down the stairs, my heart racing and my vision nearly blurred. All I can remember is being hell-bent on getting to the phone that I remembered having seen on the wall near the stove.

When I burst into the kitchen, I almost slammed into Digger, who grabbed me by both arms. "An ambulance is coming," he said. "What the hell is wrong? Is Josh okay? He ran out of here so fast."

"He's sick, too, Digger. I'm really scared," I said. My eyes began to water as I leaned into his chest. "I think Francie is dead." I was almost whispering. "I have to sit down." I was starting to feel queasy myself. Maybe Leo had been right about opening a window. The sickening odor seemed to cling to me. Or maybe fear was wrapping my stomach in knots.

Digger led me to a chair just as Josh entered the kitchen. He now looked more grim than ill, and I thought that I knew why: if Francie were still alive, Josh wouldn't have left her alone.

I found myself sitting next to Marlee, whose presence I hadn't even noticed. She was rubbing her forehead with one hand. Her face was pale and damp. "My stomach is really hurting," she said. "I've got terrible cramps, and I think I might throw up. Is there a bathroom downstairs?"

Digger moved the trash can next to her. "In case you don't make it to one," he said. "I might need it, too. I could hurl any second. I think we've got food poisoning."

"From the way I feel, you're probably right," Marlee agreed. "There's got to be a bathroom down here. Leo?"

For the first time, I noticed Leo, who was leaning against a wall as if propping himself up. He looked frozen in place, and his face was blank.

"Leo!" I said sharply. "Is there a bathroom downstairs?"

He shook himself and pointed to a doorway. "Through there." Sounding like a robot, he added, "I'm going back upstairs. Maybe I can . . ."

"Here, Marlee, I'll help you." Robin took Marlee's hand and led her out of the room.

As I watched them leave, I noticed to my horror that Nelson was standing in the dining room doorway with his face hidden behind his camera.

"Nelson, turn that camera off!" I demanded. "Stop it! This is no time—"

"Cannot do. I'm filming reality here. Raw reality! This is great!"

Glaring at him, Josh said, "Yeah, this is a great, Nelson. It's goddamn perfect."

"Nelson," I said, "the average rock would have more sensitivity than to film us right now. Turn the camera off! Unless you want me to grab it and shove it—"

Josh interrupted me. "There's the ambulance. You hear the sirens?"

"Yes," I said. "Thank God."

I'd somehow expected help to pour in through the back door, but when the doorbell rang, Josh went through the dining room, opened the front door, and took charge of directing the newcomers upstairs to where Francie lay on the bathroom floor. I felt certain that she was dead, but medical personnel and the police could hardly be expected to take my word for her condition, and there still remained a chance, I told myself, that I was wrong. The possibility made me feel guilty: what if I'd abandoned Francie when my presence might have comforted her?

While I could still hear the sounds of feet pounding up the stairs, Marlee reappeared from the bathroom. Her color was worse than it had been before. She had a greenish tinge, and her damp hair clung to her cheeks. "I heard the ambulance," she said. "Chloe, get someone to help me, would you? I'm sick. I'm so sick."

You and everyone else, I wanted to say. What I actually said was, "I'm not too well myself, and neither are—" I broke off. What if Marlee was becoming as horribly ill as Francie had been? "I'll see if I can get someone," I promised. With that, I made my way to the front hall, where the outside door stood open. Through it, I could see more official vehicles than I expected: two police cruisers and two big ambulances. As I stood there wondering how to summon help for Marlee—holler loudly? actually venture upstairs?—a handsome young EMT came bounding down, and at the same time, Josh appeared through the wide doorway to the living room.

"I'm sorry to bother you," I said to the EMT, "but there's someone in the kitchen who wants help. She's sick, too. And so are—"

"I'm going to check everyone out," he assured me, "and then we're probably going to take all of you to the emergency room."

"I'm fine," Josh claimed.

"No, he's not," I insisted. "He threw up all over the place."

"Yeah, I did throw up. I feel okay now, though. I'm fine."

"Josh, you don't know that!" I insisted. "But the one who's feeling really bad is Marlee. And Digger is sick, too."

"Give me a minute," the EMT said.

"We'll be in the kitchen," I told him. "It's in there, through the dining room."

The EMT hurried out through the front door. As Josh and I were on our way to the kitchen, we paused in the dining room to exchange a few words.

"Francie?" I asked.

He shook his head. "They had to do their thing, but . . ."

"I thought so," I said. "Oh, Josh, I was with her when she died. Maybe that's why I feel sick. Maybe I don't have the same thing as everyone else. I can't even tell."

"Hey, we've got to get these guys to take a look at you. Like he said, get you to the hospital."

"Marlee's the one I'm worried about. She looks terrible. Not as bad as Francie was, but I'm scared that she's—"

Josh held a finger to his lips. "Let the EMTs worry about her."

"I have to see how she is," I insisted.

When we entered the kitchen, I was relieved to find Marlee no worse than she'd been before. She was sitting at the table with Robin and Digger.

"Marlee, one of the EMTs will be here in a minute," I said.

Robin spoke up. "I'm really queasy, too. I don't feel right." She was slumped in her seat and was idly fingering her drooping ponytail. "I can't believe this. Is Francie really . . . ?"

Josh nodded. "Yes. Chloe was with her when she stopped breathing."

"Oh, my God, Chloe! Are you all right? Come sit down here." Robin pulled out another chair from the table.

"I'm okay." I still felt weird, but I was too embarrassed to admit that I couldn't tell whether I was sick or terrified.

Just as Josh opened his mouth to start arguing with me, the handsome EMT entered the kitchen in the company of a uniformed police officer, a large, muscular man with a neatly trimmed mustache. Before either of the men had a chance to say a word, Josh put a hand on my shoulder. "Chloe, you're not okay." Addressing the EMT, he said, "You need to take a look at her."

I caught the EMT's eye and gestured to Marlee. "I'll be okay, but Marlee's the one who really needs help."

The police officer's radio crackled loudly. He stepped to the far end of the kitchen and began muttering incomprehensible words. Interrupting the EMT, who was speaking softly to Marlee, he called out, "Where'd you get the food?"

"Natural High," I answered. "The Natural High right near here."

In an effort to be helpful, Josh began to give a detailed description of all the food we'd bought and all the dishes he'd prepared with such enthusiasm. I could hardly listen without crying for him. In the background, I heard heavy footsteps and the sound of the front door opening and closing. For a moment, everyone was quiet, as if we'd tacitly agreed to observe a moment of silence as Francie's body was carried away. My head was spinning, and everything seemed to be simultaneously happening in slow motion and at warp speed. I couldn't think clearly.

I don't know whether the EMT responded to me, to someone else, or to the whole situation, but I clearly remember that he said, "Okay, let's get you all to the emergency room." I also remember that he let Nelson have it: "And turn off that camera!"

Until then, I'd all but forgotten Nelson's existence. Wishful thinking?

"Man, look at it this way," Nelson said. "I'm just doing my job. Pursuing my art, okay? I'm a filmmaker, and I'm not going to miss this. That's what a documentary is about, right? Reality. Whatever happens. No matter what, you get it on film." The glee in Nelson's voice made me feel queasier than ever.

The cop was more effective than the EMT had been in getting Nelson to quit filming. Instead of giving Nelson an order, he did nothing but look at him, raise a hand, point his finger, and utter one word: "You!"

Nelson turned tail and vanished through the dining room.

The next thing that happened was that I stood up and . . . and . . . Well, what I definitely did *not* do was faint. For one thing, as a person who had completed a whole year of social work school and was thus a mental-health professional in training, I couldn't possibly have passed out from anxiety. For another thing, although I'd been feeling sick to my stomach, I hadn't lost any bodily fluids and thus couldn't have keeled over from dehydration. And for yet another thing, I wasn't the swooning type. So, let's just say that one moment I was rising from a chair in the kitchen, and the next moment, the next one I can remember, anyway, I was in an ambulance on the way to the hospital. But not, not, not because I had fainted.

SIX

OKAY, so I fainted. The first voice I heard when I came to was Marlee's. "I can't see right," she complained. "Everything is kind of blurry."

The second voice belonged to the handsome EMT. "You with us again, Chloe? You're going to be fine. We're on our way to the hospital, but all that happened to you was that you fainted."

It was then that I became aware of the siren and of the sensation of being in a moving vehicle. To my credit, I didn't ask where I was. In fact, although the interior of the big emergency medical service vehicle looked like my idea of the inside of a space capsule, I knew that I was in an ambulance. "Not me!" I said. "I never faint."

Besides his good looks, the EMT had a sense of humor. He laughed. "Not the type for smelling salts, huh?"

When I tried to sit up, he gently told me to keep my head down for a while, but I succeeded in looking around and saw Marlee on the opposite side of the ambulance. She was rubbing her eyes, and her face looked wet from tears. "What's wrong with me?" she asked in a feeble voice. "With us?"

Although she wasn't addressing me, I answered her. "Something in the house? Like a gas leak?"

To my surprise, it was Josh who replied. His voice came from somewhere toward the front of the ambulance. "It's got to be the food. I don't know how, but it has to." He started reciting a list of everything he'd bought today: "Lamb, halibut, olives, arugula, potatoes . . ."

The comforting rumble of Josh's voice must have soothed me. Although I didn't realize it at the time, I showed two signs of health: practicality and hunger. "I don't have my insurance card!" I said in alarm. "It's in my purse, locked in my car." I had the sense to say nothing about my empty stomach. With one person dead and others ill, this was no time to ask for a snack. Even so, the thought did cross my mind that the hospital probably had a cafeteria or at least a vending machine.

As it turned out, Josh had found my keys and retrieved my purse from my car. Although he grumbled in a sweet way about women and their purses, I was glad to have my belongings with me, especially once we were at the emergency room, which was mercifully uncrowded. By the time we arrived, even my matinee-idol EMT conceded that my case had low priority, as did the nurses responsible for deciding which of us had to be seen immediately and which of us could wait. Although I still felt shaken, I had no physical symptoms at all. Consequently, I ended up in the waiting room with Josh, Digger, Robin, and that damned Nelson, who'd followed the ambulances to the hospital, which was a small one that I'd never heard of before. Marlee, who'd felt increasingly worse, had been hustled into the exam area as soon as we'd arrived. Nelson, camera in hand, was lurking near the entrance. The rest of us were sitting together. Josh and Digger were, as usual, talking about food, but not in the way that chefs typically do.

"Dude, it can't be the food. You know that," Digger tried to assure Josh. "All the stuff you cooked would take time to produce symptoms like this. Food poisoning wouldn't come on that fast and kill somebody. You know as well as I do that it takes, like, six hours at least before you'd get sick. If this was E. coli or something, none of us would be feeling anything right now."

I saw a flash of relief cross Josh's face. "You're right. You're right. I'm just so freaked out, and I can't help feeling like this is my fault somehow. I mean, I fed Francie, and then she died! I don't know everything about food poisoning, but I think there are a few kinds that can produce symptoms in a hour or two. I wish I had my ServSafe books with me," Josh said.

"It's a program," I informed Robin. "ServSafe trains kitchen workers in safe food laws, safe practices."

She spoiled my sense of being in the know by saying condescendingly, "I already know what ServSafe is, thank you very much."

"Josh," I said, "Marlee was saying that she had blurred vision. I've never heard of that being a symptom of food poisoning. That's neurological, isn't it? Blurred vision?" An unwelcome thought occurred to me. What if the problem was not food poisoning, but poisoning? Just poisoning. My stomach clenched in knots. I hoped the doctor who must now be examining Marlee would figure out what she had and would inform the rest of us. "Robin," I asked, "how are you feeling?"

"Been better, but at least I'm not heaving up Josh's food. And you?"

"I'm okay. I'm just shaken up, I think."

I glanced at the desk, only to spot Nelson leaning against it. A second later, a nurse noticed him, too, and in an undertone ordered him to turn off his camera. I couldn't hear her words, but her irate expression suggested that she was threatening fearsome consequences.

I saw Robin smile. "I should hire her." She rubbed her stomach. "So, Chloe, talk to me about something. Anything. Distract me from my screwed-up stomach."

"Well, I'm going to be performing a wedding ceremony in a few weeks."

Robin perked up. "You are? Who are you marrying? I mean, who are you helping get married? That's so cool. How can you do that?"

Although I was a little reluctant to give Robin credit for a good idea, it did take my mind off the present nightmare to think about my best friend Adrianna's wedding to Owen. "All I did was go online, print out an application from the state, and fill out a form. It's called a one-day marriage designation. The application had to be approved by the governor, except that I don't think he has to do it personally. And then I got my Certificate of Solemnization. So now I can marry Adrianna and Owen!" That didn't sound right. Unless I wanted people to think that I was about to commit bigamy, I'd need to work on my solemnization-wording skills. "Well, you know what I mean."

"That is really neat! I didn't know you could even do that," Robin said. "They don't go to church or anything? They didn't want someone more official to preside over their ceremony?"

"No, neither of them is particularly religious, and they're having a smallish wedding. Fifty people or so. And Ade thought it would be more personal if someone close to both of them did the ceremony. They're writing the whole service themselves, vows and all. Of course, I'll do my own piece, too, but it's nice that they can control what they want in and out of the whole thing."

"Chloe?" Josh touched my arm. "They're ready to see you and Robin now. Digger is getting checked out already." Josh's phone rang. "Sorry. I have to take this." When he picked up his call, I could make out a woman's voice on the other end. "I can't talk now," he said. "I'll call you back." He clicked his cell shut. "You ready?"

"Who was that?"

Josh waved a hand. "No one. Just work stuff. Oh, there's the nurse who wants to see you." Josh pointed to a fiftyish woman with a folder in her hand.

The nurse led me into a large room filled with medical equipment and lined with little curtained exam areas. When we reached the area assigned to me and she closed the curtains, I did my best to peek through the cracks to see whether I could see Marlee or Digger and find out how they were doing. Unfortunately, the hospital was all too effective in ensuring patient privacy—I couldn't see anyone at all— but at least I didn't hear any panicked calls for crash carts or loudspeaker announcements of emergency codes, so I assumed that Marlee and Digger were doing okay.

The nurse took my blood pressure and pulse, and shoved a thermometer in my mouth. "So, young lady, tell me what's going on with you." I didn't like the accusatory tone in her voice. And how was I supposed to answer her with my mouth closed?

I made unintelligible sounds with my lips closed until she pulled the thermometer out. "I don't think anything's going on with me. But"—I started to whisper—"I was with the woman, Francie, when she died. I found her on the bathroom floor, and I, uh, I watched her take her . . . well, her last breath."

The nurse squinted her eyes at me. "Her last breath?"

"Yes. I think I'm just unnerved." At normal volume, I said, "I'm upset by the experience. Anyone would be! It was not a peaceful death. She looked like she was in a lot of pain." I looked up at the nurse. "She is dead, right? I mean . . . we heard that Francie was dead." As if the statement were somehow unclear, I said, "We heard that she'd died, but . . ."

The sour nurse stared at me before speaking. "Yes, the woman is dead." She sat down on a stool with wheels and scooted next to me. "Tell me about this party you were at."

"It wasn't a party. Although it did have a celebratory feel at one point, I guess." I briefly explained the concept of the show and told her about the food that Josh had made. "The food was really good, though. Well, except for the lamb, which tasted fine at first. But then later it tasted really bitter and strange. And that dreadful arugula pesto. Ugh."

"So the lamb changed taste as the night went on?" She eyed me suspiciously

"I guess you could put it like that."

"And what else did you people put into your bodies? You know, we can't help you unless we know exactly what's in your system, what it was that you took."

"What I *took* was gnocchi and a bit of the lamb, some vegetables."

"What *substances*?" She didn't bother hiding her exasperation.

"I did not take any drugs! I don't do drugs! I barely even drink anymore now that my best friend is pregnant. I'm supporting her by abstaining from alcohol during her pregnancy. And all the food was from Natural High."

"Natural High, my ass," the wretched nurse mumbled.

"The *market* called Natural High."

I eventually convinced the nurse that no one had snorted, injected, inhaled, or otherwise *taken* or *used* anything except food, and I was allowed to leave.

Josh was in the waiting room. "Everything okay?" he asked.

"Yeah. Either I didn't eat enough of whatever is making us sick, or it's just my nerves that were making me queasy. I'm fine. You look better, too."

"I am. I feel back to normal now. Well, as normal as I get," he teased. He pulled me close for a tight hug. "I guess they're keeping Marlee and Digger. I don't know why exactly. It's not clear if they are admitting them or not. They wanted to hook me up to an IV to rehydrate me, but I told them that was ridiculous. I'll drink some water."

I sighed. "Are you sure? There's no reason to be stubborn about this."

"Look, the last thing I feel like doing is lying down with a needle stuck in my arm all night. I just want to get out of here. I swear to you that I'm totally better."

I didn't get another chance to try to coerce Josh back into the exam room, because Robin's voice began echoing through the room.

"I am not, I repeat, *not* a drug addict!" Robin stormed over to us. "Can you believe this crap? Some idiot back there kept insisting that I must have taken too many prescription pills. Like I was mixing uppers with downers instead of producing a TV show!" She breathed out heavily. "Sorry. I'm just strung out." She turned around and yelled, "And not *strung out* in a drug-related way!"

"So," I said slowly, "I guess we're ready to go?"

"Yes. Where's Nelson? Nelson!" Robin barked.

"At your service." Nelson's tone was so cheerful and his expression so smug that the shine radiating from his damp face and scalp made him appear to be glowing with happiness.

"You need to drive us back to the house so Chloe can get her car. Chloe, maybe you can clean up the kitchen?"

Maybe you can, I wanted to say. Instead, having completed a full year of social work school, I said brightly, "Yes, we'll all pitch in. Robin, what a great idea!"

SEVEN

SO much for the benefits of a full year of social work school. During the drive back to Leo and Francie's house, Robin increasingly complained about her exhaustion, and by the time Nelson pulled the TV van into the driveway, she'd managed to weasel out of doing her share of the cleanup while simultaneously arousing my sympathy for Leo.

"We don't want Leo coming home to that mess," she'd said.

"For all we know, he's there now," I'd replied. "And if he isn't, the house is probably locked up." I'd negotiated the agreement that if we found Leo at home, we'd ask whether he wanted help in cleaning up. If not, Josh and I would leave. If Leo wanted our help or if the house was empty and unlocked, we'd stay. It was more or less a bet that I lost. When we got there, the back door was open, and there was

no sign of Leo. My only piece of luck was that Ro
sisted that Nelson had to drive her home, so at lea e
wasn't hanging around filming while Josh and I cleared up
the remains of the fatal dinner. I did the dishes while Josh
threw out food, took out the trash, and packed up the cooking equipment that belonged to him. Neither of us, however, was valiant enough to don a pair of gloves and scrub
the bathroom, which remained a revolting reminder of tonight's tragedy. I just couldn't stomach going back in there.
When Leo returned, he'd just have to use another bathroom.
Where was Leo, anyway? Someone had said that he'd ridden
in the ambulance that had transported Francie—or Francie's
body—to the hospital. I hadn't seen him there. Shouldn't he
be home by now? Maybe he simply couldn't bear to return
home without his wife?

I drove us back to my condo in Brighton. It was a one-
bedroom on the third and top floor of what had originally
been a large one-family house. My unit had a big bedroom,
a small living room, a cramped kitchen, and a tiny bathroom, but I'd never before been so happy to be in the safety
of my own little home. Josh made another trip down to the
car to bring up the cooking equipment he had so excitedly
used only hours earlier, and I put on water for tea. I wasn't
much of a tea drinker, and neither was Josh, but I felt chilled
and weak, and the idea of tea felt comforting.

Josh returned, placed a cardboard box and his knife bag in
a corner of my living room, and collapsed onto the couch. He
ran both hands through his hair and held them there, disbelief plastered across his face. "This cannot have happened.
This cannot have happened," he kept repeating. He looked up
at me with concern. "God, how are you doing, Chloe?"

I put the cups of tea on the coffee table, sat down next to
him, and moved in close when he put his arm around me.

He wrapped his other arm around me, squeezed me against him, and rubbed the back of my head. "Not very well," I said in a broken voice as I started to cry. "Oh, Josh," I managed, "I was with her when she died. She couldn't breathe right. And she was lying in her own . . . filth! She must have been in so much pain." I sat up and wiped my eyes. "I can't imagine what killed her. It must be the same thing that made everybody sick, right? I mean, the odds of the two being unrelated are . . . negligible. Zero."

My sleek, black, muscular cat, Gato, jumped onto the couch, positioned himself with his front quarters on Josh's lap, and began purring loudly. "Hi, there, my friend." Josh started patting Gato's shiny coat. That darn cat, who loved Josh to pieces, fended off most of my own attempts to snuggle with him. To me, Josh said, "I'm so sorry you had to watch Francie die. And I'm sorry I wasn't more help. I was feeling terrible, and I don't know that I was thinking all that clearly. What a horrible thing for you to have to go through."

"Josh, I can't shake the image of Francie struggling for air. And her eyes were all glassy and unfocused. What do you think happened?"

"I've got one explanation for this." He sighed. "But it's not good."

"There aren't any *good* explanations, so shoot. Tell me what you think," I said with a sniffle.

"I hate to even think it, but I wonder if Evan or Willie had something to do with it."

Josh's words shook me out of my tears. "What? You think Owen's brothers did this? What on earth—"

"Hear me out." He held out his hand to stop me from telling him he was out of his mind. "You know how Evan and Willie are. They're always pulling practical jokes and goofing around. What if they thought it'd be funny to pull off a joke that ended up on television? To pull one on me? Remember when they stuck a few pieces of fish into the engine of Owen's delivery truck? Once those things started rotting and the smell got into the driver's area, even Owen knew that was not the normal way a seafood delivery truck should smell. They could've messed with the food or the wine to make me look terrible. I don't know what they could've put in the food or maybe in the wine, but it's a possibility."

I froze. Far from hitting me as off-the-wall, the idea struck me as hideously possible. Owen swore that his brothers had always been a lot like Fred and George, Ron Weasley's twin brothers, but that once Evan and Willie had read the Harry Potter books, they'd deliberately modeled themselves on the practical-joking tricksters. Until recently, their antics had simply provided a topic of lighthearted conversation, but as Owen and Adrianna's wedding approached, I'd begun to share Adrianna's fear that Willie and Evan would pull one of their stunts at the wedding, maybe even during the ceremony. I took a sip of tea and thought for a moment. "You know, it seemed obvious to me that Evan knew we were coming to the Wine and Cheese Shop. Willie probably called him to give him a heads-up. Evan had wine bottles open and breathing, and he had that platter conveniently displaying cheeses for you to sample. Do you think he could have put something in the wine? Or on the cheese? Or Willie did something to the lamb?" Oh, God, it would've been just like one of them to lace the food with laxatives to make everyone get sick on camera. But could laxatives have killed Francie? Could an overdose be fatal? Would they cause vomiting, though? I really didn't know enough even to take a guess.

"I'm sure that Willie tipped Evan off," Josh said. "And it

would be just like the two of them to do something. But what? And what could have been so toxic it killed Francie that quickly? And, well, I don't know . . ." He paused and frowned. "The more I think about it, I don't know that they would have done something to make me look *that* bad. I don't know if ruining my episode is really their style. Now, if Evan had given me a wine bottle that had a fake snake pop out when I opened it, that wouldn't have surprised me. But I don't know those two that well."

"Ugh, I hope they don't do anything stupid at Ade and Owen's wedding. It would be just like them to pull some dumb stunt on the day of their brother's marriage." I could just imagine Adrianna's bouquet shooting water into her face or the wedding rings sending jolts of electricity through the bride and groom.

Josh said, "So maybe there was some kind of bacteria in the food we bought. Like E. coli in spinach. Remember that? The arugula could have been tainted with E. coli. We keep hearing about all those food recalls and news reports on people dying from this kind of stuff. And they always say that people with immune problems or chronic illnesses are much more vulnerable than anyone else. We don't know anything about Francie. She could've had an illness that would've made her more susceptible."

"That's true. That must have been what happened, Josh. It's the only thing that makes sense. I guess we should just be glad that we're healthy and that we're not dead, too."

"Yeah, I know. If that's what killed her, though, I still feel responsible. I mean, I chose the ingredients."

"There is absolutely no way you could have known, Josh. There must be other people who bought that food, too. We should probably call the store."

"Yeah, I'll do that tomorrow. Speaking of tomorrow, why

don't you take the day off? It's already almost two in the morning. You've got to be drained."

"That's probably a good idea. I'm sure my parents won't fire me."

During summer break from graduate school, I was working as an assistant to my parents at their landscaping and garden design company. My specialty this summer, rain barrels, tied in neatly with my studies; promoting the use of rain barrels kept me politically and socially active. I'd first heard of them when I'd read an online article. The idea was simple: Large barrels were set under gutters to collect rainwater. A spigot or hose connector was affixed to the bottom of each barrel so that the collected rainwater could be used to fill watering cans or to supply water to a soaker hose. Unfortunately, many barrels were unattractive and came in loud, obtrusive shades of red and green. When I talked to my parents about rain barrels, they said that their wealthy, house-proud suburban clients would totally reject the idea of big, garish barrels no matter how effectively they conserved a limited resource—fresh water. But instead of telling me to forget about ecological friendliness, my parents found a young carpenter, Emilio, who designed and built rain barrels that blended in with the colors and styles of individual clients' houses. My job was to accompany my parents on landscaping consults and push rain barrels into the design equation. I did some neighborhood canvassing on my own, too, but I loathed the door-to-door approach.

"Okay, Carter Landscapes' rain barrel business will have to take Tuesday off." I leaned my head into Josh's shoulder. "Can I come see you at Simmer tomorrow night?"

"You bet. I'll make you whatever you want," he promised.

I loved going to see Josh at the restaurant. Not that I

usually got to spend much time with him there, but his out-standing food made up for his absence. Besides, it was a way for him to be with me, really. He often made me special dishes that weren't on the menu, and those were some of my favorites. Sometimes he played with seasonal ingredients, experimented with dishes he was considering for the menu, or just cooked what he was inspired to make that day.

"Good. Maybe I'll hang out with Ade for a bit tomorrow afternoon, and I'll come in after that. What time are you working?"

"I should get there around nine, I suppose. I have to close, so I'll be there late, but who knows what shape the place will be in after I was gone today?" Josh stretched his arms above his head and gave a long, deep yawn. "This day is officially over, okay?"

Josh and I crawled into bed. "Josh?" I said. "What if it was poison? Not food poisoning, but poison?"

He curled his body around mine and pulled the com-forter up high. Even though it was August, we were both shivering. "I know," he answered quietly. "I've had the same thought."

EIGHT

MY mind could have used a good fourteen hours of oblivion, but my body refused to sleep past eight o'clock the next morning. When I awoke, Josh had already left for work. I knew that he must be exhausted. Even so, since he was going to be at Simmer tonight to cook me the dinner he'd promised, he'd be working a brutally long day. I brewed a pot of coffee and called my mother to let her know I wasn't coming to work today. I didn't feel ready to tell my parents about Josh's nightmare of a TV episode yesterday, so I simply said that I had a cold. In fact, I sounded so raspy that it took almost no effort to make myself sound sick.

"Chloe, you poor thing. Aren't those summer colds the worst?" My mother was so full of sympathy that I felt a pang of guilt about my lie. "Why don't I stop by later with some tissues and soup? Or, better yet, why don't you come and stay with us for a few days, and we'll take care of you?"

I was touched by my mother's offer to nurse me back to health, but even if I'd been sick, I'd have refused. I loved my parents to pieces, but it would have been impossible to get any real rest with my mother popping into the guest bedroom every five minutes to take my temperature and feed me hot broth. I'd have had to return home to recover from recovering.

"No, thanks, Mom. I'm really fine. It's just a cold. I should be much better tomorrow."

"Well, don't worry about tomorrow, either. I think it'll be a slow day around here. I'll call you if we need you. While I have you on the phone, are things looking all set for Adrianna's shower on Saturday?"

"I think so. I've heard back from almost everyone."

I couldn't believe that it was only four more days until my best friend's combination wedding shower and baby shower. Both the shower and wedding itself were going to be held at my parents' house. I'd been determined to host Adrianna's shower myself, but it would've been impossible to squeeze more than a few people into my little condo. And the wedding? Owen, who was working as a fish purveyor, was living off the commissions he made from selling seafood to restaurants, and Adrianna had just stopped working as an independent hair stylist. Consequently, the two parents-to-be were barely able to pay their bills. Owen's parents simply didn't have the money to help them, and Adrianna's mother, Kitty, had suggested that they go to City Hall for a quick service. Kitty was less than thrilled about the order in which her daughter was getting married and starting a family. Adrianna's father had vanished when she was very young, and she had no grandparents or other family members with the money or the desire to help finance her wedding.

So, a few months earlier, when it had become clear that Owen and Ade were stuck, I'd secretly approached my parents, who not only had offered to host both events at their house but were paying for practically everything. One reason for their generosity was that they knew and liked Owen and Ade. Another was that they understood how important my friends and their unborn baby were to me. A third was what felt like moral outrage at Adrianna's mother's nasty, stingy attitude. "We can afford to do it," my father had assured me, "and so we will! The wedding will be beautiful. And," he'd added, "if Adrianna's mother doesn't like it, she can sit in the back row and glower."

Once the plan was in place, I invited the bride and groom to dinner at my parents' house in Newton, where my mom and dad surprised Adrianna and Owen with their offer. Ade and Owen were completely overwhelmed at my parents' generosity, and each had thanked my parents so frequently and profusely that my dad eventually started joking about rescinding the offer if the two wouldn't shut up. Fortunately for my parents' bank balance, Adrianna and Owen wanted a fairly small, simple wedding rather than one of those over-the-top affairs with a full band, a bridal party of twenty, an expensive photographer, and an exorbitantly priced reception hall. My friends would never have asked my parents to pay for a gigantic, pricey wedding, which wouldn't have been Ade and Owen's style, anyway.

Ade's mother was flying in from Arizona on Friday, the day before the shower, and would be staying for over a week—in other words, until after the wedding. Although my parents were footing the bill for the shower and the wedding, Kitty had done nothing but complain about how much everything was costing her. Adrianna and Owen had had a hard time convincing Kitty that there was no room for her in their tiny apartment, which barely had room for the two of them—the nursery was a converted closet—and they'd suggested that Kitty skip the shower and just come to the wedding. Eventually, Kitty had decided to stay at a hotel for the week, but not without asking, "Do you have any idea what that's going to cost me?"

Thank God that Ade had my dad and mom, Jack and Bethany Carter, to act as substitute parents!

"So," my mother said, "Josh still can't cater the shower, right?"

"No. He got Gavin to give him the day of the wedding off so he can cater it, but Gavin wouldn't give him another Saturday, too." To maintain the illusion of illness, I pretended to blow my nose.

"Well, darn it, Josh works so hard at that restaurant! You'd think that this Gavin would have the sense to keep his executive chef happy. Anyhow, we can handle the food. The shower won't be that big. Is Adrianna excited?"

"Very. Mom, she is so overwhelmed by everything you and Dad are doing for her. Thanks again." My parents' help meant as much to me as it did to Ade and Owen.

"Of course. We'd do anything for them. With the baby coming in a few weeks, the last thing they need to worry about is trying to pay for a wedding. And I can't stand the idea a tiny civil ceremony with no real celebration to go along with it. We wouldn't have it any other way. So let's talk food!"

We finalized the menu for Saturday's shower. I hung up feeling guilty for feigning a cold, but if I'd told my mother about Francie's death, we'd've had a whole long conversation that I didn't feel like having right now. And all this wedding talk was so fun! While making all these plans over the past few months, I'd spent my fair share of time fantasizing that I was planning my own wedding to Josh. Not that I was expecting an engagement anytime soon, but it seemed like marriage could be a possibility for the two of us.

As soon as I'd put down the phone, it rang again. I looked at the caller ID window and saw the dreaded words *Private Call*. Answering the phone when caller ID had picked up no information about the incoming call was risky: for all I knew, I'd be stuck talking to someone who'd coerce me into responding to a long survey about tile cleaning products or about my infomercial-watching preferences.

"Hello?" I said tentatively.

"Hi. Why aren't you selling rain barrels? Do you want to come over?" Phew. It was Adrianna, whose new number was still unlisted. I'd have to get on her about having her number published, or I'd be missing a lot of calls.

"I'm playing hooky. Yeah, let me just throw on some clothes, and I'll be over soon."

When Ade and Owen had moved in together last spring, I'd been glad that their apartment was within walking distance of my place. Today, I actually wished that Adrianna lived a bit farther away than she did, because a good, long walk would've helped shake off some of yesterday's tragedy. I tossed on a pair of gray yoga pants (not that I actually *did* yoga) and a white top, and yanked my hair into a ponytail. Knowing that Adrianna wouldn't have any caffeinated coffee, I filled a travel mug with my own and left to see my incredibly enlarging friend. On the way, I resolved not to make any more jokes about how many babies she was carrying. *Quads? Are you sure it's not at least triplets?* Well, I'd try very hard not to. The last time I'd made a joke about multiple births, she'd thrown a stuffed bear at me. Next time it could be something painful, like a bottle warmer or a diaper bin.

Like me, Ade and Owen lived on the top floor of a house.

Trudging up the stairs to their place, I once again lamented the steepness of the steps my friends would have to manage with a baby. Now, while she was pregnant, Ade needed to stop for a break when she climbed the stairs, but once she had a baby or toddler in her arms, the staircase would become perilous. At least the apartment looked attractive. It was minuscule but charming, with hardwood floors and original molding around the doors and windows.

I knocked on the door while simultaneously opening it and announcing my arrival. "Ade?"

The heavenly smell in the apartment made me suspect that Adrianna was once again cooking. Now that Ade had stopped work, she was doing the whole nesting thing: she spent most of her time organizing and reorganizing the apartment, baking decadent cakes with elaborate icing, and putting together scrapbooks using strange craft tools I'd never seen before.

"Hi, Chloe. Come in," my friend called.

I stepped into the hallway and into the bright living room–kitchen area. All I could see of Adrianna was her backside popping out from the open door of the refrigerator. "Yeah, I know. I'm cooking again. But wait until you see what we're having."

"No complaints from me," I said happily, peering into a pot on the stove. "What are you making?"

"I already baked a coffee cake, and now I'm starting the artichoke and spinach eggs Benedict with a spicy hollandaise sauce on croissants. And potatoes with rosemary, onion, and garlic. It's going to be bang-up." Ade emerged from the depths of the fridge, her arms loaded with half its contents. Her blonde hair cascaded down her back in soft curls. Even hugely pregnant, she was stunning. Her face was bare of makeup, and she wore black stretch pants and an oversized tank top over a sports bra, but she still looked better than anyone else I knew.

"Look at you!" I practically squealed. "You've become so domestic and cute!" The change in Adrianna was incredible. The prepregnant Adrianna never appeared in front of anyone without makeup. As for cooking, she'd been the queen of takeout—high-end takeout, admittedly, but takeout nonetheless. Not that I objected: a warm, comforting meal was just what I needed to soothe my nerves.

"Shut up. I'm not domestic, and I'm certainly not cute. Have you seen my feet?" She kicked a leg out for my viewing pleasure. "I mean, I haven't seen my feet in weeks, but I imagine they are monstrous, swollen blobs. Grab a mixing bowl for me, will you?"

I complied and then helped her to mix spinach, artichoke hearts, mayonnaise, sour cream, garlic, mozzarella, and Parmesan cheese. She poured the concoction into a ceramic baking dish that I popped into the oven. While the oven door was open, I got a glimpse of the aromatic potatoes that were crisping beautifully.

"Now the hollandaise sauce," she said.

I watched in awe as Adrianna heated a double boiler and began melting butter. This from a woman who adored food as much as I did but who, until now, had had zero cooking skills!

"Here, separate the eggs for me." She pushed the carton toward me.

"Yes, ma'am!" I dutifully began cracking eggs, separating yolks and whites, and tossing the shells into the sink.

"Oh, so I want to hear about Josh's filming yesterday, but get this," Adrianna began as she cut a lemon for the sauce. "Owen called me earlier and said that someone from the Department of Public Health went into Natural High and

Evan's cheese shop first thing this morning to investigate a serious case of food poisoning. How gross is that?"

"Oh, God, really?" When I turned from the sink to look at Ade, I broke the yolk from the egg I was trying to separate. "Well, I can't say the filming went smoothly." Gross understatement.

"Why? What happened? Josh didn't panic and burn everything, did he?"

I handed Ade the bowl of egg yolks and watched as she mixed them with an electric beater. "No," I yelled over the din, "he didn't do anything wrong. But the guest's wife died during dessert."

"She cried? His food was that bad? Screw her. Who cries over a dessert?"

"Died, Adrianna! Died!" My loud voice filled the room when Ade abruptly turned off the mixer.

"Someone died eating Josh's food? I guess she did get screwed." She started adding small portions of the egg to the melted butter and lemon. "Did she have a heart attack or something?"

"No, I wish," I answered. "Not that I wish she'd had a heart attack! It's just that . . . that the situation is complicated."

I told Adrianna all about yesterday's events as she finished making the hollandaise, which was now spiked with hot sauce, and began to poach four eggs. "Francie died while I was with her. She looked horrible, Ade. She was so sick. And it happened so fast. Right in front of me." My stomach clenched in knots, and I tossed my head as if trying to shake out the image of Francie dying on the floor of that filthy bathroom. "Ade, I have to know what happened to her! I was right there, and I couldn't do anything to help her. I *didn't* do anything."

I was ashamed of not having made some sort of heroic effort to revive Francie. At a crucial time, I had completely frozen; in the worst possible way, I had let Francie down. The ugly thought came to me that since I'd done it once, I might do it again. I was Adrianna's backup birth coach! What if Owen was unreachable when Ade went into labor? And I was the only person she had to depend on? Owen's fish truck could break down, his cell could be out, and I would be Adrianna's sole support. Some help I'd be! To judge from my reaction to Francie's crisis, if Adrianna relied on me to help her through labor, I'd stare dumbly while she pushed a human being out of her body. I had to get it together! There was no way I was going to fail my best friend.

"Chloe, it doesn't sound like there was anything to do. She was obviously incredibly sick. Whatever killed her, killed her very quickly. I can't imagine anyone could have saved her." Ade ladled the eggs from the simmering water and began assembling our plates. She scooped the melted artichoke and spinach mixture onto the croissants and placed an egg and hollandaise sauce on top of each. "So you think it was food poisoning? That's why the health department wanted to talk to the stores where the food came from?"

We carried our plates to the coffee table in the living room, which also served as the dining room. "I guess," I said. "I don't know what else to think. The police were there, and they didn't . . . well, they didn't do much of anything." Although I couldn't entirely dismiss Josh's speculation about Evan and Willie, I avoided telling Adrianna that her fiancé's brothers might have perpetrated a prank with a very unfunny outcome. "Now that I'm saying it out loud, it does seem weird that the police just assumed it was food poisoning and didn't want to investigate any other possibilities. Even Josh and I wondered for a minute whether Francie had been poisoned. Whether all of us had been poisoned, really." In spite of the unappetizing topic of conversation, I was still able to savor Ade's cooking. The delicious eggs were exactly the comfort food I needed.

"I bet I know," Ade said as she stuffed her mouth full of the outstanding if unorthodox Benedict. "Look at the neighborhood you were in. Who the heck gets killed in a wealthy upper-class town like Fairfield? Plus, when the cops showed up, most of you were sick to some degree. I watch cop shows, you know, and it's the job of the first police officer on a scene to determine if it's a crime or not. At first glance, it definitely looks like food poisoning, so I guess he felt he had no reason to think of it any other way. See, the good thing about being pregnant and slothlike is that I've been reading tons of mysteries and watching TV. It's paid off, don't you think? So who would want that poor Francie dead?"

"I have no idea. I don't know anything about her. But after watching what she went through as she died, I want to know what killed her. Or who killed her. No one should have to die like that." I shuddered. "What else did Owen say?"

"He said he talked to Willie, and Willie told him that everyone at the store was furious because, of course, no one wants to be blamed for selling nasty food, right? What business wants that kind of notoriety? I guess they had to yank a bunch of stuff from the shelves, and it's causing a big stir there. If I walked into an expensive market and saw employees pulling tons of food, I'd turn around and walk out. And Evan is closed for the day, now, and since it's his store, he's losing money while they check out everything he's selling. A reputation for selling deadly food could destroy his business."

I took a deep breath and blew it out. "Let's change the subject," I said with as much cheer as I could muster. "Let's talk about the wedding."

"Chloe, you're traumatized and depressed." Adrianna said matter-of-factly. "I'm sorry you and Josh had to go through all of this. Let me take care of you." Ade picked up a piece of croissant and wiped the plate with it before popping the last bite in her mouth. "The best route to feeling good is looking good. So I'm going to do your hair. A run-through for the wedding, okay?" She stood up as gracefully as she could. "I need the practice so I don't lose my touch before I have to do my own hair. I'll do your hair the way I'm going to do mine. So try to look like me."

I almost shoved a couch pillow under my shirt but didn't want to risk one of Ade's mood swings. I cleaned up the kitchen and helped myself to some freshly baked coffee cake while Adrianna gathered her styling tools. Although the temperature in the little apartment felt comfortable to me, Ade decided that the thermometer that read a mere seventy-two degrees was horrendously inaccurate, so she cranked up the air conditioner while I huddled under a blanket. "Besides, the AC will dry out the air in here and make for better hair," she insisted. "Now, go stick your head in the sink and then sit in front of me. And this reminds me. Tell your mother I'm doing her hair, too. I don't want to take the risk that she might stick something weird in it. Seriously, I love Bethany to pieces, but I really don't want her wearing one of her craft projects on top of her head."

This wedding had become a Carter family affair. I was performing the ceremony, my mother was to be Adrianna's matron of honor, and my father was walking the bride down the aisle. Josh was doing double duty. Besides serving as Owen's best man, he was catering the reception. Digger was going to help in the kitchen, but I had no idea how Josh was going to coordinate the food preparation while simultaneously being a member of the wedding.

We watched *Veronica Mars* on DVD while Ade began blowing out my hair. "Oh, ick, Chloe! Look at your roots!" My highlights had grown out enough to horrify the bride-to-be. Consequently, after my hair was thoroughly dry, she started covering my head with foils and lightener. "And you need a trim. Your hair has got no shape left in it."

I resigned myself to sitting in one spot for the next few hours while Adrianna brought my hair up to her wedding standards. After toying with a variety of complicated updos involving curls and twists pinned to my scalp, Adrianna decided on a looser, more flowing style with gently shaped curls that would work beautifully with her simple veil. When the predicted hours had finally passed and I was finally allowed to look in the mirror, I was speechless. I'd almost forgotten about the veil affixed to my head. I'd never before worn a veil, and I have to say that all of a sudden, I was a princess! I was about to start twirling when Ade saw me wide-eyed in the mirror. "Don't get all dopey on me now. Let's get through *my* wedding first. You look like a lovesick puppy."

"It's just so fun to wear a veil. There's really no good excuse for wearing a veil except for when you're a bride, so let me enjoy myself for two minutes. Please?" I was *so* not taking off the veil. A short headband piece that had been wrapped in bright white material was affixed to the top of my head, and sheer layers of fabric fell to just below my shoulders. I looked at my reflection and imagined myself traipsing down the aisle, headed toward wedded bliss with my chef.

"All right," she agreed. "But don't get anything on it."

I crossed my heart with my finger. "Promise. Hey, I'm going into Simmer for dinner tonight. You want to come?" I leapt up and down the narrow hall, letting the veil fly out behind me, while Adrianna shook her head at my lunacy.

"No, thanks. Owen is going to be home soon, and I want to take a nap, and then we're finally going to put the crib together."

The baby's room was actually a walk-in closet with a window and a radiator. Once a crib was in there, it would occupy so much space that there might not be room for an adult to stand. To get the kid into the crib, Adrianna and Owen would be able to open the door and toss the baby in. But how would they ever get the baby out?

"Come here," Adrianna said. "Let me do your makeup, too, and then you'll really knock Josh's socks off tonight."

I reluctantly let Ade remove the veil. By the time she'd painted my face with M•A•C cosmetics, I was ready for this in-home salon to close. I hugged her good-bye, thanked her for the spectacular job she'd done on my hair, and rubbed her belly.

I went home and admired my newly blonde-streaked hair in my own mirror. My scruffy clothes looked silly with my fancy hair and makeup, but I didn't care. Adrianna had certainly cheered me up and distracted me from dwelling on Francie. And tonight I would see Josh! I tried to take a short nap, but visions of Francie danced unpleasantly in my head. The ringing of the phone rescued me from the atrocious images. Caller ID showed my favorite number.

"Hi, Josh," I said happily into the phone. "How's it going there?"

"Good. Good," he answered. "Um, how are you?"

"You know, as well as can be expected after yesterday."

"So . . . what else is going on? You know . . . you doing anything?" Josh sounded strange.

"No," I answered hesitantly. "Josh, is something up?"

"What? Oh, no. It's just, um, do you want a cat?"

"A cat? No, not really. I already have Gato. Why? Do you know someone giving away a cat?"

"Sort of. Yeah. This guy is giving away this Persian cat, and . . ." Josh's voice trailed off.

"Spit it out, Josh."

Josh coughed. "When I went out to get a coffee on my break, I walked past this guy outside the T station who was stopping people and asking them if they wanted a cat. He stopped me, too. He said he just broke up with his girlfriend and moved, and he didn't want the cat anymore, so he was trying to give it away."

"Josh, I'm sure someone will take it. Especially a Persian. Or he'll take it to a shelter."

"Maybe," Josh said skeptically.

"Josh?"

"Yeah?"

"Josh, did you take the cat?"

There was a long, long pause. "Yeah."

I sighed. As much to myself as to Josh, I said, "You took the cat." Turning practical, I asked, "Where are you? You didn't bring it into the restaurant, did you?"

"No, I'm sitting in my car behind Simmer, and it's in a cat carrier next to me."

"Oh, my God." Josh was hardly ever at his own apartment. He certainly wasn't there enough to take care of another living creature. In other words, I knew whose cat this was going to be.

"Chloe, I asked the guy what he was going to do with the

cat if nobody took it, and he said he was going to throw it in the river! The Charles River is only a few blocks from here, and I think he was serious." Josh was talking a mile a minute now. "He was a totally normal-looking guy, too, which was weird, but he said it was his ex-girlfriend's cat, and they broke up, and he didn't want to deal with it, and so I took it. Her, actually. She's a girl. And she is so beautiful. She's got white fur and orange ears, and she's just sitting here looking at me, and I feel so bad for her."

I was momentarily torn. On the one hand, I was irritated with Josh for taking in this strange cat that would end up with me. On the other hand, I felt overwhelmed with appreciation of how sweet and adorable my boyfriend was. How many men would even have stopped to listen to some idiot on the street trying to give away a cat? And Josh hadn't just listened but had gone on to rescue the cat from her heartless owner.

"Do you know how old she is? Has she been to the vet?" I asked.

"He said she's not even a year old. And I don't know if she's been to the vet, but I sort of doubt it. Her fur is all matted, Chloe, and she looks so scared and sad. I had to take her."

I smiled. "Of course you did. Should I come get her?"

"I guess I could take her to a shelter if you don't want—"

"No!" I cut him off. "We are not taking her to a shelter. Do you know how overcrowded those places are? Who knows what would happen to her! I'll come get her."

I was suddenly excited. In the wake of Francie's death, I suddenly had a new pet, a rescued cat to smother with love. I kissed my quirky black cat, Gato, and did my best to explain to him what was about to happen. "Now listen, mister.

Someone is moving in with us, and you're not going to like her right away. I accept that. But I expect you to be on your best behavior nonetheless."

Gato rubbed his head against my cheek, swatted my hair, and then ran off. Maybe a feline companion was just what he needed.

NINE

I flew down Newbury Street into the heart of Boston, my heart racing with eagerness at the prospect of meeting my new housemate. I pulled into the alley behind Simmer and parked next to Josh's car.

"Hi, babe." He grinned sheepishly at me. "You're the best."

"No, you're the best. I love that you saved her from a Sopranos-style death. Let me see her!" I demanded happily.

Josh reached into his car, lifted out a beige plastic cat carrier, and gently lowered it to the pavement. I bent down, peered through the little wire door of the carrier, and found myself looking into the round blue eyes of a small white cat with a darling little smooshed-in face. Eager to get a better look and also eager not to get scratched, I asked, "Do you know if she's friendly?"

"Oh, yeah," Josh said with a smile.

Careful to avoid giving the little cat the chance to escape, I eased open the wire door and tentatively reached in. After giving the cat a few seconds to adjust to the presence of my hand, I stroked her face. When I reached in and gently touched her back, my hand encountered a heartbreaking combination of thick mats and palpable bones. "Oh, Josh! The poor cat!" I said angrily as I removed my hand and closed the carrier door. "Look at her fur! She's never been groomed. And she's starving. What kind of monster would do this? That bastard!"

"I know. I know. That's why I had to take her. But look at her gorgeous blue eyes! She's so sweet, too, Chloe. I took her out and let her walk around in my car, and she let me hold her. She even started purring a little bit." Josh's eyes were glistening. "So, you'll keep her?"

"Yes, I'm going to keep her! This poor thing has had a rotten life so far, and we're not going to let anything else happen to her. Ever! I'll take her to the vet and get her checked out and make sure she's okay."

"I'm really sorry, but I have to get back to work. Gavin is going to kill me as it is for taking such a long break. I'll still see you tonight, though, right?" Josh handed me the cat carrier and kissed me, lingering just a bit. "Thanks, Chloe." He turned and bounded up the back steps to the restaurant.

"Hey, Josh," I called, "what's her name?"

"The jerk didn't say. But she told me her name was Inga." He grinned and disappeared into the restaurant.

I lifted the carrier up to eye level and looked into those amazing blue eyes. "Inga, huh? It actually suits you. Come on, Miss Inga, let's get you out of here."

I called Gato's vet as I maneuvered my way through the downtown traffic. Once I'd given the receptionist a capsule version of Inga's story, she agreed to have the vet see the cat right away. As much as I wanted to take little Inga home immediately, I knew it would be unfair to Gato to expose him to whatever bizarre cat disease the neglected Inga might be carrying. And if she had fleas? Well, neither Gato nor I wanted them.

An hour later, Inga and I arrived at my Brighton condo. Aside from being severely underweight and in need of spaying, Inga seemed to be fine. When the vet had subjected her to shots and had taken a blood sample for tests, she'd peed all over the vet's assistant and squirmed so much that she'd pulled out one of the needles and spattered herself with blood. The tests were still being run, but for the moment, she was given a clean bill of health, and I'd been told that it was safe to take her home.

When I arrived in my apartment, opened the carrier door, and released Inga, Gato acted downright furious. He took one look at Inga, put up his hackles, leapt to the top of the fridge, and positioned himself in his favorite pissed-off Halloween-black-cat stance. I sat the frightened Inga on a towel in my lap and tried to work on getting the knots out of her fur. After only a few minutes with a metal grooming comb, I gave up. Her body was covered in matted snarls that almost seemed to grow like tumors from her skin. I imagined that she must be terribly uncomfortable; I knew how I'd feel if some mean person were yanking my hair twenty-four hours a day. "You will have to go to a groomer tomorrow, my little friend." Unready to get up and explore her new home, Inga remained motionless in my lap.

I ran my hand across the top of her head and scratched under her chin, the only places without tangled clumps. "I couldn't help Francie, but I can help *you*." The little cat rewarded me with a small purr. In spite of a disapproving glare from Gato, I offered Inga a small dish of his dry cat food. When she had eaten hungrily, I carried her to the living room, flicked on the television, and held her until it was time to get ready to go out for dinner.

Newbury Street, where Simmer was located, isn't just any old ordinary Boston street. Especially around Simmer, near the Boston Public Garden—home of the Swan Boats and the setting of *Make Way for Ducklings*—it's lined with art galleries, high-end clothing stores, fancy cafés, and trendy restaurants. On my graduate-student budget, I couldn't afford the outfits that would've let me be mistaken for one of the beautiful people who spent money on Newbury Street, but I did change into something more worthy of Simmer's fancy location than the hanging-around-and-grooming-a-cat clothes that I had on. In other words, I wore black. Because I was hesitant to leave Inga alone with my cranky Gato, I'd put her in my bedroom with food, water, and a litter box, and shut the door. I wouldn't be gone all that long, and I hoped that she'd eat and take a good nap while adjusting to her new, safe home.

Then I drove downtown and scanned the street for a space. Parking in this congested area of Boston was always a challenge, but it was a bit easier on a Tuesday night than it would've been on a Saturday night. It had been a while since I'd eaten at Simmer, but with Josh's work schedule what it was, visiting him at the restaurant was sometimes the only way to catch a glimpse of my overworked chef. I had Inga to thank for the rare chance to see him twice in one day. Since the parking garages and lots in the area were breathtakingly expensive, I'd gotten good at spotting legal spaces on the street, at finding spots on side streets, and at squeezing my car into miniature spaces. Tonight I snagged a place around the corner from the restaurant. I had to pin myself between two BMWs, but getting an actual metered space at all was a good sign.

The patio outside Simmer was packed, but inside there were only a handful of customers. Although Josh said Mondays and Tuesdays were typically slow nights at most eateries, I found it disheartening to see the large room so empty. The tiled floors and the warm colors of the walls softened the angularity of the modern light fixtures, the square tables, and the high-backed chairs. The room's earth colors were welcoming, and I was pleased to see candles lit on each table and in sconces on the walls. Keeping candles in stock and replacing the ones that burned down was a challenge. Simmer used dozens every day, and no one who worked there wanted to add candle duties to the already long list of tasks to be done daily.

I waved to the hostess and helped myself to a seat at the bar. I wished that Ade had come with me. Eating out alone was lonely, but if I'd stayed home, I'd have moped in front of the television by myself watching Bret Michaels in reruns of *Rock of Love*.

The general manager, Wade, strolled behind the bar and checked for empty bottles. Because Wade was salaried, he often ended up working the bar so that the owner, Gavin, didn't have to pay another employee. "Hey, Chloe. I haven't seen you here in a while. You here for dinner?"

I nodded. "You know I can't resist Josh's cooking." I smiled, partly at the thought of Josh's feeding me and partly at the sight of the elaborate gel work formed by Wade's dark hair. Wade's hair was always a sight to gawk at, if not to admire. Today, he must have taken extra time to sculpt the poofy clumps that sat high off his scalp. Still, since Wade spent as much time working out at the gym as he did styling his hair, I couldn't complain about how he looked in the fitted black T-shirt that was standard for Simmer employees.

Wade handed me a menu, and I scanned the familiar items. At one time or another, I must have tried everything on the menu, but I never tired of the food. Besides, in addition to the standard dishes, there were specials that Josh ran a few times a week. They were always wonderful, but tonight I was hungry for two of my favorites from the regular menu, the crab and corn fritters that came with a lemon-cilantro aioli, and a Caesar salad with homemade dressing. Josh's Caesar dressing was based on egg yolk and anchovies. I could practically drink it by the bucket. He also offered a less fishy—and very popular—version for those who didn't like the strong anchovy taste, but I preferred the powerful version.

Wade took my order, brought me a lemonade, and told me that Josh would be out in a few minutes. As I watched Wade shine glasses with a towel, I started wondering what Josh had told his coworkers about the filming yesterday, but my thoughts were interrupted by Gavin Seymour's unhappy voice.

Simmer's owner was glaring angrily at a server. Gavin was in his late thirties, quite handsome, and dressed exclusively in clothing purchased from the high-end shops on this street. His usually toned physique looked neglected, though, and even his overpriced outfit couldn't hide that. "Now what is it?" Gavin demanded of a quivering young male server. "Can't we ever get anything done around here without a problem?" Gavin stormed away from the server and beckoned to Wade.

Before responding to Gavin's summons, Wade rolled his eyes and imitated Gavin. "Now what is it?" he echoed with an exaggerated whine.

Although Gavin caught my eye, he otherwise ignored me and, after speaking briefly to Wade, he disappeared into the kitchen.

I turned away and glanced uncomfortably at Wade, who was again polishing glasses.

"Don't worry about Gavin. He's all worked up tonight. Everyone is trying to stay out of his way today because he's in such a salty mood. I guess some guy from the Department of Public Health came in to talk to Josh." Wade shrugged.

If DPH was wandering around Simmer, the staff must know something about the disastrous *Chefly Yours* episode. "What did he want with Josh?" I asked.

"I guess to find out more about the food he'd made for the show. I was sorry to hear about that, by the way. Really sucks. Anyhow, Josh told Gavin that the issue had nothing to do with Simmer, but Gavin has been insisting all day that if it has to do with Josh, then it has to do with Simmer. 'I'm not interested in excuses, Josh,' is what Gavin must have hollered twenty times." Wade again mimicked Gavin and waved his hands around in no-no gestures. "Whatever. Gavin will get over it. Everyone is just trying to steer clear of him today."

Josh appeared with a plate of the deep-fried corn and crab treats. "Hi, babe," he said, kissing me on the cheek. Josh looked more worn-out than usual but, as always, he was putting on a happy front for my benefit. Flipping a dish towel over his shoulder, he covered half of a huge food stain on his once-white chef's coat. "How is Inga?"

I briefed Josh on the vet visit and explained that Inga would need some serious time with a cat groomer, who, I hoped, would get out the mats in Inga's coat without shaving her entire body. "She's had enough humiliation for one lifetime. I couldn't bear to see her with no fur."

"I'm just glad she's alive and not at the bottom of the Charles," Josh said. "Oh, guess who called me today?"

"Who?" I asked through a mouthful of fritter. I loved the fritters, with the crispy batter fried to perfection on the outside and the gooey, creamy crab mixture on the inside. Heaven on a plate.

"Two calls, actually. Robin and then Leo."

I nearly choked. "What did they say?"

"Well," he began, perching himself on the stool next to me, "Robin is insisting that the series won't be affected by what happened. She says we'll just tape another episode." He raised his eyebrows in doubt. "I don't know how she thinks this isn't going to be a problem. I mean, word is going to get out about Francie, the show, and me. No one is going to want me to go to their house after hearing that I'm the one who killed Francie—"

"Josh! Don't say that. You know that's not how it was." I put my hand on his and gave a good squeeze.

"I know, I know. Obviously I didn't kill her, but I'm going to be associated with her death, and that's less than appetizing, so to speak. So it's not going to be smooth sailing." He paused. "Maybe if the television station makes a public statement? If we can really clear up what happened, then things might blow over for the show. I don't know." Josh exhaled deeply. "Oh, and then Leo called the restaurant an hour ago to get your phone number."

I wrinkled my brow. "He wants to talk to me?"

Josh nodded. "He said he wants to talk to you about Francie. I hope it's okay, but I gave him your number."

Ugh. If Leo wanted to hear about Francie's last moments, what could I possibly tell him? "Yeah, that's fine."

"There's more. He told me that it turns out that Francie had definitely been poisoned and that the police are involved.

So it wasn't food poisoning. It wasn't something I did or bought. I knew that, but it's a relief to have it confirmed."

"So she *was* poisoned! What was it?" I nearly shouted. "This means Francie was murdered for sure. Who did it? Have the police talked to you?"

"Leo didn't say what the poison was. He said that the police are investigating who could have done it. A detective called me earlier, and I'm going to talk to him tomorrow morning, but I'm pretty much in the clear since practically every second of that day is on film. And I don't have any motive. So I'm not worried."

Josh might not be worried, but I was—and would be until Francie's murderer was locked up in a cell. Why would someone murder Francie? And during Josh's cooking episode?

"I have to get back to the kitchen. Gavin made me send home all the hourly employees, so I'm alone except for Santos tonight. I'll go make your salad and get that out to you in a few minutes. Love you." Josh kissed me again.

"I love you, too."

I took a big drink of my lemonade and tried to process what I had just learned: Francie had been poisoned. Someone had intentionally killed that poor woman and let her die a painful, grotesque death. I shivered. Lost in thought, I jumped at the sound of a dish breaking behind me.

"Your job isn't that hard. It's quite simple, really." Gavin's voice echoed throughout the restaurant as he marched across the floor. "Pick up dishes. Take them to the kitchen. Seriously, it's not tough. Break another dish, and I'll take it out of your check."

I spun around on my stool. Standing before Gavin was a young Brazilian busboy who held a plastic tub filled with dirty dishes. The busboy hung his head while Gavin continued his tirade.

"Do you know how much those dishes cost? Do you? Clean up this mess and get out of my sight."

Aha! I finally got it. To my surprise, I realized that Gavin was drunk. I could hear it in his voice. Josh's boss wasn't normally my favorite person, but he and I had no problems with each other, and he had always been pleasant to me. According to Josh, Gavin could be tough to work for, but Josh had never mentioned anything like what I was seeing and hearing now. Yelling at a busboy? Creating a drunken scene that was bound to drive customers away? Never. Or never before.

"Like I was saying," Wade said as he refilled my lemonade, "best to stay out of Gavin's way today."

After what I'd just witnessed, I was hardly going to get *in* Gavin's way. Avoiding him was evidently going to be easy, since he was continuing to ignore my existence. When he appeared a few seats down from me at the bar and leaned over the counter to grab some lime slices for his drink, he barely looked my way before dropping lime into his cocktail and again disappearing.

"What's going on with him?" I asked Wade.

"Oh, you know, typical owner bullshit." He spoke while he adjusted his gelled hair in the mirror that walled the back of the bar. "Josh must have told you some of it, though, right? Gavin has been hanging out here after hours with customers, drinking free from the bar, going home with college girls, snorting a little here and there. He's become a pain in the ass."

What? I'd heard none of this from Josh. And using cocaine? Stupid, stupid. "No wonder he's so moody, then, huh?"

Wade leaned against the bar. "No kidding. We can always tell when Gavin's been here late at night, because we open the restaurant to find dirty glasses, spilled drinks, half-finished beers. Then we have to clean the place again after the night crew already did it. It's disgusting. Plus, Gavin is losing money on all that alcohol he's drinking, and then he complains about having to reorder more liquor. I just ignore him."

A waitress brought out my Caesar salad, but it was hard to enjoy it as much as I usually did. In fact, it occurred to me that most of what I was being served tonight was one piece of bad news after another. What happened next confirmed that impression: Gavin popped out of the kitchen, again summoned Wade with a gesture, spoke to him for a few seconds, and then slumped down at the end of the bar and pulled out his cell phone. Wade returned to me with an apologetic look on his face. "I'm sorry, Chloe, but Gavin is making me give you a bill for your dinner. He says he's tired of his staff bleeding him dry."

I'd never before paid for dinner at Simmer. Gavin had never expected me to pay. And it wasn't as though I were in here every day ordering lobster and foie gras. All along, from the time Simmer had first opened, I'd assumed that Gavin knew how hard Josh was working to make Simmer a success and that Gavin saw my occasional meals as a small symbol of thanks. Hah! Apparently not.

I finished my salad, thundered off the stool, slammed my purse on the counter, and pulled out some cash. Gavin showed zero reaction, but Wade absolutely refused the tip I tried to give him.

"I always tip, even when the food is free," I protested. "Wade, please!"

Although Gavin was still at the far end of the bar, Wade spoke softly. "Not tonight. Consider it my apology for Gavin's behavior."

"If Gavin continues acting like this in front of customers,

pretty soon he's not going to have any." I thanked Wade again, grabbed my purse, and rushed out of Simmer.

Josh always painted a pretty picture of everything about the restaurant, but over the past few months I'd been learning more and more about the downside to life at Simmer. Despite Gavin's early promise that when Simmer began to do well, Josh would do well, there'd been no improvement in Josh's brutal schedule or in his pay. On the contrary, although Simmer had now been open for eight months and had, I thought, done very well, it seemed to me that Gavin's demands on Josh were becoming more extreme and more unfair than ever. I wondered how long Josh would put up with his increasingly impossible boss.

Ten

I spent Wednesday morning at home going over rain barrel orders, of which there were a surprisingly large number. Considering that this summer had been my first attempt at jumping into the world of sales, I was pretty pleased with how many barrels I had sold. Of course, I hadn't done it alone. Each time my parents landed a new landscaping job, they sent me to meet with the client to suggest the addition of an environmentally responsible rain barrel to the project.

Because my parents ran an eco-friendly company, many of the clients were receptive. These were people who lived in Boston's wealthy suburbs, where environmentalism was just beginning to influence landscape design and maintenance. Many of them had seen Al Gore's film and were aware of the environmental impact of traditional landscaping and lawn care. Noise pollution was impossible to miss. There were days when I went to my parents' house and found that we could barely have a conversation over the roar of the leaf blowers and gigantic lawn mowers that attacked the neighbors' yards. Those machines guzzled gas. And then there were the ubiquitous sprinkler systems that sprayed water on every available surface, including sidewalks and streets, at preset times, even during torrential rainstorms.

My parents discouraged large, water-hungry lawns. They encouraged clients to plant shrubs and flowers that could survive with minimal watering, to install solar lighting, and even to make compost. As much as possible, Mom and Dad used recycled materials and herbal pesticides and herbicides. Fortunately, Jack and Bethany Carter's switch to green design had been good for their business. Environmentally friendly gardening did not come cheap, but in their affluent area, homeowners could afford to go green.

And I was enthusiastic about something related to school! I'd spent my first year of social work school frustrated, irritated, and lost. My uncle Alan had stuck a clause in his will that required me to get a master's degree in anything in order to receive my inheritance. The requirement, which had originally felt outrageous, was finally beginning to make sense. I'd been floundering through my early twenties, and it turned out that forcing me into school was the kick I needed to get me focused. Although a lot of the students at social work school were exclusively interested in one-on-one counseling and mental health, the school pushed us to get involved in what was called "organizational social work," a field that included politics and larger social issues that trickled down to affect individuals on a daily basis. I'd discovered this summer that the one-on-one therapy tricks I'd acquired this year were incredibly helpful in talking with landscaping clients about their plans. Using my newfound people skills, I engaged clients in discussions about water conservation without sounding like an annoying, pushy salesperson who was just trying to make money.

I leafed through the pending jobs. A few of the clients were going to have prefab rain barrels installed and didn't mind the large green plastic containers that would catch water from the gutters. Most clients, however, were going to have our new carpenter, Emilio, build encasements to cover the unsightly barrels. I hadn't yet met Emilio, but from what I'd heard, he could do just about anything. In particular, he worked with eco-friendly materials and was skilled at making the barrels blend in with a house and its garden design. I was meeting up with my mother and Emilio later at my parents' house, after I dropped Inga off at the Fancy Feline, a nearby cat groomer. The owner, Glenda, had promised me on the phone that she'd try to preserve as much of Inga's fur as possible.

As I was reviewing the rain barrel projects that needed to be installed first, the phone rang. I reached behind me and blindly picked up. "Hello?"

I heard a man clear his throat. "I'm trying to reach Chloe. Chloe Carter."

"Speaking," I said as I scanned the installation requirements for a house in Needham.

"Oh, hi. Chloe, this is Leo. From the other day." He spoke unsteadily.

I dropped my papers. "Leo. My . . . my gosh, how are you?" Under normal circumstances, I don't go around saying *my gosh*. The circumstances of Francie's death had, of course, been anything but normal. "I mean, how are you holding up?"

"I guess I'm doing the best I can. I'm not sure if the shock has worn off yet."

"Well, I'm awfully sorry about Francie. I don't even know what to say. Of course you're still in shock. Josh said you might call. Is there something I can help you with?"

"Actually, there is. You were with Francie upstairs. You were the last person to see her before she lost consciousness and then . . ." His voice trailed off. "I am just wondering what she might have said. Did she have any . . . ? Did she . . . I don't know. Did she say anything?"

I shut my eyes and tried to invent something comforting or profound to pass along. In truth, Francie's last words had been "Oh, shit," whereas it seemed to me that her poor husband needed her to have said, "Tell Leo I love him," or, "It's okay. I've lived a long, wonderful, fulfilling life with the man I adore." Not only would Francie's actual last words fail to ease Leo's sorrow, but who in her right mind would want to be remembered for Francie's real exit line?

I racked my brain for what to say to Leo. The first thing that came to mind was what Oscar Wilde had reputedly said on his deathbed: "Either that wallpaper goes or I do." I sighed. The walls of the fatal bathroom, so to speak, hadn't even had wallpaper, and if they'd been covered with some ghastly palm-and-flamingo pattern, Leo would hardly find solace in learning that Francie had departed this life while expressing discontent with the home they had shared. It suddenly came to me that someone—who?—had sat bolt upright on his deathbed and demanded, "Who is that?" Francie had been far too weak to sit up and had shown no sign of perceiving the approach of the Grim Reaper. Even so, I went ahead and attributed the words to her.

"She said that?" Leo asked dubiously. "Wasn't that what Billy the Kid said?"

Damn. "Maybe she was quoting him. Or maybe she imagined she'd been shot." I did my best to backpedal. "She wasn't terribly lucid. And of course, I didn't know her well. Maybe she was making a joke." There. That put a positive spin on it!

"Francie had many . . . many good qualities. But a sense of humor really wasn't one of them." Leo paused. "Maybe she was asking who poisoned her? Or asking who you were? Or who Death was?"

"Well, if Billy the Kid was serious, I guess that she might've been, too. But, yes, she certainly might have been asking who poisoned her." I took the opportunity to gather information. "Leo, do you know what the poison was?"

"I'm told that it was something called digitalis. That's what the autopsy showed."

I talked with Leo for a few more minutes but managed to hang up before I had to lie about anything else. Thank God he hadn't asked me whether Francie had suffered. I wouldn't have been able to tell him the truth about that, either: that she had indeed suffered an excruciating, humiliating death, a death that was apparently the result of digitalis poisoning.

What was digitalis, anyway? I had a half hour before I had to go to my parents' house to meet with them and with Emilio. I Googled *digitalis* and quickly scanned Web pages for information. According to the first few pages I read, digitalis was a drug used mainly to treat congestive heart failure and some arrhythmias. Could someone with access to the food have added digitalis to one of the ingredients or dishes? Did anyone with access to the food have a heart problem? Everyone was too young for heart failure, I thought, and I'd noticed no one who seemed less than healthy. An arrhythmia? That condition might not be obvious. But what did I know? I was in social work school rather than medical school. I did know that Owen and his brothers had grandparents who lived near Boston. Maybe one of them was taking digitalis? It would've been just like Willie or Evan to swipe some of a grandparent's medication to use in playing a practical joke.

I called Adrianna under the pretense of asking about Saturday's wedding shower and baby shower and also about the wedding itself.

"I think we're in good shape for the wedding," she said. "Josh is doing the food, we have our dresses, the music will play over the speakers, and we've solicited various people to take pictures for us. No way would I pay some professional photographer five grand for a wedding album. With everything you can do to digital pictures on the computer, I think we'll end up with great photos. And the shower is all set, too. I told your mom I wanted to keep it pretty simple and low-key. I'll have enough to worry about with my deranged mother in town. I think the brunch idea was perfect. That way it won't turn into an all-night event with everyone drunk and dancing on couches."

"Will Owen's mother be there?" I asked in my most casual voice.

"Yeah, his mother, grandmother, a few cousins, I think. Grampa will be at the wedding. Why?"

"Just wondering. I know he has a big family."

"You're not kidding. Owen's mother, Eileen, isn't totally happy about everything, but he thinks she'll come around. The family as a whole is pretty relaxed, but Eileen is more traditional and still not completely rooting for me. The rest of them are all so excited about the baby that I'm afraid I might not even see my own kid for the first year. They've all got plans for holidays and birthdays, and they're fighting over who gets to take the kid to Disney World first. Nut jobs," she said, but I could hear the affection in her voice.

"That's great, though, Ade. Your baby is going to have so

many people in his life that love him. Or her. I can't believe you haven't found out if it's a boy or a girl!"

"Yeah, Owen's losing his mind over that, but I want to be surprised. All I care about is if the baby is healthy."

"Of course," I agreed. "You don't have any reason to worry though, right? Is there, you know, any family history that you need to worry about?"

"What do you mean?"

"Oh, you know . . . diabetes, heart disease. Anyone in the family with a condition like that? Anything treated with medication?"

"What? Are you saying my baby is going to be born with a congenital heart defect? What a sick thing to suggest!"

"No! No!" I was backpedaling again today. "I'm sorry! I didn't mean that at all. It's just, don't they ask you family history stuff when you get pregnant? I didn't know if there was anything you were worried about."

"Oh. Well, no. There's nothing. Not that I know of. Everyone in Owen's family seems to live well into their nineties. They're all healthy as horses. What the hell is wrong with you?"

"Seriously, Ade. I'm sorry. I really didn't mean to alarm you." God, I was an idiot. "I know your baby is going to be the most gorgeous, healthy, bouncing baby in the world. I don't know what I was thinking."

I hung up feeling appropriately mortified; I had really messed that up. In simply trying to find out whether Evan or Willie had had access to heart medication, I'd unintentionally suggested that there might be something frighteningly wrong with Ade and Owen's baby.

Especially after that fiasco, I wasn't about to call up everyone who'd been present at the filming to inquire about family health histories. Besides, the only person there I knew well enough to interrogate was Josh, who would be willing to answer any weird, prying questions I might ask but who would never, ever have poisoned food he was preparing. He'd never met Francie before and had had no reason to kill her. And if—inconceivably—he ever did decide to murder someone, he'd use a gun or a knife or any other weapon except the food in which he took such pride. I'd met Digger before the filming, but I knew him only as one of Josh's chef friends. When I'd been with Josh and Digger, they'd traded anecdotes about restaurants where they'd both worked and about the local restaurant scene. It was possible, I guessed, that Josh knew something about Digger and his family. Not that I was aching to prove that Digger was a poisoner! But Francie's death had been no accident. Furthermore, her killer had been willing to risk having any of the rest of us eat the poisoned food and die, too. Some us had been sick. For the first time, it occurred to me that the murderer had benefited from having people besides Francie get sick. When the police and the EMTs had arrived, it had been easy and natural for them to assume that the cause of Francie's death and other people's illness was food poisoning. I had a vivid image of Josh and me as we'd cleaned up the kitchen. Unknowingly, we'd been tossing out evidence! But the food wasn't the only evidence. That annoying Nelson had had his camera going almost every second. Who had his film now? Nelson himself? Robin? Or maybe the police?

I called Josh while I was in the bathroom putting on makeup. Besides wanting to see what I could learn about Digger, I wanted to hear Josh's voice.

"Yup?" Josh sounded as if we'd been in the midst of a conversation.

"Hi, honey. It's me."

"What's up, babe?"

"Not much. Inga is going to the Fancy Feline later to get cleaned up. And I just wanted to thank you for dinner last night. Everything was delicious, as always."

"Anytime. You know that."

Josh clearly didn't know that I'd paid for my dinner, and I wasn't about to break the news to my overstressed chef that Gavin was no longer letting him comp food. "Hey, I heard someone from the health department was in to see you yesterday. How did that go?" Leaning against the basin, I practically had my face in the mirror as I tried to apply mascara without dropping the phone. Driving isn't the only thing it's risky to do while having a phone conversation. Applying makeup has its hazards, too. I should probably get a hands-free phone for the bathroom.

"Oh, fine. He asked me a lot of questions about the fresh herbs that I used on Monday. What kinds I bought, did I use them all, did I use anything from Francie and Leo's house? Questions like that. Stupid questions, if you ask me, because there is no way anything I used was tainted. I told him the truth about everything, since obviously I have nothing to hide. I assume he's going to go check out Natural High and pull some of their produce and herbs, though. Hold on a sec." Josh must have covered the phone because I heard a very muffled *I told you not to dress the salads now because they'll be wilted by lunch. Come on!* Then Josh said to me, "Sorry, I'm back. Hey, has a detective called you yet? "

"No. Did someone call you?"

"Actually, a detective showed up while the health department guy was here. He made me run through every detail of the day. Nice guy, but I had to repeat the same answers three times while I was trying to work. He may call you, too, and I assume he'll talk to everyone else who was there."

"Josh, did the detective tell you . . . Josh, what killed

Francie was digitalis. It's a heart medicine. She was poisoned. Leo called me, and he told me. So, I hope they'd want to talk to everyone there. Do you know if they have the video footage? I was thinking there might be some useful evidence on there."

"The cops do have it. They made sure I knew they had it, and they reminded me I better be telling the truth, since they had a detailed record of the day."

So much for getting my hands on the video. I changed the subject. "Is everything going all right at Simmer? Gavin seemed to be in a bit of mood last night."

"Yeah, just the usual bs around here. It's all good."

"Seriously? Because it seems like things have been pretty rough for you there. I know Gavin has been riding you pretty hard about food and labor costs, and you're still working such long days—" I started.

"Look, I don't want to talk about this, but trust me. Everything's going to work out."

"If you say so," I said with some doubt. "Hey, it was good to see Digger the other day. Except for the circumstances, I mean. How's he been doing?" I asked.

"Good. Same old grind at his restaurant, too, but I think he's doing great."

"Oh, good. I guess I thought he looked a little off the other day," I hinted. "Even before everyone got sick. Kind of pale."

"Pale? Well, you know us chefs. No one gives us a day off to go relax in a hot tub or lie in the sun."

"I just thought maybe he wasn't feeling well. Maybe a virus." I cleared my throat. "Or a heart problem."

"What are you talking about? Digger doesn't have a heart problem, you kook." I recognized the sound of a pan hitting the professional-sized gas range in Simmer's kitchen.

"Oh, good. Is there anyone in his family with a heart condition? Maybe he should be careful about—"

"Are you out of your mind?" Josh started laughing. Meanwhile, I poked myself in the eye with the mascara wand, smearing dark brown goop all over my eyelid. "I don't know what you're up to, but Digger is the same as ever, and I don't know the slightest thing about his family. Is this about this poison? The heart medicine? Whatever you're doing, you're not being subtle. So, what's going on?"

"Um, nothing. Forget it. I don't want to talk about it yet."

"Chloe? Spit it out."

"Then tell me what's going on at Simmer," I countered.

"Fine." He laughed again. "We'll call it a draw."

"Agreed."

"Give Inga a kiss for me, and tell her I said good luck at the groomer's."

I shut down the computer, gathered my client files, and got Inga into her carrier. On the way to my car, I repeatedly assured Inga that everything she was about to endure was for her own good. Once we got to the Fancy Feline, the owner, Glenda, confirmed what I'd been telling Inga; Glenda was as horrified as I was about the state of Inga's coat. "What monster did this to you, sweetheart?" Glenda asked as she gently examined the little cat. But Glenda had goods news: she thought that she'd be able to shave off the mats rather than Inga's entire coat.

I apologized to Glenda for the blood and urine that remained on Inga. I'd done my best to get the mess out, but I'd wanted to avoid hurting or frightening her; I was playing good cop, and Glenda was stuck playing bad cop. When

Inga was back in her carrier, I poked a finger through the grated door and wiggled it at her. She looked pathetic and scrawny.

"I promise I'll come back for you. I promise." I wiped tears from my eyes as I left the shop.

ELEVEN

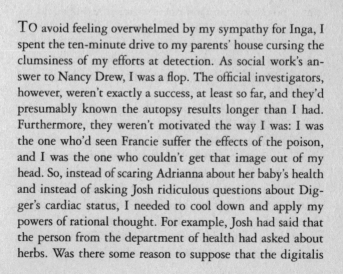

To avoid feeling overwhelmed by my sympathy for Inga, I spent the ten-minute drive to my parents' house cursing the clumsiness of my efforts at detection. As social work's answer to Nancy Drew, I was a flop. The official investigators, however, weren't exactly a success, at least so far, and they'd presumably known the autopsy results longer than I had. Furthermore, they weren't motivated the way I was: I was the one who'd seen Francie suffer the effects of the poison, and I was the one who couldn't get that image out of my head. So, instead of scaring Adrianna about her baby's health and instead of asking Josh ridiculous questions about Digger's cardiac status, I needed to cool down and apply my powers of rational thought. For example, Josh had said that the person from the department of health had asked about herbs. Was there some reason to suppose that the digitalis had been added to the herbs that Josh had used? Or was there some other connection between digitalis and herbs? I'd scanned only a few of the Web pages that my Google search had produced. I'd return to the task when I got home. In the meantime, I decided, I'd do my best to avoid discussing Francie's murder with my parents. Their house was going to be my safe harbor. My happy place.

My parents' white Spanish stucco house did look happy— or at least improbable and whimsical, belonging as it did in Santa Barbara, California, rather than where it actually was, in Newton, Massachusetts. I let myself in the front door and found my mother and a young man huddled over the dining room table. My mother, Bethany Carter, was decked out in virtually every piece of hideous jewelry she owned, and she owned a lot. I could never reconcile my mother's good horticultural taste with her astoundingly awful taste in almost everything else. Despite the vile adornments, my mother was a pretty woman, and not the tiniest wrinkle had appeared on her face, so I had high hopes for aging well. She'd recently cut her hair into a wash-and-wear style that fell in soft waves around her face and had colored it a chestnut brown to erase the four gray hairs that had dared to grow on her head.

Hearing me enter, she popped her head up. "Chloe, come meet Emilio. Emilio, this is my daughter, Chloe."

Whoa. Happy place, indeed! Emilio was hot. Not just good-looking or handsome but downright hot: sexy, rippling biceps, broad chest, dark skin, and a strikingly gorgeous face. Think Mario López meets John Stamos. All coherent thoughts flew out of my brain, and I stood there thunderstruck and mute as I fought off the mental video I'd inadvertently created of a tan, sweaty, half-naked Emilio playing beach volleyball to the *Top Gun* soundtrack.

Miraculously, my knees did not buckle out from under me as I stepped forward to shake Emilio's hand. "Hi, I'm Chloe," I said breathlessly. "Oh, my mother already said that. It's nice to meet me. You! I mean you! I already know me. Myself. I know myself, of course. Ha-ha!" I laughed idiotically. "Should we talk about rain barrels?"

When Emilio the God smiled, dimples appeared. As if this guy needed any more alluring physical traits! "It's really nice to meet you, Chloe." Although my mother had told me that Emilio was Colombian, he sounded totally American. If he'd had a Spanish accent, I'd have been totally gaga. "I heard you've drummed up a lot of business this summer," he continued. "I'm ready to get going on this with you."

"Yes, I'm ready to get going on you, too." *Oops.* "On the projects!" I said quickly. "I'm ready to get going on the rain barrels!" One hot guy, and I fell to pieces. *Get it together, Chloe!* I already had a good-looking boyfriend. But there was no denying that Emilio was more than drool-worthy.

Okay, I just wouldn't look at him.

"So," I started as I sat down next to Emilio and across from my mother, "Anna Roberts is our first client. She's going to have three rain barrels installed, and she'd like them to be enclosed in a rounded rock wall to match the existing rock walls she has in her yard." I handed Emilio the photos I'd taken of the house and grounds. I relied heavily on my digital camera for these projects, because my drawing skills were limited to stick figures, and sloppy ones at that. "Do you think you can come up with some sort of top to go with this? Maybe a wooden one that would coordinate with her deck? And something environmentally friendly, of course."

Emilio nodded enthusiastically. "Absolutely. I could do bamboo, for instance. That's a great wood to use because it's an easily renewable natural resource. There are also really beautiful materials made from recycled plastics that I could use. I can show Mrs. Roberts a few options and let her decide."

"Perfect."

My mother went into the kitchen to get us some lemonade, and I pulled out the next client's specifications. "So, Emilio, my mother told me that your family owns a large nursery and garden center nearby. My parents do business there. You came back to Boston after college?"

Emilio flashed his dimples. "That's right. One of my interests at Princeton was environmental studies, and after I graduated, I spent a year working with my family at their business. I did a lot of work on their property, finding ways to save energy and turn their business green. We actually won a local award from the Small Business Association." More dimples. "Then I spent a few years interning with an architect in Boston and learning about green design. It's amazing what can be done now with eco-friendly design. It used to be that anything made from recycled products was . . . something you wouldn't want to look at. But not anymore. So I wanted to bring some of what I'd learned back to my family's business and keep them on the cutting edge. The problem is still the initial investment costs, though. The people who can afford to install things like wind turbines and solar panels aren't the people who need four-dollar electric bills."

Handsome and politically conscious to boot. I could be in trouble.

I nodded in agreement. "You're right. We really need to get energy-efficient structures into low-cost housing areas. We need to get costs in the reach of the middle class. I think over time we'll see the costs come down, but for now it's the wealthy who are benefiting from these kinds of resources."

My mother returned with tall glasses of iced lemonade.

As she set a glass down in front of me, I noticed a hint of makeup on her usually bare face. Ah! Apparently my mother wasn't immune to Emilio's looks, either—hence her overzealous display of jewelry today, too. I was feeling a bit guilty for admiring Emilio, but knowing that my happily married mother wasn't resistant to his charms made me feel better. There was nothing wrong with looking, right?

Look but don't touch! Look but don't touch! I repeated in my head.

"Chloe, did you know Emilio's family is from Colombia? He's been a great translator for me. My Spanish is quite rusty. Last month I asked Fernando and Matias to dig an ocean in the Marberrys' backyard."

Emilio waved away my mother's compliment. "Glad to help, Mrs. Carter. Listen, I hate to rush us here, but I just moved into my new apartment. I'm right by the Hynes T stop, near Newbury Street and Mass. Ave. It's a cool location, even if the apartment is pretty small. Anyhow, I've got loads of work to get done there, and I'm hoping to finish unpacking today so I can start building tomorrow. Can we run through the other projects?" An apologetic Emilio looked hopefully at us.

"No problem," I said. "There are four more, and they are all pretty straightforward."

Fifteen minutes later, when we'd run through the last of the clients, Emilio left to finish his unpacking. "It was nice to finally meet the carpenter you've been talking about. He seems nice," I said casually to Mom.

"Yes, and isn't he positively gorgeous?" my mother said exuberantly.

"Mom!"

"Well, he is. There's no denying it. No harm in admiring, is there?" She took a sip of lemonade and skimmed over the schedule for constructing the rain barrels. "I guess he and his girlfriend just broke up, and he moved out of the apartment they shared. I'm sure it won't be long until he finds someone else, though."

"Probably not," I agreed.

"Are you and Josh doing all right?"

"Yes, we're fine," I said quickly. "Why would you even ask that?" I glared at her.

"Just checking. Emilio is a great catch, that's all. Don't misunderstand me, Chloe. I adore Josh, and I think you two have a wonderful relationship. It's just that I know how much he works, and I imagine that must take a toll on you. It's hard enough for couples who've been together for years, but you two have only been dating for a year. His schedule must present some challenges." Mom rose from her seat and picked up our glasses. "And that damn restaurant world is not the most conducive place for cultivating a romance, right? Josh is under tremendous stress a lot of the time, and I just hope you're not getting shortchanged in the relationship."

"I'm not. Everything is okay, Mom. I'm used to his schedule, and we always manage to find time for each other." At least we *tried* to find time for each other.

"Oh, did I tell you that Emilio and a couple of his cousins are going to help out at the wedding? They're going to carry out food, serve drinks, that sort of thing. I thought we'd need a few extra sets of hands, especially people who aren't in the wedding and aren't guests. Maybe Emilio can help Josh with the food, too."

Emilio and Josh. Josh and Emilio? An interesting combination. I shrugged my shoulders. "I think Josh will be fine. Digger will be here to help him out." Digger was not only Josh's friend, of course, but a chef who could be counted on to put out delicious food. Besides, I had no visceral reaction whatever to Digger, whereas the prospect of having Josh work next to the hunky Emilio was all too . . . visceral, let's say. "But we could definitely use Emilio's help with all the other work that will need to be done that day. Anyhow, I've got to get going. I have to go pick up Inga."

"Who is Inga?" my confused mother asked. "A new friend from school?"

I laughed and explained how Josh had rescued the white cat from death by Charles River. "She's at the groomer's right now. I'm just hoping the owner there didn't have to shave all her fur off."

"Josh is an angel, isn't he?" Mom said warmly.

I had to agree. Josh was an angel. I felt scummy for even noticing Emilio. Would Emilio ever save a pitiful cat from death? His dedication to finding solutions to a multitude of environmental crises might save the world, but I couldn't say for sure that he'd have rescued Inga.

But I did want to think so.

TWELVE

"HERE is Miss Inga!" Glenda beamed as she lifted the cat carrier onto the counter. "She looks like a whole new cat, doesn't she?"

She truly did. Even peeking through the grated door, I could see she looked clean and beautiful. "I told you I'd come back, little girl, didn't I?" I cooed to my cat.

I swear that there was gratitude in Inga's big blue eyes. Sticking a finger into the cage for her to smell, I felt her touch me with her wet nose. Then she rubbed her head against my finger.

"How was she, Glenda? Was she a monster?" I was sure that Inga had peed all over the groomer as she had the vet, but I was wrong.

"She was fine. No trouble at all. I think she knew I was trying to help her. Those were some nasty mats she had, but

I managed to just shave off the clumps and let her keep the rest of her coat."

"Thank you so much for fitting her in today. How much do I owe you?" I reached for my purse. Even though Glenda gave me a discount because of Inga's escape from death, I still shelled out a hefty sum. But my money bought me a clean cat no longer tormented by mats that yanked at her skin. As if to celebrate Inga's rehabilitation, Glenda had tied a silly pink bow between the little cat's ears. I waved thanks to Glenda and drove Inga back to my condo.

When we got home, Gato was sitting on the couch, but one look at Inga sent him back to the top of the fridge to mope. I knew that he'd come around in a few days, but I hated to see him even crankier than usual. Gato normally ate dry food, but I kept a small reserve of canned food for special occasions and bribes. I opened a can of salmon and chicken, dumped it in a bowl, and placed it on top of the fridge in an effort to cheer my boy up. Gato didn't share my opinion that the cat food smelled like garbage. On the contrary, it elicited a steady purr. As Gato scarfed down his meal, I reached up to pet his shiny black coat.

Then I went to my bedroom, which was the largest room in my small condo and hence doubled as a work space for school and for my summer job. Sitting at my desk, I checked my e-mail, sorted through a few messages about rain barrels, and decided to do another search for information about digitalis.

Wham! Digitalis was a genus of perennial plants, the most common being foxglove. As the daughter of two horticultural experts, I should have known! In fact, my parents would've been horrified to realize how little botanical information I'd absorbed over the years. In particular, I liked the common names of plants and had never bothered to learn botanical names. So, digitalis was a stranger, but foxglove was an old friend. I'd always adored the tall, spiked plants with their showy, tubular flowers.

Digitalis in the form of foxglove was obviously much easier to obtain than was digitalis in the form of a prescription medication. In fact, as I read about foxglove, I had to wonder why such a dangerous plant was positively all over the place: offered in seed catalogs, sold at garden centers, and grown in backyards. Every part of the foxglove was poisonous, and especially toxic were the leaves from the upper stem. The symptoms of having ingested foxglove were identical to those that Francie had shown. Furthermore, it had a strong, bitter taste. So that was why Josh's arugula pesto and lamb had tasted so putrid! Dear God, all of us who'd tasted it could have died! I remembered how sick Josh had been. It was a blessing that in vomiting up everything in his system, he'd rid himself of most of the poison.

Damn. Instead of pestering people about possible cardiac conditions, I should have been asking about gardening. My questions about heart problems and family health histories had been awkward and unwelcome, but gardening was an ordinary topic that was easy to introduce in a casual conversation. My mother was always saying that gardening was the most popular hobby in America. Had anyone present at Leo and Francie's house pursued the hobby?

Evan and Willie shared an apartment. I hadn't been there, but they could be growing foxgloves in pots on a balcony or in a yard, and they might well not have realized how lethal a practical joke involving digitalis could be. Leo and Francie's house had some kind of a disheveled garden, but I hadn't really paid attention to it except to notice that it was a weedy mess. Foxglove was a biennial rather than a perennial. In its first year, it produced leaves, but it didn't blossom until its second year. Then, I thought, it died. But it self-sowed. In other words, if someone had planted foxglove in Leo and Francie's yard a long time ago, the descendants of the original plants could still be growing there. Although it was obvious that neither Francie nor Leo had been maintaining the garden, Leo might have known all about foxglove and might have known that it was growing right outside his house. Murders were often family affairs, weren't they? They were on TV. So Leo had to be a suspect. What's more, the rest of us had just met Francie. What possible motive could Robin, Marlee, Digger, or Nelson have had for killing her? None, so far as I could tell. Except possibly Nelson? Not that the cameraman had had anything personal against Francie, but he'd certainly been the weirdest person there. He'd kept spouting off at the mouth about the power of reality television, and he'd ghoulishly kept filming when Francie had fallen ill and after she'd died. He'd even tried to film the aftermath of the poisoning in the ER. Could Nelson have killed Francie only to have "reality" to film? If Nelson was, in fact, the murderer, he probably hadn't cared which of us died. Maybe he'd even been disappointed to have only one victim. Sick thought, yes, but especially as a social-worker-to-be, I knew that there were sick people in the world.

I remembered something else potentially important. When Josh and I had both sampled some of the food before it had been served, there had been nothing wrong with it. But when we'd tasted the same food after Francie had complained so forcibly, it had been horrible. In between those two times, there'd been chaotic activity. The food had been served, returned to the kitchen, and served again. The scene at the dinner table had been filmed and filmed again. Everyone, or almost everyone, had had the opportunity to contaminate the food with poison. Marlee and Digger had handled the food when Robin and Nelson had accompanied them to the kitchen to reshoot the plates. Leo had had his hands all over the food, hadn't he? To complicate matters, it seemed possible that the digitalis had been added either to what was originally on Francie's plate or to one of the bowls or pans used to replenish her plate before the dinner-table scene was reshot.

It's typical of me that the thought of food, even food loaded with a fatal toxin, made me hungry. I was in the kitchen getting myself a snack when the phone rang. "Hello?" I managed between bites of garlic-stuffed olives. I really needed to go food shopping.

"Hi, Chloe. This is Robin. From the TV show."

"Robin. Hi. How are you?" I couldn't imagine why Robin was calling me.

"Fine. Fully recovered. Well, I'm fine considering the hellish week it's been. The station is having a fit about what happened. They're trying to spin it in a way that doesn't get our show off the air forever. It's a nightmare, actually. But the reason I'm calling is that I wanted to find out more about this wedding ceremony you're performing for your friend. Angelica, is it?"

"Adrianna. Adrianna and Owen."

"I thought I might be able to do a piece on getting a license to perform a wedding ceremony. It's such a fun idea that a friend of the couple can officiate. After Monday's disaster, I'm trying to find other pieces to do for the station in case they yank the chef series. This wedding business sounds like a great human interest story. I was thinking that we could film the wedding, if your friends don't mind. But maybe they already have a videographer."

On their budget, Ade and Owen most certainly did not have a videographer. My parents had mentioned the possibility, but there was no way that my friends would accept more than my parents were already paying for. Adrianna and Owen did, of course, want a video of their wedding, but all they intended to do was to shove a recording device into a guest's hands and hope for the best. "Robin, that would be wonderful," I said. "I'm really excited about doing this wedding. Ade and I have been friends for ages, and I just adore her. And Owen is a good friend of mine, too. I know they'd love to have you film their wedding. I don't even have to ask."

"Listen, I have to run, but how about we meet for dinner tomorrow? Have the bride and groom come with you, and I can talk to you more then about how you got licensed. I'll bring Nelson, and we can talk about filming the wedding."

Although I wasn't dying to spend an evening with that creepy Nelson, I was eager to find out more about him. What's more, sometime during the dinner, it would be easy to slip in a subtle reference to gardening and to find out whether Robin or Nelson had a garden.

"Okay," I agreed. "I'll have to run the idea by Adrianna and Owen first and make sure it's okay with them, but I'm sure they'll love it. Where do you want to have dinner?"

"Why don't we meet at Marlee's restaurant? Alloy, it's called."

"It's in the South End, isn't it?" So were dozens of other trendy restaurants.

"Yes. Tomorrow at seven? The food is fantastic. Very contemporary. You'll love it."

The choice of Alloy didn't surprise me, since Marlee was one of the chefs in rotation on *Chefly Yours*. I assumed that her food must be good. She was, after all, competing against Josh and Digger, both of whom I knew to be talented. "That sounds great. I'll see you there."

I scrounged around in the kitchen for something else to eat and came up with nothing good for dinner. Too bad I wasn't meeting Robin tonight.

I called Adrianna and explained Robin's idea for filming the wedding. "It wouldn't cost you a thing, and you'd have the entire day on tape. Isn't this cool?"

"That sounds really nice. Please tell Robin we accept her offer. But I'm not eating at Alloy, I can tell you that. I have a client who ate there once, and she said it was the worst."

The real reason for Adrianna's refusal suddenly occurred to me. "My treat," I said casually. Not that I had all that much money! But Ade and Owen had practically none.

"No, it's not that, Chloe. Really, she said that it was pretentious and snobby, superexpensive, and the food was nasty."

"Oh," I said, disappointed. If I was going to shell out money for a pricey dinner, I expected the food to be delectable. I hoped that Ade's client had lousy taste buds.

"Didn't you read the Mystery Diner's review a few months ago? He totally panned the place. Said it was one of the worst restaurant experiences he'd ever had. Not only was the food a disaster, but he wrote that it was dirty and probably broke every health code in the book."

The Boston Mystery Diner, who wrote a popular column for a local paper, was genuinely mysterious: nobody knew who he was. Josh told me that restaurant staff around the city were forever wondering, worrying that the patrons on a given evening included the elusive reviewer.

"I'm surprised he wasn't sued," I said. "I didn't see that one, but you know how unfair some of his reviews are. He said Pinnacle serves a revolting basket of fried clams, and I think it's the best seafood place in Boston."

"True enough," Ade agreed. "Can you imagine what an

awesome job that would be? Eating in restaurants with no one knowing who you are? And eating everywhere and having the paper pay the bills? I'd do that job in a heartbeat."

"Join the club. You sure you don't want to talk to Robin yourself?"

"No. I'm sorry, Chloe. I can't eat at that place after what I've heard. Besides, I'm too huge to leave the house. I'll probably end up having the baby in my apartment because they won't be able to push me out the doorway."

"Very funny," I said. In spite of Adrianna's joking and protestations, I remained half convinced that her real reason for refusing to come with me to Alloy was money. Or money and pride. I was sure that she already felt indebted to my parents and wanted to avoid feeling like an object of my charity. She was not, in fact, totally housebound. And Alloy was surviving in the South End, where competition among restaurants had to be ferocious. How bad could it really be? "Do you have any requests for how the wedding is filmed?" I asked. "Anything you want me to pass on to Robin or Nelson?"

"Tell them not to film my goddamned mother. I just know she's going to be difficult, and I don't need a visual reminder of her stinky attitude when I watch that video twenty years from now. If they accidentally get her on tape, have them put one of those blurry circles over her face and remove her voice from the audio. What's today? Wednesday? She's coming in on Friday, so the countdown to doom has officially started."

"Don't worry about her. There'll be enough people around to keep her under control," I assured Ade while reminding myself to designate someone to head the official Kitty Patrol.

I hung up and searched the Web for reviews of Alloy. The

ones I read were far from fantastic. A local arts and entertainment magazine called Alloy's food "undeveloped and mundane" but admitted that the dishes were helped by the bountiful use of fresh herbs. The reviewer was not ready to dismiss Alloy and hoped that time and experience would improve this little restaurant's fare. Online customer reviews were mixed, with some people raving about simple ingredients and dramatic presentations, and other people complaining about small portions and an overemphasis on elaborate style at the expense of flavor.

I looked up Alloy on Boston's Mayor's Food Court, a Web site that was, I thought, a bane to restaurants and a great boon to consumers. Posted on the site were the results of every Boston restaurant's health inspections, and not just general results, either, but details about every violation, no matter how minor. According to the home page, "The Mayor's Food Court provides consumers with current information about Boston's restaurants so that they can make informed decisions about where they will eat." In other words, I could make an informed decision not to eat at Restaurant X, which was infested with rodents and cockroaches, and routinely stored food at temperatures meant for growing a plethora of bacteria.

I have to admit that out of curiosity, I'd looked up Simmer a couple of times. Because Josh was an absolute fanatic about keeping his kitchen sterile and up to code, I'd never found any violations. As I soon discovered, Alloy, on the other hand, had been repeatedly cited for improper cooling of cooked or prepared foods, unsound equipment maintenance, toxic items not properly labeled, and evidence of—ewww!—rodents.

All I could think of was the Monty Python sketch about rat tart. Still, I absolutely couldn't cancel the dinner. One point of it was to get a free professional wedding video for Adrianna and Owen. Another was to ask about gardening and thus to find out who might be growing foxglove. The third point was frivolous: being in a "human interest story," to use Robin's phrase, would be a hoot. Being in? Well, as the official solemnizer, I wouldn't just be in the story, I'd be one of the stars. So rat tart or no rat tart, and Nelson or no Nelson, I had to go. I wondered whether Nelson would have his camera at the restaurant. From what I knew of him, I had to assume that yes, he would, so I'd better dress accordingly. Never having been the subject of a human interest piece before, I wasn't sure exactly what was involved, but if I was going to discuss my role as a one-day solemnizer at a wedding ceremony, I presumably shouldn't wear a tube top and stilettos.

I tried to reach Josh on his cell at Simmer but just got his voice mail and didn't feel like leaving a message. I parked myself on the couch, ordered in Thai food, and lamented the crummy schedule that kept Josh chronically exhausted and separated him from me.

While washing down yum nuah and drunken noodles with a few bottles of beer, I dealt with a phone call from the same detective who'd questioned Josh the other day. With my mouth half full of food, I reeled off my account of Francie's death to a man who sounded less interested in figuring out who had killed Francie than he was in learning where he, too, could get good Thai food. In his view, was her horrible death just one more murder? Or maybe the authorities felt hopeless about solving the crime. If so, I could understand why. After all, the crime scene had been compromised, and a great deal of the evidence had been destroyed.

"You know," I said, punctuating my words by jabbing my fork in the air, "I heard that digitalis is what killed

Francie. That's foxglove. It's a common biennial. I hope you're finding out who does and doesn't have a garden. I, for one, don't. I live in a condo. There's a yard, but it's just a lawn, really, with no flowers."

"Ma'am, I really can't comment on the investigation, but we're doing everything we can," the disembodied voice said unconvincingly.

"I watched that woman die, and let me tell you, it wasn't a pretty sight." I took a big swig from my beer. "And why didn't that police officer think something fishy might be up when he got to the house and there was a half-dead woman and a bunch of other people sick and vomiting all over the place, huh? That was a mistake, wasn't it?"

Okay, my alcohol tolerance was negligible, presumably because in a show of solidarity, I'd had almost nothing to drink since Adrianna got pregnant. With Ade out of commission—she was the only girlfriend I ever went to bars with—abstaining from alcohol had been an easy sacrifice. Somehow the lure of the beer that Josh kept in my fridge had sucked me in tonight, and the alcohol was hitting me hard.

Even so, I answered as many of the detective's questions as I could, but I knew almost nothing about the people who'd been at Leo and Francie's. The exception was, of course, Josh. I'd never seen either Francie or Leo before, I knew Digger only through Josh, and I'd met Robin, Marlee, and Nelson only a few times. I hung up and polished off the spicy beef salad.

"Damn detective," I said to Inga, who was perched on a windowsill, eyeballing my noodles. Inga licked her paw in response.

I heard a thud as Gato leapt down from the fridge and casually strolled into the living room as though he hadn't been hiding out for the past few days. He gave Inga the hairy eyeball and hissed spitefully before hopping onto the couch and curling up a foot away from me. I reached over, patted him, and whispered, "That's a start, buddy."

THIRTEEN

THURSDAY was a day of rain-barrel activities: researching designs that I could pass on to hunky Emilio, returning phone calls from potential clients, and preparing written materials on the environmental benefits of watering gardens with rainwater. I was pretty pleased with the pamphlet that I came up with to pass out to clients. I gave myself extra credit for printing it on recycled paper. I was building an e-mail list, too, so that we could keep clients posted on new developments in the exciting world of rain barrels without using more paper than necessary.

I worked steadily, with hardly any interruptions, and by early evening I was starving and ready for my dinner with Robin and weirdo Nelson. The grilled cheese and tomato sandwich that I'd eaten for lunch hadn't satisfied this gourmet girl, and I was really hoping that the fare at Marlee's restaurant would be better than the Boston Mystery Diner claimed.

I showered, dried my hair, and stood disgruntled in front of my closet, unable to find anything I was in the mood to wear. Then I remembered that I still had a bag of Adrianna's prepregnancy clothes to root through. In spite of my loyalty to Adrianna, I dreaded the inevitable day when her fabulous clothes would once again fit her, and she'd demand their return. In the meantime, I was making the most of the goods. Until now, I'd been wearing her summer things, but it was relatively cool this evening. In almost no time, the fall clothes that had been stashed in a large bag in my front closet were strewn all over my bed, and within minutes, I was wearing a brand-new outfit. Ade's pants were a mile too long for me, so I opted for a camel-colored wrap skirt that could've been meant to be long and an off-white scoop-neck top. I pulled on some nylons and shoes, and feeling like a crazy cat lady, ordered Gato and Inga to behave themselves. Then I left for Alloy.

On-street parking in the South End can be tough to find, but I lucked into a legal spot about a block away from Alloy—a block away according to Google Maps, anyway. Still, I had a hard time finding Alloy, mainly because I expected it to occupy one of the charming old brick town houses that are typical of the South End. In fact, the outside of the restaurant was so modern that I couldn't even figure out how to enter the building. Large metal-framed glass panels covered the face of the eatery. Peering in, I saw Robin and Nelson seated at a stainless-steel table off to the left. Robin was talking on her cell phone but caught my eye and waved. I casually waved back and pretended to inspect the architecture. The glass panels all looked the same to me, and I could not for the life of me determine which one was the entrance. No welcome signs, no door handles, no overhead awning! Metal light fixtures that hung equidistant from one another across the length of the restaurant facade provided not a hint about where to enter the restaurant. I walked slowly to my right and watched Robin's face pinch in confusion. I then headed left and, in desperation, ran my hand along the side of the building in hope of discovering a tactile clue about how to get in and have dinner here.

Aha! I touched a barely noticeable keyhole and pushed. What was presumably the door hardly moved, so I gave a kick and, at last, found myself in the interior of Alloy, which was so hard to break into that it should have been named Fort Knox. If the food was as crummy as the reviews claimed, maybe the owners were deliberately trying to keep customers out.

Finding no hostess up front to greet me, I simply joined Robin and Nelson at their table. "Hello," I said but was unable to take a seat because there were no more chairs at the table. "Oh, I guess I better ask for a chair." I whirled around to find a staff member to help me.

"No, Chloe, you have a seat. There's a stool under the table," Robin explained.

Indeed, hidden beneath the table was a backless stainless-steel stool. Doing my best to hide my surprise, I pulled it out. "I see. How . . . modern."

Who the heck wanted to eat while sitting on a cushion-less, backless metal stool? First I'd been unable to come in, and now I didn't want to sit down. The entire room was so heavily decorated in metal that I wondered whether I should have worn the Tin Man's outfit out to dinner. Perching on the stool, I silently vowed to avoid alcohol tonight lest I get off balance and tumble off my seat.

"So," Robin said with a bright smile, "Marlee should be

out any minute. As soon as she gets a break." I looked at Robin's beady eyes and was struck by the realization that she quite strongly resembled a hedgehog: a cute, delicate little body that you just wanted to pick up in your hand and cuddle. Except that I knew what a nasty bitch she could be while directing a shoot.

Despite the unusual and, I thought, unfriendly decor, Alloy was about three-quarters full of diners. I suspected that the would-be patrons who'd have made up the fourth quarter had been unable to locate the door.

"How are you, Chloe?" I barely recognized Nelson without his camera pointed in my face. His plaid golfer's cap, which concealed his bald spot, seemed to violate Alloy's unofficial dress code, which evidently called for trendy formality. And the hat made it unattractively obvious that Nelson's ears were three sizes too big for his head. I was glad that I'd raided my cache of Ade's fall outfits. "You doin' okay after what happened with Francie?"

"I'm all right, I guess. Still in a state of shock, I think, but I'm okay." I really did not want to rehash the details of that fatal day. Besides, to ferret out anything incriminating about Robin or Nelson, I'd need to use subtle methods; I couldn't just blurt out the questions I actually wanted to ask, such as whether either one of them had murdered Francie. Thankfully, we were interrupted.

A waitress approached our table to deliver menus. She held up a pitcher of ice water. "Would you like me to refill your drinking vessels?"

Our *drinking vessels*? You had to be kidding me. But the pretentious phrase was oddly appropriate: the cylindrical metal tubes that sat on our table certainly were not glasses. "No, thank you. I'm fine," I said while sucking in my cheeks to hide my smile.

The waitress poured water for Nelson and Robin while she robotically recited the specials. "Alloy uses herbs that the chef grows in her own garden. All of our dishes are complemented by fresh herbs. Tonight we have a cucumber soup made with organic cucumbers, crème fraîche, and homegrown dill, and garnished with a spiral of lemon zest." She looked down and flicked a piece of lint off her apron. "Then there's a farm-raised chicken leg encrusted with fresh herbs and roasted with a mélange of organic mushrooms and topped with a truffle foam."

Are the herbs fresh? I wanted to ask. *Could you tell us one more time?* I also refrained from asking whether it was only the *leg* of the chicken that had been raised on a farm, whereas the rest of the bird had grown up elsewhere. And no way was I going to eat *foam*. I'd seen enough *Top Chef* episodes to know that gastronomic foam meant a substance that looked like spit. The waitress left the table without so much as a nod.

Robin raised her glass. Whoops! Pardon me. Robin lifted her drinking vessel. "Cheers to the wedding!" She took a sip and opened the menu. "Let's take a look at what else Marlee has for us." Addressing me, she advised, "Sometimes it's best to order off the menu."

The menu had such long, grandiloquent descriptions that it was all I could do to decipher what was actually being offered. Also, I had the sense that I was reading a culinary version of the "The Twelve Days of Christmas": nearly every dish included numbers: *Six Clams Simmered in White Wine and Five-Herb Garlic Butter, Two Slices of Pork Loin Seared and Served with a Three-Potato Gallette,* and *A Tower of Four Shrimp with Seven Seasonal Vegetables.*

"Fiiiive golden rings!" I sang in my head.

Because I wasn't sure whether Robin was paying for dinner, the high prices had me scanning the menu for the cheapest items. Furthermore, the reports on the Mayor's Food Court had left me leery. Under no circumstances did I ever go out of my way to order a dish garnished with food-borne illness—*Salmon with Salmonella*, let's say, or *Sole on a Bed of E. coli Spinach*—but now, a few days before Adrianna's shower, I especially wanted avoid the risk. I decided on the cucumber soup and roasted cod. As I decoded the description of the fish, the dish had something to do with pureed chickpeas and, needless to say, a mountain of fresh herbs.

"So I gather that fresh herbs are the theme of this restaurant, huh?" I asked the table.

"Absolutely," Robin answered.

"I wonder how Marlee finds time to garden? Considering that she must work here all the time."

"Oh, she's an avid gardener. And the herbs are very important to her."

Hmm. An avid gardener who might grow more than just herbs? "Does either of you garden?"

Nelson shook his head. "Nah. I don't care about flowers and all that. I've got a small apartment with no yard, anyhow."

"Same here," Robin said. "I've got a black thumb when it comes to flowers. Not that my apartment has a yard or a balcony, even, but I can't keep so much as a houseplant alive. I forget to water them. Marlee!" Robin stood up and smiled as Marlee made her way through the dining room.

The female chef looked even pastier than the last time I'd seen her, and her soiled white chef's coat did nothing to flatter her stocky figure. "I heard you were out here, Robin." Marlee tucked her short hair behind her ears, a move that only exaggerated her round face. I caught sight of her dirty fingernails and desperately prayed that she was cooking with gloves on. "I'm so glad to see you. Hi, Nelson. Hi, Chloe. I have to get back in the kitchen, but I wanted to say hello and let you know that I'll send food out for you, so don't bother with the menus, okay? I'll pop out again if I can." Marlee smiled curtly and waved.

Robin reached under the table and pulled a yellow notepad from her bag. "Now, I want to talk about the process of obtaining permission to solemnize a marriage. This is going to be a great piece. We're not filming today, because I want to run the story by the station first, but they're just going to love it."

Phew! So I'd continue to be spared Nelson's camera. I went over the simple process of solemnization with Robin, while Nelson munched on a green bread stick that, according to Robin, was flavored with pureed fresh thyme.

"Adrianna is really excited at the idea of having her wedding filmed," I said. "If it weren't for you, the only footage she'd have would be from a home video camera, and the result would be shaky images and bad lighting. With the baby coming so soon and the shower this weekend, this is one less thing she needs to worry about."

Robin's eyes lit up as I talked. "So, wait! Adrianna is giving birth soon after the wedding?" She looked at Nelson.

"Cool. Now I'm really interested in filming the wedding. Maybe she'll go into labor! Talk about good film." Nelson's eyes brightened, probably in the hope that Adrianna's water would break in the middle of her vows.

"Well, we must film the shower then, too! What an exciting time for your friends, Chloe. And maybe I can use some of the footage of the shower in the piece on solemnization. This will be wonderful!"

"Sure. I guess that would be okay with Adrianna." I

made a mental note to add two more people to the guest list for Saturday. "And Adrianna will still have a few weeks before she's due. So," I said lightly as I eyed Nelson, "let's plan on filming the shower and the wedding and *not* the delivery on the same day." As if Nelson's hopes could induce labor! Still, I had the superstitious sense that his greed for dramatic events to film could jinx Adrianna.

Robin's cell phone rang shrilly. When she pulled it out of her purse, its color—metallic hot pink—should have told me that she had no desire to use it unobtrusively. Foolishly, I expected her to turn it off. Instead, she not only answered but spoke loudly. "Hello? What? I can't hear you. Speak up. This isn't really a good time. Not now." Although the people at the next table glared at her, Robin kept talking. Meanwhile, Nelson and I sat in uncomfortable silence, unable to converse even if we'd wanted to over Robin's noisy phone call. She finally snapped her phone shut.

Food began to arrive. Mindful of the Mayor's Food Court, I looked nervously at my plate as I inspected its contents for signs of improper storage or rat poop. Finding nothing noticeably wrong, I picked up my fork and stared in disbelief: the fork had only two tines. I looked at Robin and Nelson, and then glanced around at other customers who were eating. Was I the only one who found it completely bizarre that we were expected to use this *prong*? Evidently so. Reconciling myself to impaling my food or possibly balancing it, I turned to a dish that Marlee had sent out, a shrimp tower of sorts that initially resisted the attack I mounted with the not-a-fork. After a couple of failed efforts, I had to use my fingers to yank out a rosemary spear that elevated the shrimp above a mountain of thick brown mush almost covered in what appeared to be grass clippings.

Although the shrimp were terribly overcooked, I managed to chew and swallow a few bites, but I nearly choked on a small prongful of grass.

"It's got a kick to it, huh?" Robin handed me my water. "That's the jalapeño Marlee puts in her mushroom and sprout puree."

"Very unusual," I sputtered.

Robin's cell phone went off again, and she began another loud exchange. A male server approached our table. "Ma'am? I need to ask you to turn off your phone." He pointed to a prominent sign on the wall requesting that all cell phones be turned off in the restaurant.

"Oh, all right," Robin said sharply to the server. "Shit, I'll go outside." She made quite a display of stomping across the floor and rolling her eyes as she marched out of the restaurant. At least she found the exit. I made a mental note of its location. Looking embarrassed, the server left the table.

"Just you and me, Chloe." Nelson chomped happily on the vile food. "I've been hoping to get a chance to talk to you. Maybe we can find some time to talk on Saturday at the shower."

Eeek! To cut Nelson off, I signaled the server who had asked Robin to leave. She'd been so rude to him that I felt compelled to apologize, as I couldn't do in her presence. "The sign about not using cell phones is pretty clear," I said. "I'm sorry for what happened."

He shrugged his shoulders. "Friend of the chef. That's how it is. Thanks, though. Excuse me, I have an order to bring out."

Nelson was gazing at me with strange intensity; he almost seemed to be in a trance. In what I intended as a startling tone, I said, "I didn't know that Robin and Marlee were friends. I thought they just knew each other from *Chefly Yours.*"

"Oh, yeah. They've been good friends for a while. Robin wants to keep that quiet, though, because she doesn't want it to look like she's playing favorites on the show."

Well, Robin most certainly *was* playing favorites! And having a chef friend of hers in the competition was bad enough, but keeping the friendship secret was even worse. Granted, Robin couldn't control the number of viewers who actually called in to vote for each chef, but for all I knew, she could falsify the voting results. What if Marlee ended up winning the show because Robin had tinkered with the numbers?

I was fuming. It ticked me off to realize that Josh could lose to a chef who served such disgusting food at her restaurant. In the single episode that Marlee had done, the food had looked better than the revolting stuff I'd eaten tonight, but Josh's cooking was incomparably better than Marlee's, and his on-camera personality outshone Marlee's by light-years.

Nelson's hand slithered across the table toward mine. I swiftly yanked my hand away while desperately looking around for Robin. Mercifully, she was on her way back to her stool.

"Sorry about that. That waiter is an asshole."

I pushed my food around on my plate and watched in awe as Robin polished hers clean. Nelson ate all of his food, too, but he struck me as someone who'd be unable to discriminate between a dinner at a run-down roadside shack and one at La Tour d'Argent. When the entrées appeared, I repeated the process of pushing my food around and managed to ingest only a tiny portion of the lavender-and-oregano-infused salmon that Marlee had chosen for us. Chosen for us? Inflicted on us, I should say.

To avoid Nelson's ogling, I shifted around to face Robin and concentrated on giving her a detailed description of the wedding plans. Robin sounded delighted to have the opportunity to produce Adrianna and Owen's wedding video and assured me she'd edit the footage down and set it to whatever music the couple wanted.

"Another delicious meal!" Robin pronounced as the waitress cleared our plates. "After that, I think I'm too full for dessert tonight."

"I agree. Stuffed. I'm absolutely stuffed." The last thing I wanted was cilantro-scented ice cream or whatever other vile dessert Marlee would send out. I was already brainstorming about where to stop on the way home to buy an edible dinner.

"Would you like to go see the kitchen? I know Marlee wouldn't mind." Robin put her napkin down and gestured to the depths of the restaurant. "Nelson, we'll be back in a minute. Here's my credit card. Will you get the check?"

"I'd love to see Alloy's kitchen," I said cheerfully. I went on to thank Robin for treating me to dinner. Thank God I hadn't paid out of my own pocket for that terrible meal.

A restaurant kitchen was no novelty to me—I already knew the ins and outs of Simmer's—and I was less than eager to examine the source of dishes that had made me gag, but I could hardly say so to Robin, who was Marlee's friend and who was footing the bill. Still, a visit to Alloy's kitchen would give me the chance to see for myself whether there were any signs of all those code violations I'd read about. There presumably wouldn't be rodents or insects in sight, but I was so used to Josh's exceptionally sterile kitchen that I should be able to detect iffy conditions in Marlee's.

As it turned out, no experience was required to spot unhygienic areas in Alloy's kitchen. Chicken pieces lay uncovered on a plastic cutting board, their juices running onto the counter and floor. The floors were wet and filthy, and the one drain I could see was covered in gray gunk. In contrast to the minimalist metallic dining area, the entire kitchen had an air of chaos. I did notice a spray sanitizer, but its nozzle hung over containers of chopped vegetables that sat on a long stainless counter. The soap dispenser over the sink was empty, its drip spout clogged. I shuddered to think of the bacteria that must already be growing in my poor gut.

"How was your meal?" Marlee rounded the corner from behind a high shelf that held teetering pots and pans. "Not too shabby, was it?" She smiled at what she assumed to be her outstanding culinary skills. She wiped her forehead with a dish towel and then slapped it onto the counter, where it landed in the chicken juice.

"Brilliant, again, Marlee," Robin chirped.

"Thanks. Business has been up and down." Marlee shrugged and examined her filthy hands with no visible alarm. "What're you going to do, right? I just do the best I can and put out a great product. Anyone who wants to complain can get out."

"Thanks so much, Marlee," I said politely, resisting the impulse to douse her with a bottle of sanitizer. "And, Robin? I'll give Adrianna your number so she can call you tomorrow and talk to you about the shower." I couldn't wait to escape. "I should get going," I said. I gave Robin quick directions to my parents' house and said good-bye.

As I turned to leave, I noticed a large corkboard by the doors to the dining room. Pinned to it were the usual permits and postings from the state, but what stuck out was the Boston Mystery Diner's damning review of Alloy. The article was covered in black marker: a large X ran across the typeface, and "Eat Me!" and "Screw You!" were printed in angry letters at the top of the page.

Most noticeable, however, was a gleaming, stainless-steel knife that had been plunged into the center of the review.

FOURTEEN

I spent most of Friday afternoon and evening at my parents' house, and I was back there again at nine on Saturday morning to finish the preparations for Adrianna's shower. I'd already finished some of the work: the table linens had been washed and ironed, the white dishes set out, the flowers arranged in vases. The candles were ready to be lit. Fortunately, an eleven o'clock shower meant brunch: it was much easier for three amateurs to do brunch food than it would've been to cook and serve lunch or dinner. Dad was going to be kicked out of the house when the guests started to arrive, but for now he was busy arranging a fruit platter.

"Why did I get stuck with the fruit platter when there are four boxes of perfectly delicious pastries I could be setting out?" My dad eyed the white cardboard boxes tied with red and white string.

"Jack, you cannot be trusted with the pastries. That's why you're in charge of cantaloupes and kiwis." My mother walked across the kitchen with a tray of bagels, cream cheese, lox, red onions, and capers. "I'll try to save you some tiramisu if you promise to stay away until after the girls have gone. Chloe, watch your father," she instructed me as she disappeared into the dining room.

"Dad? What does Mom think she's doing with that *thing* on her head?" I was referring to a silk-flower headpiece my mother wore.

"Ah, yes." He cleared his throat. "That's her latest craft project. She seems to believe that floral headwear is going to be the fashion hit of the year." He spoke with amused resignation.

I shook my head in disbelief. "She looks like she's going to a Maypole dance." I'd have to make sure that she didn't accessorize with that monstrosity on the day of Ade's wedding. "Dad!" I yelled. "No!" I practically had to tackle my father, who had grabbed a pair of scissors and was on the verge of breaking into the pastry boxes.

"Oh, all right. Some help you are," he teased. "I did my dumb fruit platter, so I'm going to get out of your hair and go to my yoga class. Did Mom tell you about it? It's wonderful! Watch this."

Dad raised his arms while teetering awkwardly on one foot. Even while he was striking a ridiculous pose, I had to admire how muscular my middle-aged father was. He still had a full head of hair, most of it gray, and with his fit build and those Paul Newman blue eyes of his, he was quite a handsome man.

I laughed. "Okay, Dad. Go work on your chakra or whatever, and we'll see you later."

Dad grabbed a gym bag and blew me a kiss. "I'm trusting you to snatch a few of those treats for me."

"Hey, Dad?" I stopped him. "Thanks so much for everything you're doing for Adrianna and Owen. Especially walking her down the aisle. It means a lot to her. And to me."

"You got it, kiddo. We love those two. It will be an honor for me to stand in for her father." He smiled and went out the back door.

I mixed up a yogurt dip for the fruit platter and then put puff pastry shells in the oven to bake. They'd eventually be filled with a sweet cream filling and topped with strawberries.

At about quarter of eleven, when I was finally finishing up, my mother answered the doorbell and let Robin and Nelson in. Ushering them into the kitchen, she said, "Chloe, your friends are here."

Not friends, exactly.

"You'll never believe it," my mother exclaimed, "but Robin and I know each other!"

Nelson, hiding behind his camera, panned to my face.

I said, "Oh, really? How?"

"Robin produced a show on gardening at a house where your father and I had designed the landscape. Small world, isn't it?"

"That was what? Two years ago?" Robin asked.

"I think so," Mom agreed.

"Come on, Nelson," Robin said. "Let's get some footage of the rooms and the decorations." She directed her cameraman to the dining room. Robin wore a bright floral dress, and an eighties-inspired wide white belt hugged her small waist. She stomped away with Nelson, and her skirt flounced decisively.

A few minutes later, at five before eleven, the doorbell rang again, and I welcomed Naomi, who'd supervised my school internship during the past year, into the living room. When Naomi engulfed me in her usual bear hug, I had to blow her long braids out of my mouth. Since I'd known her, Naomi had chosen a version of the Bo Derek hairstyle; her entire head of hip-length hair was braided into chunky strands.

Naomi barely knew Adrianna, but Adrianna had so few female friends that I'd had to pad the guest list. Including men wouldn't have worked, since almost all of Adrianna's male friends were ex-boyfriends. The women who disliked Adrianna were fools. They envied her looks and were put off by what they saw as her haughty manner. Little did they know what a loyal, generous person she really was. In any case, Naomi belonged at the shower and at the wedding because she'd written the letter of recommendation for me that was required by the commonwealth before issuing a Certificate of Solemnization. Attesting in writing to my "high standard of character," as the instructions phrased it, had made Naomi feel intimately involved with everything about Adrianna and Owen's wedding and procreation. Among other things, she'd mistakenly gained the impression that Adrianna and Owen were following her advice about what she called "alternative birthing" methods. Naomi, who was a big fan of the alternative, the natural, and the New Age in all its forms, had had a long conversation with Adrianna about the benefits of acupressure, hypnosis, water birth, and guided imagery during labor. It was typical of Naomi to have misinterpreted the gasps of horror that Adrianna emitted during the discussion as exclamations of enthusiasm. In reality, Naomi's arguments in favor of drug-free birth had done nothing except fuel Ade's desire for a super-strength epidural.

"What an exciting day!" Naomi was glowing with enthusiasm. "Wait until you see the gift bag I have for our mother-to-be! It's full of aromatherapy oils that promote relaxation during labor. And all sorts of other goodies! In a bag made from natural hemp, I should add. Just like my dress." Naomi spun around, sending her braids flying horizontally off her head while showing off her clay-colored pinafore. I ducked before I got smacked in the face but complimented her on her politically correct attire. "What a beautiful house!" she exclaimed after her three hundred sixty-degree spins.

My parents' stucco house did look wonderful. In keeping with Adrianna's fall theme, my mother and I had run red, orange, and brown ribbons along the traditional Spanish archways that ran between rooms on the first floor. Last year, my parents had refinished the wood floors in the large living room and had put in terra-cotta and decorative hand-painted tiles in the dining room to enhance the style of the house. The walls had been painted in soft earth colors, and at times I felt as if I were actually in New Mexico instead of in a Massachusetts suburb.

Adrianna arrived dressed entirely in hot pink, her nails painted to match her above-the-knee maternity dress and her chunky shoes. "I swear on my baby's life that I'm going to kill my mother," she hissed into my ear as I hugged her.

Adrianna was soon followed by her mother, Kitty, who appeared to be in deep mourning. She wore a black pantsuit with no accessories except a watch that she was already checking. Her badly tinted blonde hair hit her shoulders, where it rolled under in a perfect curl. Her expression suggested a combination of dissatisfaction and grief. Despite Kitty's funereal garb and air, it was hard to miss her incredible figure and easy to see where Adrianna had gotten her modelesque looks.

"Chloe, it's lovely to see you. Where shall I put this?" Kitty held up a white gift bag.

"I'll take it. It's wonderful to see you, too." Knowing that Kitty did not like to be touched, I leaned in and gave her air kisses. "I know my mother is eager to catch up with you. Why don't you go find her in the kitchen?"

"Wonderful, darling." Kitty brushed past me to seek out my mom.

I went to shut the door and nearly slammed it in Owen's face. "Owen? What are you doing here?"

Poor Owen's disheveled appearance made me suspect that Kitty had put him through the wringer since her arrival yesterday. No matter what, Owen was always incredibly handsome, but today his black hair was messy, and his fair skin had a sickly pallor.

"I drove Ade and Kitty here. I can't leave Adrianna alone with that woman! Please let me stay." His expression was pitiful.

"No, you can't stay, dummy. This is a shower just for the girls. I promise I'll mediate the Kitty situation. Ade will call you when it's over."

"But what if—"

"It'll be fine," I said as I shoved the groom-to-be out the door.

I introduced Robin and Nelson to Adrianna and then left the three of them to discuss the video.

Next to arrive were Owen's mother, Eileen, his grandmother, Nana Sally, and his cousin Phoebe. Moments later, two women from Simmer showed up: Isabelle, a shy young cook whom Josh had taken under his wing, and Blythe, a waitress. My sister, Heather, who had let herself in the back door, deposited a gigantic box on the coffee table. Heather had curled her hair into a mass of Shirley Temple ringlets. As usual, Heather was vibrating with such energy that she made the rest of us look like slugs. The mother of a one-year-old and a five-year-old, Heather always looked as if she'd just emerged from fourteen hours of sleep followed by a trip to a spa.

"Give me a hug, Sis." Heather wrapped me in her arms and held me tight. "So I hear that young Emilio caught your eye. Any chance you're finally done with Josh?"

I pushed her away and glared at her. "Don't start," I warned her.

"Don't get all pissy. I'm just asking."

Unlike my parents, Heather was anything but a fan of Josh's. Her idea of the perfect man for me was a money-maker who had gone to a four-year college and who worked a traditional job with regular hours.

"Well, stop asking," I snarled. "And today is about Adrianna, anyway, not about me. Or Josh. So we are not getting into it now."

She smiled sneakily. "But Emilio is hot, isn't he?"

I couldn't help grinning back. "Well, duh!"

I didn't notice Nelson until he quickly turned his camera away. The exchange with Heather was a segment that would have to be edited out of the final video. I hoped, of course, that there would be few such segments. But at least the video would show that a satisfying number of people had attended the shower. Desperate for guests, I'd expanded the list by including a couple of my fellow students from social work school, Julie and Gretchen, who must have been bewildered about why they had been invited to a shower for someone they didn't know, but who showed up nonetheless.

The guests helped themselves to plates of food from the dining room. My parents had sprung for champagne, which was poured, served, and sipped by most of the guests. Adrianna avoided it, of course, as did I, but Owen's grandmother, Nana Sally, compensated for our abstemiousness by quickly drinking her first glass, refilling it, downing that one, and then getting yet another refill. "Mother, go easy!" I heard Eileen whisper.

Kitty sat down next to Eileen on the living room couch and nibbled on a shortbread cookie. I sighed, hoping that they'd manage to converse without bashing the wedding. In particular, I hoped that Eileen would refrain from voicing her belief that Adrianna had tricked Owen into marrying her by getting pregnant. Nelson and Robin stood a few yards from the couch with the camera focused on the two women. If my fears were realized, here was another segment that would have to be edited out. Alternatively, maybe Robin could replace the audio throughout the tape with music, thus obliterating forecasts of marital doom.

"Chloe?" Adrianna handed me a cup of tea. "Who are those girls over there?"

"Oh. Um, well . . ." I faltered. "That's Gretchen and Julie. You remember them, don't you?" Raising my cup of tea and taking a sip, I tried to act as casual as possible. In other words, I tried to avoid having Ade realize that she had never even seen either of them before. "They were so happy to hear about your wedding and the baby that I just had to invite them."

"Uh-huh." Ade looked at me doubtfully.

"Come on! Let's open presents."

I signaled to my mother, who joyously clapped her hands and addressed the entire group. "Everyone? Let's all gather over here while our guest of honor opens her gifts."

The older women sat on the couches, while most of the

younger women seated themselves on the floor around the coffee table. I reserved a big, soft, upholstered chair for Adrianna.

"I'm never going to get out of this seat," Ade said as she sank into the deep pillows.

"Open this one first," I ordered, handing her my present.

Adrianna unwrapped my gift and looked totally boggled.

"It's a BabyBjörn," I had to explain. "You strap the baby to your body and voilà! Hands-free! Like a backpack for your front. I got the leather one so you'd be the most fashionable mommy out there."

"This is so cool!" Ade beamed happily. "I really think I'm going to like this. I'm still learning about all this baby stuff. I've never even heard of this."

Next she opened a box packed full of small baby items, gifts from my sister, Heather, who said, "I know these might not look exciting, but they're all things you'll use. See? Teethers, rattles, baby blankets, bottle brushes, onesies, wipes. Seems boring, but they'll be useful." My niece, Lucy, was one, and my nephew, Walker, was five. Heather prided herself on having nearly every conceivable baby and child gadget ever invented.

"Wow, Heather. This is amazing." Ade rooted through the gift box, her eyes wide with interest at all these never-before-seen infant supplies. "This is so thoughtful of you. Thank you."

Adrianna had never been one to fawn over babies—worse, she'd actually seemed to dislike children—and her surprise pregnancy had thrown her for a good loop. Early on, I'd given her some books about pregnancy and about baby care, but I was far from sure that she'd read them. Owen was the one who'd hurled himself into stocking up on kid paraphernalia. Only as Ade opened the baby presents with little apparent recognition of everyday baby items did I understand how hard it was for her to come to terms with the prospect of motherhood. The gifts were, I thought, giving her the boost that she needed to get through to the end of her pregnancy; the fun stuff was a better choice than my books had been. Remarkably, Adrianna even looked interested in Naomi's aromatherapy oils and in the big inflatable ball that Ade was supposed to sit on during major contraction time. Cousin Phoebe and Nana Sally jointly gave Ade a Baby Jogger stroller that looked as if it could be propelled over rock-strewn mountains without jostling the child, and Gretchen and Julie from my school were generous enough to give a stranger three adorable unisex baby outfits. Shy Isabelle and Blythe the waitress had put together a collection of board books for babies that would endure hours of the kid gumming and chewing the hard pages.

I handed Ade the gift from Owen's mother. Unwrapped, the package turned out to contain a voluminous white cotton nightgown with a high ruffled neck. Staring at this chaste garment, I realized that it should have had a prominent monogram that read Not Adrianna. Ade shot me a look out of the corner of her eye, and I refrained from laughing out loud.

"This is lovely, Eileen. Thank you." Ade spoke politely.

"Isn't it?" Eileen said cooly. "You can think of me every time you wear it."

"Yeah, every time I return to the convent," Ade muttered in my ear as she noisily scrunched up the wrapping paper.

Adrianna had seen what I'd missed: the nightgown was suitable for a nun and must have been chosen to keep Owen as far away from Adrianna as possible. Dream on, Eileen!

Adrianna could wear a chicken costume, and Owen would still find her the sexiest woman in the world.

"I'm sure it will be beautiful on you when you lose all the weight you've put on, dear," added Kitty, passive-aggressive as ever.

I hurriedly put Kitty's gift in front of Adrianna. "Now, your mother's present."

When Adrianna had removed the wrapping paper, I could hardly believe my eyes. Or maybe I just didn't want to believe what I was seeing. To Adrianna, to her own daughter at this wedding and baby shower, Kitty had presented a cheap-looking basket that held a small assortment of cheese balls and dried sausages. Bad? Bad enough if the basket had been new, but the terrible gift had already been opened: one of the sausages was obviously missing.

"Thank you, Mom," Ade croaked.

My heart broke for her. Of all the stupid, meaningless, idiotic gifts to give to a daughter on any occasion! But now? Oh, I was furious. Goddamn it. Kitty soared to the top of my official shit list. So what if Adrianna was pregnant before her wedding? Couldn't her own mother have the decency to fake understanding? Kindness, generosity . . . and even love? Evidently not!

Robin reached out to push Nelson's camera down. Amazingly, for all the cameraman's greed for his notion of reality, he actually looked sympathetic.

Adrianna's eyes were glistening. Before she had time to shed tears, I put the presents from my mother in front of her. One was in a big box on the coffee table, the other in a long, wide package too bulky to lift off the floor. I knew what Mom was giving Ade and saw the lavish gifts not just as expressions of celebration but as tokens of the maternal devotion that Ade's own mother withheld. Adrianna opened the Cuisinart food processor and then a fancy high chair with an adjustable seat, a dishwasher-safe tray, and all sorts of decorative doodads, baubles, and bells.

Kitty leaned over for a better view of my mother's gifts. "My, how extravagant."

Adrianna pulled herself up from the chair and gave my mother an enormous hug. Ade was not one to get sappy or weepy, but I saw her wipe her eyes.

Naomi's voice rang through the room as she happily leaped off her seat. "Hasn't this just been a touching display of female bonding? Really, the power of a group of women coming together to celebrate the impending arrival of another life!" She placed her hands on her chest. "My heart is overwhelmed with the love in this room."

I smiled at Naomi, who was totally oblivious to the family drama that had just transpired. Although this couldn't be the first baby or wedding shower that my supervisor had ever attended, I suspected that it was rare for her to find herself in a gathering of women not associated with some sort of political movement.

Nelson was standing five or six yards from Naomi with his camera fixed on her. He briefly peered around the camera to gaze at her with such clear interest that I spotted an opportunity, pounced on it, and pushed him in her direction. As far as I knew, Naomi was still involved with her boyfriend, Eliot, who owned a gallery on Newbury Street right near Simmer. Still, it wouldn't hurt to have Naomi see that other men noticed her.

"Why don't you go interview Naomi?" I suggested to Nelson. "I'll bet she'd give you some really good material to include in the video."

Nelson responded immediately. He practically skipped

across the room to position himself smack next to a surprised Naomi.

I cleaned up wrapping paper, moved gifts into one area of the living room, and then helped my mother to replenish the supply of coffee and pastries. When I returned to the living room and took a seat, Nana Sally was narrating a tale about Owen's brothers, Evan and Willie. From the look on Cousin Phoebe's face, I gathered that this sort of recitation was a family ritual.

"Hee hee!" Nana Sally shrieked. "And remember when those two set up that skateboard ramp for Owen?" She had a fit of laughter. "Owen was fifteen, but he still could barely stand on the skateboard without falling off. Love him! But athletic he is not. Well, Evan and Willie built a ramp and told him it would be easy as pie for him. They got poor Owen standing on the skateboard at the top of a hill, and then the pair of them sent him flying down onto this ramp contraption that they'd thrown together out of old plywood. I don't know how Owen managed to get all the way to the ramp without falling off, but he did. As soon as he hit the top of the ramp, he fell crashing down!" Nana Sally again squealed with laughter. Covering her eyes with a napkin, she finished the story by saying, "Those damn kids had rigged the ramp to crumble when Owen hit it!"

Eileen crossed her arms and frowned. "It wasn't funny, Nana. Owen still has a scar on his forehead from that incident. Four stitches, he needed!"

Ade perked up her head. "Owen told me he got that scar from a fistfight he had in ninth grade."

Phoebe took a turn at storytelling. "Then there was the time those two rascals balanced a bucket on top of the door so it would fall on their dad's head," she said. "Remember that?"

I chimed in. "That doesn't sound so bad. It's an old trick. Did they fill the bucket with water or something?"

"No!" Nana giggled. "Rocks!" She exploded into uproarious laughter.

Rocks? The prank didn't strike me as the least bit funny. In fact, both of the supposedly hilarious practical jokes sounded cruel and dangerous. Nana Sally's and Phoebe's stories, far from convincing me that Willie and Evan were harmless pranksters, fueled my theory that Owen's brothers could have perpetrated a horrible joke that had turned deadly last Monday. I hated to have Adrianna's shower end on such an ugly note.

By the time Owen arrived to pick up Adrianna and Kitty, Ade looked exhausted. Owen loaded the gifts into the car and did his best to be polite to Kitty, who issued nonstop criticism disguised as advice.

"Owen, I don't understand why you're putting the bags in the car first," she said. "You ought to start with that overpriced high chair." Kitty shook her head as she spoke. It seemed to me that she might as well have come right out and voiced the opinion that her daughter had chosen to procreate with an idiot.

"Thank you for that very sage advice, Kitty. I'll reload the car in the proper manner." Owen winked at me and picked up the last of the gifts.

"I can't thank you enough for all of this, Chloe." Adrianna engulfed me in a hug. I rubbed her back with my hands as I squeezed her.

"I'm so sorry about your mom, Ade," I whispered. "I don't know what in the world is going on with her."

"What's going on with her is that she is a bitch." She pulled back from me. "It's just the way it is. She's done nothing but complain since she got here. The hotel is crappy, she hated the restaurant we went to last night, and she is one hundred percent put out that she has to stay in town for the week until the wedding. Believe me, I'm put out by it, too. And the kicker? My due date is a major pain in her ass. She has herself in knots because the birth might interfere with a work conference she has in Chicago. I informed her that no one invited her to the delivery room anyhow, and after that, we had a particularly obnoxious exchange. What are you going to do, right?" Adrianna waved her hand in the air. "I'm going to go home and inhale some of those aromatherapy oils Naomi gave me. Maybe they'll actually work."

Before the tipsy Nana Sally was helped to the car by Phoebe, she slipped me an envelope for Adrianna and Owen. "Give this to the proud couple at the rehearsal, okay? I don't want Kitty and Eileen to know about it." Nana Sally kissed me sloppily on the cheek. "You're a good friend, Chloe."

When everyone had left, my mother started on the dishes while I cleaned up the living room. Under a napkin on an end table I came across the distinctive cell phone that Robin had used at Alloy, the metallic hot pink phone that was as loud and obtrusive as her phone conversations had been. I tucked it in my pocket to take home.

"Well, that went pretty well, don't you think?" My mom threw a dish towel over her shoulder and somehow managed to get it caught on her Maypole hair wreath. "Oops, there we go." She untangled the towel and surveyed the room. "Looks like we're all set in here."

"Aside from Kitty, it was perfect." I couldn't bring myself to mention Nana Sally and Phoebe, who'd done their share, too. "Adrianna looked really happy. You and Dad have been amazing to her, and I know how much she appreciates you guys."

"Our pleasure, Chloe. With a mother like that, Adrianna needs all the support she can get. Oh, before you leave, I have a bag of clothes to donate to that women's shelter you volunteered at."

"Haven't you done enough good in the world today?" I teased. "Now you're just showing off!"

FIFTEEN

WHEN I got home, I hauled the bag of clothes up to my apartment and put it in the living room, where it served as a reminder of what a lovely person my mother was: kind and generous to her family, her friends, her daughters' friends, and even to the strangers at the women's shelter; considerate to everyone; respectful of privacy; and, in short, the kind of fine human being who would return someone's forgotten cell phone without so much as thinking of turning it on and exploring its contents. Bad luck for Robin that it hadn't been my mother who'd found her phone. I should've been calling the shelter to arrange to drop off the clothes, but first things first: I turned on Robin's cell, plopped down on the couch, and started scrolling through her list of contacts. Inga settled in next to me and began purring melodiously. I stroked her with one hand as I tapped through names on the phone.

One stood out: Leo.

Unless Robin knew Leonardo DiCaprio, I had a strong suspicion that this Leo was Francie's husband and not a famous movie star. Because Leo's number was still stored on my own caller ID, it took me all of thirty seconds to confirm that Robin's Leo was, in fact, Leo the widower. When had Robin added Leo to her list of contacts? On the day of the filming? In other words, on the day of his wife's murder? Or could Robin have known Leo before the show?

Leo. Hmm. As I knew from carefully studying thousands of TV shows, murderers were often spouses or lovers, so unless Francie had had a lover, Leo should have been the prime suspect from the beginning. Did the police agree? Did they watch as much TV as I did? And what about motives? What about love and money? Maybe Leo had wanted to get rid of Francie because he had a lover or because he stood to inherit oodles of cash when Francie died. As to access to digitalis, for all I knew, he had foxglove growing right in his weed-choked garden. Under other circumstances, I could have gained access to his yard by trying to sell him a rain barrel, but as it was, I couldn't very well call him up and say, "So sorry your wife died a grisly death, but would you like to conserve water by recycling rain?"

Still, I could follow him to see whether he did anything suspicious. Such as? I didn't know exactly. But there was nothing wrong with my keeping an open mind. And how hard could it be to tail someone? I was too wiped out from Adrianna's shower to set out on a spying expedition today, but I resolved to pursue the investigation the next morning.

I checked my messages. There was a brief one from Josh to ask how the shower had gone. He said that tonight he was again working late and working an early shift on Sunday, but could he come by in the late afternoon? I returned his call and left him a voice mail saying that unless he showed up tomorrow, I was going to kidnap him from Simmer and, like some sex-starved cave woman, drag him back here. I was on my way out, I said, to buy a loincloth, a club, and a bone for my hair, so he'd better watch out.

Early on Sunday morning, I drove to the warehouse in Waltham where my parents stored equipment and supplies. They did most of the landscape design and planning work from home, but the rest of the company ran out of the second location, which was only a twenty-minute drive from my place. The deep red building gave the impression that a tornado had dropped a barn in the middle of Waltham, and the stacks of hay and the smell of garden manure only fueled that fantasy. I can't say that I was a fan of the manure aroma, but I did love the smell of hay and soil and the sawdust aroma from Emilio's lumber. I parked my Saturn in the small parking lot, let myself into the building through a large red door, and got the keys to the oldest of the five vehicles used for deliveries, a beat-up gray Chevy van with seats in the front and all sorts of shovels, rakes, and hoes in racks on the walls of the rear. The other two vans were new, as were the two pickup trucks. As I drove toward Leo's house, the stick shift gave me a hard time, and I regretted my choice of the beat-up gray van, which I'd picked because it was the smallest of the vehicles and would presumably be the easiest for me to maneuver. As it was, although I'd driven the gray van a few times before, everything about it felt unfamiliar, and I hated having to rely on the side-view mirrors. Whoever had driven it last had left half-empty coffee cups in the holders. With each passing mile, the trip seemed more and more like the stupidest idea ever. I was hardly Veronica Mars. But by the time I'd decided that the whole undertaking was a mistake, I'd passed the Natural High market and was almost at my destination.

I parked the van a few houses down from Leo's place and sank into my seat. Vans used for real surveillance had equipment such as listening devices rather than gardening implements, but I had eyes and ears, I reminded myself. Besides, the old van really did belong to a landscaping company, and if anyone questioned my presence, the Carter Landscapes logo on the side of the van and the garden equipment would show that I was who I said I was. Few landscapers would be working on a Sunday morning, of course, but I could always claim that a resident had been stricken with a crisis of environmental conscience and desperately needed information on rain barrels.

I felt like an idiot sitting there parked on the street, periodically looking at a clipboard I'd found on the passenger seat and wrinkling my brow in false concentration as I read and reread my parents' pamphlet on their company. An hour after my stakeout began, Leo finally drove his car out of his driveway and zoomed to the end of the street. No one else was visible in Leo's car, so unless someone was flattened on the floor, Leo was alone. Following him proved to be nothing like what I'd seen in movies and on TV, probably because the streets were almost empty and because he wasn't going very far: I just stayed a block behind him and trailed him to a large chain supermarket.

Disappointed that I hadn't caught Leo pulling over to burn evidence or stopping to engage in a scandalous love affair, I debated about whether to get out of the van and follow Leo right into the supermarket. Feeling disappointed, I decided that the risk of being seen was just too high, so I stayed in the van and waited for him to emerge from the market. I consoled myself with the thought that I couldn't be missing much: the probability was slight that he was having a clandestine amorous encounter among the cabbages, the steaks, or the cartons of milk.

After thirty minutes, I reconsidered: Leo still hadn't appeared. Then my hopes rose when I caught sight of a police cruiser in a side-view mirror. I watched excitedly as it slowly passed by. Maybe Leo was about to be arrested! Eager to witness the capture of a murderer, I stuck my head out the window, but the cruiser moved past the entrance to the store and continued along.

A few minutes later, Leo exited the supermarket and pushed a full shopping cart to his car, where he transferred his shopping bags to the trunk and got into the car. The only vaguely suspect action he took was to fail to leave his cart in one of the designated areas, but irresponsibility with regard to shopping carts obviously didn't prove him guilty of true crimes. As he backed out of his parking spot, I started up the van's engine and shifted into reverse. Before I'd even put my foot on the gas, however, I was stopped by the presence of a police cruiser right behind me. The lights were flashing. Seconds later, that first cruiser was joined by a second one.

A uniformed officer slowly approached and through the open window of the van said, "License and registration, please."

I smiled brightly at the officer, who looked old enough to be my great-grandfather. I prayed that my winning grin would send him away. "Is there a problem?" I asked as I fumbled through my purse. What was I thinking? Of course there was a problem! Why else was this cop talking to me? I handed him my license, shuffled through papers and maps in the glove compartment, found the registration, and passed it to him. I couldn't be in that much trouble since this officer looked so ancient and scrawny that I had a hard time picturing him chasing down violent, gun-toting criminals. I could probably knock this man over with one push of my pinky finger.

Without even examining the registration, he wrinkled his wrinkles and said, "This vehicle had been reported stolen."

Crap.

I hate the kind of robotic pretense at politeness that's more offensive than honest rudeness, and that's what I got. It took twenty minutes to straighten out the mess, but the officer did eventually call my parents, who convinced him that I hadn't stolen a beat-up van that no one would even dream of stealing. Giving up on Leo for the day, I left to exchange the supposedly stolen van for my Saturn. On the way, I called my mother and fed her an improbable tale about scouting out neighborhoods where people might be interested in rain barrels.

"You're not even working this week, Chloe," my mother said with exasperation. "You have the week off to help with the wedding. And the next time you take one of our vans, you'd better let us know!"

"Promise." I said. And meant it! I wanted never again to face the kind of public humiliation I'd just experienced.

"While I have you on the phone, I had a call from Robin. She thinks she left her cell phone at our house."

"She did. I have it."

"Chloe! Why haven't you let her know? She is a producer for a television station, and I'm sure she needs it back. What is going on with you?"

"Nothing. I'll call her as soon as I get home."

I hung up feeling grumpy and frustrated. While learning nothing about Leo, I'd pissed off my mother. When I reached my condo, I dug up Robin's home number and left her an apologetic message saying that I had her cell phone and would be happy to return it anytime. Then I cleaned the apartment and spiffed myself up for Josh's arrival. The first half of the day had stunk, but maybe the evening with my boyfriend would compensate.

SIXTEEN

WHEN Josh arrived, I threw my arms around him and kissed him deeply. When we finally came up for air, he said, "Well, it's nice to see you, too."

I ran my hands through his hair and looked into his blue eyes. "I was beginning to forget what you looked like. You're very cute, you know that?" He did look cute. Cute and tired.

Josh pulled me with him as he collapsed on the couch. "You're not so bad yourself." He snuggled me into his body and shut his eyes.

I sighed inwardly. Maybe if I let him take a nap, he'd perk up.

Josh's phone rang. He growled and sat up. "Now what do they want? I've been gone twenty minutes!"

When Josh wasn't at Simmer to supervise, the staff routinely called him about supposed emergencies. Despite having a strong sous-chef, Snacker, the restaurant seemed practically unable to function without Josh. Our romantic moments were forever being interrupted because someone couldn't find the order sheets or because the stove wasn't working properly or because the produce bill hadn't been paid or . . . The list was endless.

"Oh, it's not them," Josh said, meaning his staff. To me, he said, "Hold on, I have to take this." He stood up and walked into the kitchen as he talked. "Hi, this is Josh Driscoll."

I trailed after him and wrapped my arms around his waist. I could make out the sound of a woman's voice coming from the phone.

"Yeah, that sounds good. Can I call you back, though?" Josh sounded strange. Embarrassed, maybe? "Okay, thanks." He hung up.

"Who was that?" I asked.

"No one. Don't worry about it. I'm going to take a shower, if that's all right." He loosened my arms from his body and slipped his phone into his pocket.

"Sure. What do you want to do for dinner? I could make something, if you trust me to feed a chef of your caliber."

"Actually I'm meeting up with Digger later."

"Oh," I said, unable to disguise the disappointment in my voice.

"It's just kind of a guy thing tonight. That's all." Josh went into the bathroom and ran the water in the shower while I sat dejectedly at the kitchen table. "Are you upset?" he called from the shower.

I poked my head into the bathroom. "Kind of. I mean, I feel like I've hardly seen you." After a pause, I said, "That's because I *have* hardly seen you."

It was quiet for a moment, and then Josh spoke. "I guess it would be all right if you came."

Irritated, I said, "I don't want to be a third wheel or any-thing."

Josh pulled the curtain back and peeked out. "You won't. I want you to come." He puckered his lips and blew me an exaggerated kiss.

I blew a kiss back and planted myself on the toilet seat to talk to him. How pathetic is that? I was so desperate for time with my boyfriend that not only was I going to barge in on his guys' night out, but I was stalking him while he took a shower.

"So how has work been?" I asked. "I'm getting the impres-sion that there have been a lot of problems recently." Prob-lems? If a restaurant's dining area is noisy, and the service is a little slow, and a couple of menu items are unavailable, there are problems. If the owner is meandering around drunk in front of the patrons and using cocaine with them after hours, there aren't just problems with the restaurant, there's a catastrophe in the making. But I deliberately used the weak word.

"Ah, just the usual crap."

"Obviously Gavin's been cranky and difficult lately, but I can't tell how bad things are for you there."

"It's nothing, okay? And like I told you, Robin told me we can just film another episode for the TV show, so that won't be a problem either. She's just going to pretend it never hap-pened."

I didn't inform Josh that I, at least, intended to remem-ber that the murder certainly had happened. Furthermore, since I was sure he'd disapprove of activities such as driving around in a stolen landscape van tailing a suspect, I said nothing about my morning's adventure.

"Josh, you know you can talk about work with me if you want. Maybe I could help you," I suggested.

"Lay off, okay?" Josh sighed audibly. "It's fine. Leave it alone."

"Fine." I shut the bathroom door and let him finish his shower. Maybe he'd wash off some of his grumps.

This was hardly the romantic start to the evening that I'd hoped for. Something was up with Josh, but I didn't know what. And who was that woman on the phone? I'd heard Josh deal with a lot of calls from Simmer. This hadn't been one of those. Josh would never cheat on me, would he? If not, why was he was getting secret calls from unknown women? But this was clearly not the right time to push him on the subject of her identity; although I hadn't tackled him about her, we were already verging on the seriously irritable.

While I was changing clothes, I heard Josh turn the water off and then heard him talking. He had his phone in the bathroom with him, and I couldn't help sticking my head into the hallway to eavesdrop.

"Dig? It's me. Just FYI, Chloe is coming out with us. So just don't say anything, okay? Cool. We'll see you there in an hour."

Don't say anything about what? I didn't like Josh's odd behavior one bit, but I had to trust him not to keep anything important from me. I'd just have to suck it up and act maturely; he'd talk when he was ready.

"Babe? How's La Morra sound to you?" When Josh opened the bathroom door, he looked totally normal, as though he hadn't just made that cryptic phone call to Digger.

"Good. I love that restaurant."

While I finished getting ready to go out, Josh spent twenty minutes snuggling Inga and cooing to her. "Who's so pretty now? Who is all clean and cute and gorgeous? Aren't you lucky to be living here with Chloe instead of with that nasty shithead who starved you and didn't brush you? We won't talk about what might've happened to you, okay? Gimme a kiss." I heard goofy kissing noises coming from the living room.

Josh and I got to the restaurant a few minutes early and were seated at a table near the bar, where we had a view of the semiopen kitchen. La Morra was a northern Italian restaurant on Boylston Street in Brookline. Wood beams ran across the ceiling, and the wood tables were set with colorful place mats and white dishes rimmed with a warm yellow. The staff at La Morra were consistently warm, and the whole restaurant had a wonderfully cozy and rustic feel to it. Also, as I knew from previous visits, the food was fantastic. My mood improved the second we sat down.

"S'up, kids?" Digger's rough voice echoed across the restaurant.

We waved to him, and then Josh stood up to shake his hand. Digger leaned in and gave me a kiss on the cheek before grabbing the seat next to Josh.

Our waitress welcomed us, handed us menus, and took our drink orders. The menu here began with cicchetti, which were preappetizers, little mouthfuls of amazingly delicious snacks. Digger, who was working at a small tapas restaurant in the South End, was bound to become a fan of these small dishes.

I looked up from the menu. "We have to get the Tuscan meatballs with porcini and prosciutto. And also the fried risotto balls."

"Fried olives, too," Josh added.

"Nice!" Digger agreed. "And then for antipasti, we're getting the savoy cabbage salad with pomegranates, hazelnuts, and bagna càuda." The bagna càuda was a strong anchovy and garlic dip that I could practically drink. "Do you guys mind sharing the soup?"

The lobster soup with spaghetti squash and toasted pumpkin seeds was another of my favorites. I certainly didn't mind sharing a bowl with Josh and Digger.

Josh added his request. "And I pick the shaved sunchoke salad with pickled mushrooms and frisée."

We spent a few more minutes deciding on main courses before placing our order and returning the menus to the waitress.

"Digger, you've recovered fully from Monday's fiasco, I hope?" I asked the chef.

"Tough as an ox." He thumped his chest with his fist. "I could've used a few days off from work though, so maybe it's too bad I got better so quickly." He grinned slyly.

"Why? What's going on there?"

"Ah, it's a wreck. The servers suck, and they're totally obnoxious. Every night they let the orders sit out until they're practically bone cold, and then they get sent back. It's crap, I tell ya! I can't even believe I'm off tonight. I've worked the past two weeks straight, except for last Monday, and the goddamn owner is on my case about keeping food costs down." Digger took more than a sip of his wine. "Did you see the Mystery Diner's write-up about us? Frickin' hated the place. Hated everything about it. The food, the decor, the staff. Everything. And you know what? He was half-right, too. The service is awful, and the customers get treated like shit."

Digger's colorful language reassured me that he'd recovered from any digitalis poisoning that he'd had.

"I didn't see that review." Josh furrowed his brow. "Your food is great. What could the reviewer find to pick on?"

Digger shrugged. "The usual stuff. This was too oily, that was underseasoned, this wasn't spicy enough. And my favorite? The portions are too small. It's tapas for Christ's sake! Obviously the portions are small!"

"That's not fair." Josh shook his head. "Some of these reviewers . . ." His voice trailed off.

I had to agree. "I saw that Marlee and Alloy got a pretty nasty review from him, too. That one might have been on target, but it was still vicious."

Digger continued. "That dude is one mean son of a bitch. Do you know how much power reviewers have? People come into a restaurant and say they read a great review, and so they wanted to try us out. Nobody comes in and says, 'Hey, I just read a crappy review of this place, but I thought I'd give it a shot anyhow.' The Mystery Diner may have been right about the service, but not about the food. And I'm not just saying that to be cocky. The food really is good. That Mystery Diner should be strung up, if you ask me." Digger took another drink and then looked sheepish. "Sorry. But you know what? Bad reviews happen. And the review didn't single me out. The reviewer just hated the whole place. It's part of the business, and it makes the good reviews all the better. Still, I'm not gonna say it doesn't sting like a bastard when I read the awful ones."

"And then you get blamed for it, right?" Josh gave Digger a knowing look. "The owner rides you for a bad review and takes all the credit for a good one. What're you going to do? That's the life we chose." Josh lifted his glass in a sarcastic toast.

"Actually, I'm looking for another job. *That's* what I'm gonna do. When things reach a certain low, we chefs have to move on and find something better. There's only so much punishment I can take on a daily basis, you know?"

"Wow," I said, stunned that Digger was thinking about quitting. "Do you have any leads?"

"A couple. I got a headhunter I use. Actually I gave—"

"The food is here," Josh cut in.

The waitress set down the cicchetti we'd ordered. I inhaled the aroma and couldn't wait to taste the meatballs. As I knew from a previous visit, when I'd practically interrogated the server about the meatballs, they had been seared and then simmered in the oven with white wine. I popped one in my mouth. Heaven!

Inevitably, we talked about the murder. Digger hadn't known about the digitalis found in Francie's system. "It's a heart medicine," I said. "It comes from a flower. Foxglove. Don't some people garnish dishes with flowers?" I bit into a risotto ball.

"Ugh, yeah. Nasturtiums and shit. Ick." Digger blew a raspberry. "I've never done that, have you, Josh?"

Josh shook his head. "Nah. That was sort of trendy for a while. Some flowers are edible, but I never got into that. Seriously, nobody wants to eat a flower."

I'd had nasturtiums in salad that had been pretty good, but I felt unqualified to argue flavor with two chefs, so I kept quiet.

Digger pointed his fork at me and spoke with his mouth full. "Flowers belong in a garden or in a vase, if you ask me. Just don't make me grow 'em for you. I've never touched a garden in my life."

By the time I finished my entrée, lasagna con coniglio brasato (braised rabbit and crispy polenta lasagna with shaved raw mushrooms, thyme, and gremoulata), I was so stuffed that I didn't know whether I'd be able to eat dessert. As usual, though, my appetite returned quickly, and I managed to squeeze in a ricotta cheese tart with Marsala sauce.

When Digger went to the bathroom, Josh reached across the table and took my hand in his. "I'm sorry I was so snappy earlier. Really."

Since Josh looked so genuinely apologetic, I squeezed his hand back. "How early are you working tomorrow?"

"Not that early." Josh winked at me.

SEVENTEEN

"IT'S not possible that I got bigger since Friday!" Adrianna's yell shot through my phone's receiver. "What in heck made me think it was a good idea to alter my own wedding dress?"

"I don't know," I said helplessly. "I wish I could do your alterations, but I'm not particularly adept with a needle and thread. Do you want me to come over anyway and see what I can do?"

Adrianna had bought a discount wedding dress for herself in a much larger size than she normally wore. The supposed point was to alter it to fit her pregnant shape.

"Yes, I want you to come over and help! Can't you hear the anxiety in my voice? Get over here!"

I told Bridezilla I'd be over in a few minutes.

Even though Josh and I had more than made up the

previous night, things between us still felt strained. That stress, combined with the experience of having Francie die in front of me and my so-far-unsuccessful investigation of the murder, left my spirits low. I worried that my mood might rub off on Adrianna. She was already nervous enough about the wedding, the baby, and her future in general, and it was supposed to be my job to calm her down. I'd need to muster every ounce of cheer I could.

As I was about to head out the door, Robin called. "I'm so glad I caught you. I really need to get my phone back. Can I stop by and get it this afternoon? Around three?"

"Absolutely." I gave Robin my address and directions, and promised to be home.

When I arrived at Adrianna's, she had her wedding gown half on. It was inside out, and most of the material was gathered around her middle, where her waist had once been.

With despair on her face and in her voice, she said, "I can't deal with this right now, Chloe. I can't."

"Calm down. Let me help you."

I pulled the front of the dress up over her chest, which had practically doubled in size, and tied the halter top around her neck.

"No one told me I was going to get Pam Anderson boobs," she seethed. "I look trampy. I can't wait to hear what my idiot mother has to say about it."

"Here," I said handing her a box of pins. "Start pinning and stop whining. You can do this. Just pin and sew, okay?"

"Okay." Ade started pinning the sides of her dress. I helped in the spots she couldn't reach. "This is not exactly the image I had of how I was going to look on my wedding day," she said with a sniff.

"What? You didn't picture yourself beautiful? Stunning? Radiant?"

"No," she barked at me. "Stressed out, bloated, huge, and busty like a porn star."

"Ade, stop," I said firmly as I pinned the hem. "Everything is going to work out perfectly."

"Your mom has her dress all set, right? And your dress is ready?" I nodded, petrified about how she might have reacted if I'd said no! Ade continued. "I have to call today to confirm the arrangements for renting the tables, chairs, and linens. Oh!" She snapped her fingers. "And I have to finalize the flowers." She exhaled deeply.

"I'll do all that for you. Just give me the numbers. You don't need to do anything except finish the dress and then rest. My mom is taking care of the tent, and the company is going to set it up on Thursday afternoon. You'll be able to see it Friday at the rehearsal dinner."

The rehearsal itself was going to be a quick run-through rather than an elaborate, formal affair. My dad, with the best of intentions, had promised to grill dinner. It was remotely possible that he'd fulfill his promise without charring everything.

I spoke with pins clamped between my lips. "And I want you to try to keep Kitty from driving you insane. Where is she, by the way?"

"I'm trying to keep my distance from her, so I sent her off to Faneuil Hall to do the tourist thing. And there's enough shopping down there to keep her occupied. Who knows? Maybe she'll find another smoked sausage basket for me."

"I'm so sorry about that, Ade." I moved to the front of her dress and continued pinning, doing my best to keep the hemline straight.

"I shouldn't have been surprised. I should be used to my mother by now. But it does hurt. I'm pregnant and getting married, and I need my mother. Or, rather, I need a less insane mother. Kitty is never going to be who I want her to be, so there's no use trying to change her. I don't have the energy for it anyhow. Bless your parents for taking such good care of me. And you, too, of course." Ade looked down at me and smiled.

"I'd do anything for you. You know that." I smiled back.

When I left, Ade was running her dress through the sewing machine. Although she seemed to have relaxed a little bit, I was reluctant to go. But I had to get home to meet Robin and return her cell phone. I still hadn't thought of a way to ask her whether she'd known Leo before the filming without accusing her of rigging the show and also, of course, without revealing that I'd explored her cell phone. Once I got home, I hurriedly scanned through her phone again in search of recently dialed or received calls. Everything had been erased; there were no call records. The absence meant nothing. I routinely erased all of my own calls.

Following the directions I'd given her, Robin knocked at my back door, which opened to a wooden fire escape that doubled as a miniature patio. "Hello?" She cupped her hand over her forehead and peered through the window.

I opened the door. "Hey, Robin. I bet you'll be glad to get your phone back. Come on in."

"Sorry about this. I can't believe I left my phone at your parents' place. It's been driving me crazy not to have it."

"Here, grab a seat. Pardon the clothes everywhere. My mom gave me a ton of stuff to donate to a home for women in transition. It's a temporary place for homeless women to stay while they're trying to find jobs and housing. My mom gave me some great stuff that could be worn on interviews." I'd spread everything out on the couch. Feeling embarrassed about the mess, I started folding the outfits and putting them neatly in bags.

Robin's eyes lit up. "That's a wonderful idea. You know, Leo could probably use some help in clearing out Francie's belongings. I'm sure that the last thing he feels like doing is going through all of her clothes. Maybe he'd want to donate them to this women's place."

"You've been in touch with Leo?" I asked casually.

"Obviously I called him to offer my condolences. I guess there isn't going to be a funeral. He said maybe a memorial service later. I'll give you his number." Robin took a scrap of paper from her purse and jotted down Leo's home number. "I'm sure he'd appreciate some help. Sort of a grisly process, I'd think, going through your dead wife's clothing." Robin grimaced.

"I'll definitely give him a call. Thank you."

It distressed me to realize that poor Francie was going to disappear. No funeral? And nothing more than the possibility of a memorial service? In no time, I thought, it will be as if Francie had never existed. But the possibility of going through Francie's clothing did offer the hope of learning something—anything!—about her murder.

As soon as Robin left, I called Leo, who picked up after a few rings. His voice sounded raspy and weak.

As I explained why I was calling, I felt grateful for my social work training. "I'm sorry if this is premature on my part, but I've done some volunteering at a shelter that helps homeless women to find jobs. Do you think that Francie would have liked the idea of donating her clothing? I just thought I could be of some help to you. Maybe you're not ready, though. "

"You know what? I do like that idea. I've been trying to figure out what to do around the house. Do I throw out anything that reminds me of her? Do I keep the house set up as though she were still here? No one gives you an instruction manual that tells you what to do when your wife dies. But this feels right."

"Do you suppose that I could come by tomorrow morning?" I tried to suppress my excitement at the prospect of getting to peek around his house.

"Sure. How about nine o'clock?" Then he asked the last question you'd expect to hear from a grieving widower: "Uh, by the way, not that it matters, but do you know if these donations are tax deductible?"

"Yes," I said. "Yes, they are."

Eᴉɢʜᴛᴇᴇɴ

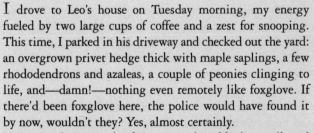

I drove to Leo's house on Tuesday morning, my energy fueled by two large cups of coffee and a zest for snooping. This time, I parked in his driveway and checked out the yard: an overgrown privet hedge thick with maple saplings, a few rhododendrons and azaleas, a couple of peonies clinging to life, and—damn!—nothing even remotely like foxglove. If there'd been foxglove here, the police would have found it by now, wouldn't they? Yes, almost certainly.

I opened the trunk of the car and grabbed a cardboard box and the garbage bags I'd brought for Francie's clothing. Feeling superstitious, I avoided the front door, the one through which Francie's body had been carried, and went to the back door. I rang the bell and waited several minutes for Leo to answer.

"Chloe. Hi. Excuse my shirt. It never occurred to me to

learn how to do laundry. Isn't that stupid?" Leo looked dreadful. His eyes were puffy, his hair unruly. His shirt was not only dirty but buttoned wrong. Had he relied on his wife to align buttons and buttonholes? Once I'd entered the kitchen, it was clear that laundry was far from the only kind of housework left undone. Every surface of the kitchen was piled with dirty dishes, empty and half-empty take-out containers, newspapers, junk mail, and tons of other debris, including four grocery bags that hadn't been unpacked and, scattered all over the floor, what must have been at least two pounds of coffee beans. Leo waved his arm around. "Sorry about this. I had no idea how much Francie did around the house."

"Really, it's no problem. I don't know what to say after what you've been through. I'm glad I can do something," I said in my best social worker voice. "Why don't you show me where Francie's closet is, okay?"

"Sure. It's up here," he said as he started for the stairs. "But I've got to warn you. Avoid the bathroom where, uh, where Francie, you know . . ." Leo stammered. "The police spent hours up there, but they didn't . . . It hasn't been cleaned. Can you believe that? It's their job to find out what happened to my wife, and they leave that filth in there for me?"

As if it were a police job to scrub the bathroom for him! Leo might reasonably want to avoid sanitizing the area himself, but couldn't he have hired a cleaning service? Or some sort of company that specialized in hazardous waste? It was obscene that the mess had been sitting there for over a week now. Was Leo just going to seal off the bathroom forever? I tried to remember the exact words I'd used in offering Leo my help. I prayed that I hadn't been foolish enough to tell him that I'd do absolutely anything. As we passed through the dining room and the front hall, I noticed yet more litter as well as the need for dusting and vaccuming. The mess seriously detracted from what was otherwise a beautiful house. The multitude of large and brightly colored art pieces on the walls were so cheery that I momentarily forgot this was the scene of the crime.

"Leo," I said speedily, "there are companies that can be hired to clean anything. I can help you find one, if you like."

"Really? That would be wonderful. I just haven't known what to . . . Here you go." We entered the master bedroom. "Thank God there's another bathroom off the master suite. That's Francie's closet." Leo pointed to an oversized walk-in closet with sliding doors that were partly open. "Please, take anything you think these women could use. Francie has enough clothes to outfit a hundred homeless women. I'll be back in a minute." Leo left the room.

Because of the condition of the rest of the house, I was surprised to find the bedroom tidy. Amazingly, the bed had been made, and Leo had taken care to arrange the bright blue bedding and pillows to resemble a guest room at a Vermont inn. Expensive off-white Berber carpeting was stain-free, and the four windows that let bright light into the room gave it a fresh, unsullied appearance.

Leo's promise to be right back suggested that he intended to stay while I gathered Francie's clothes. Since I couldn't order him to leave so that I could tear the house apart looking for clues, I had to make the most of my time. Leo's return would require me to go through the closet. Consequently, I took advantage of his absence to peer under the bed, where I found nothing but a few dust bunnies, and to take a quick look at the night tables, on each of which sat a small lamp. The table on the left-hand side had nothing else. The second night table had, in addition to the lamp, an empty bottle of mineral water, a box of tissues, a clock radio, and a stack of magazines, with a recent issue of the *New Yorker* on top.

Afraid of getting caught, I turned to the closet, which was jammed full of women's clothes. Every one of its many shelves, drawers, hangers, and shoe racks was occupied by some item of clothing. Tall boots and plastic storage containers teetered at the edge of the top shelf; I resolved to keep an eye out for falling objects. I set down my cardboard box, shook out a garbage bag, and started to remove clothes from hangers. Francie had had a large wardrobe in a narrow range of colors and styles. The predominant shades were brown, beige, and gray. The boldest color was dark navy. Many items were conservative pieces from Talbots. I was learning nothing that would contribute to my amateur investigation, but the good news was that many of Francie's things would work perfectly as interview outfits for the women at the shelter. I folded simple sweaters, blazers, and dresses and collected at least twenty-five pairs of nondescript dress shoes.

Toward one end of the heavy wooden rod that supported the hanging clothes were several large zippered plastic clothing bags. Unzipping one, I was nearly blinded by color. The outfits in this bag were radically different from everything else I'd seen. Yanking the bag open, I fingered through a slinky pink outfit, an ugly flower-print dress, a series of short skirts, and even a man's suit. I unzipped the next bag and found additional outfits as outrageous as those I'd just examined. I stood on tiptoe and pulled down a printed storage box that turned out to contain hats. Checking another box, I found high-heeled shoes, brooches, eyeglasses, and scarves, all in styles radically different from the dull, conservative look of the clothing displayed openly in the closet. Yet another box contained wigs: long hair, short hair, curly hair, blonde, brunette—you name it, and Francie had a wig for it. I sat on the floor of the closet surrounded by a mound of bizarre . . . outfits? No, not outfits. Costumes. These had to be costumes. But why? Why had Francie been dressing up as other people?

"Francie's little secret." Leo's voice made me jump. "I guess I should have warned you," he said. "The things in the boxes won't work for the homeless women, will they?" He produced an almost hysterical-sounding laugh. "Or maybe they will! Oh, what the hell does it matter now?" Leo tossed his hands up as he spoke. "Maybe you'll think it's funny. What the heck! Francie wrote restaurant reviews. You may have heard of her. The Boston Mystery Diner? She got the idea for the costumes from Ruth Reichl. You know that food critic from the *New York Times*? Francie made reservations under false names, and she'd go to dinner all gussied up in one of these outfits. Sometimes I'd go with her. I've got some, uh, costumes, I guess you'd say, too." Although I tried to keep my face neutral, my expression may have been what prompted him to add, "She wanted to do fair reviews and not get recognized as a reviewer every time she walked into a restaurant."

Francie? Francie, of all people, was the notorious Mystery Diner? Unbelievable! And fair reviews? Those I'd read had been ruthless, unforgiving, and cruelly unfair.

"Wow," I said. "I had no idea. For some reason I'd always assumed that the Mystery Diner was a man. Everyone does, I think. I don't know why. Wow," I said again.

"She was the most prominent food critic in Boston. She was very astute and had high standards, so her praise meant a lot to local restaurants."

Praise? I wanted to ask. *What praise?* Well, maybe in reviews I hadn't seen.

"Please, Chloe," Leo continued. "Don't tell anyone." He spoke earnestly, even urgently. "Francie was proud of what she did and so proud of not being recognized. She took her job seriously, loved what she did, and there's no reason to spoil her game now."

"Of course. Sure." I nodded.

Nothing about Leo's statements or demeanor even began to hint at any comprehension of how violently his wife was hated in the restaurant community. As far as I could tell, he believed that Francie's reviews had been admirably honest, and he failed to comprehend the damage and devastation they had inflicted on the hardworking staff of the restaurants she had trashed.

As quickly as possible, I finished packing the clothes I wanted and left behind the wild costumes. No woman at the shelter needed to set off for a job interview sporting a neon dress and a blonde wig or, heaven forbid, a man's suit; the shelter did not encourage employment in prostitution, nor did it seek to promote cross-dressing. Before I left, I thumbed through a phone book that Leo dug up, copied down the numbers of a few cleaning services that could take care of the bathroom situation, and left Leo the task of making the calls.

During the entire drive home, I puzzled over the revelation that Francie had been the Mystery Diner. I'd previously seen Francie as a harmless, innocent victim. In contrast, the Mystery Diner's reviews I'd read had been downright vicious. Of course, I hadn't looked at the Mystery Diner's complete works, so to speak; maybe from time to time she'd lavished praise on a chef. And I was baffled by Leo's apparent obliviousness to the impact of the reviews and the anger they generated. Or was he playing dumb? And if Leo had murdered his wife, why was he keeping her secret identity a secret? The Mystery Diner's reviews had provided many chefs and restaurant owners with a potential motive for murder. If the Mystery Diner had torn Josh to pieces, I'd have felt like killing her myself! Why wasn't Leo pointing the finger of suspicion at the restaurant people whom Francie had enraged? Why wasn't he deflecting suspicion to people who'd hated her?

Marlee had a defaced copy of the Mystery Diner's beastly review of Alloy pinned up in her kitchen. Someone, probably Marlee herself, had stabbed that review with a knife. Digger, too, had had a rotten review. His attitude was more mixed than Marlee's; he seemed torn between anger at the review and acceptance of it as an inevitable part of the restaurant business. Still, Francie's reviews had excoriated both Marlee and Digger, both of whom had had the opportunity to add digitalis to the food that Francie had eaten. According to Leo, Francie's identity as the Mystery Diner was a secret. Oh, really? Just how secret had her secret been? Leo had revealed it to me readily enough. Had he told others during Francie's lifetime? Had she?

Robin. Yes, if Robin had had a prior relationship with Leo, he might have told her that Francie was the Mystery Diner, and Robin absolutely could have passed that information on to her good friend, Marlee. What's more, Robin could have let it slip to Marlee that Leo was going to be the shopper chosen for the filming of *Chefly Yours*. If so, Marlee would have known ahead of time that she'd be in Francie's kitchen and would thus have the opportunity to poison food that Francie, the despised reviewer, would eat.

I peeled into my parking space, left the clothes in the car, flew up the stairs to my condo, rushed to the computer, and searched for Francie's reviews online. I'd only glimpsed the review posted in Alloy's kitchen; I hadn't really read it, in part because the knife sticking out of the center had distracted me. The review I found on the Web was worse than I'd imagined, far worse than merely scathing. As I read it, one damning sentence after another hit my eye:

What is meant to be a sleek and artful presentation is instead an exercise in pretension . . . Each dish is comprised of unsightly lumps; not only do these lumps not relate to one another in any conceivable way, but each is inedible on its own . . . Despite the chef's effort at contemporary plate arrangement, I found the micro-green and herb-stem garnishes unattractive; far from whetting my appetite, they destroyed it. My roasted chicken had what appeared to be a small branch poking out of its thigh. I appreciate fresh herbs as much as the next diner, but there is no need to overwhelm a guest with what amounts to piles of shrubbery . . . The service? Worse than what one would expect at a fast-food joint . . . The trio of beef was enough to convince this reviewer that I would rather stick kabob skewers in my eyes than return to this restaurant.

Good God! What a horrible review! And, unfortunately for Marlee and Alloy, it was all the more horrible for being accurate—or at least consistent with my own experience. Perhaps the Mystery Diner's reviews—Francie's reviews—had, after all, been fair, just as Leo had claimed. Mean and nasty, yes, but on target. Still, it would have been possible to critique Alloy honestly yet tactfully, whereas Francie had clearly prided herself on snarky, savage reviews that titillated readers and sold newspapers.

But the piece on Alloy might be an aberration. Consequently, I looked up Francie's review of Digger's restaurant. After tearing apart the whole notion of small servings and declaring tapas to be a lame excuse to overcharge patrons for the supposed novelty of minuscule plates, the review went on to blast the quality of the food. It was one thing for a chef to hear that the service was poor or that restaurant was unacceptably noisy, but to attack the taste of the food was to hit a chef where it hurt. In contrast to the review of Alloy, this one didn't ring true. Although I'd never been to the tapas restaurant where Digger worked, all the meals that he had ever cooked for me had been delicious. The Mystery Diner had made some direct assaults on Digger. For example:

> *Whoever cooked the smoked sausage with olives and tomatoes should throw in his knives and not even bother returning to culinary school. In the opinion of this reviewer, the dish was a pure insult.*

Ouch! Digger had given me the impression that the review was a harsh critique of the restaurant as a whole and not a personal attack on his skill as a chef. In reality, Francie had slung insult after personal insult at Digger. She'd called him, among other things, an "untalented fool" and an "ordinary hack." My close reading made me question Digger's apparently mellow attitude about the review. Maybe Digger had simply been saving face. Still, at La Morra, Digger had repeatedly referred to the Mystery Diner as "he" and had given no indication that he knew the reviewer's true identity. Plus, Digger had seemed genuinely clueless about gardening.

Stinging with empathy for chefs who'd been Francie's victims, I struggled to be unbiased. Digger was Josh's friend and therefore my friend. Marlee was not. Even when I took my bias into account, it remained true that Marlee was the one who'd shown outward hostility to the Mystery Diner. Hard though I tried, I couldn't shake the image of that knife in the corkboard.

Nineteen

AFTER reading those beastly reviews, cooking was the last thing I felt like doing. For all I knew, Francie's spirit might appear in my kitchen and criticize my efforts! But Adrianna and Owen were coming for dinner to go over the wedding ceremony. They were writing their own vows—at least they were *supposed* to be writing them—and I'd put together some ideas for the rest of the ceremony. All of a sudden, I felt a sense of urgency: unless I finalized my part, I'd find myself standing in front of an expectant crowd and babbling incoherently about the joys of marriage.

I ran out to the store and returned with everything I needed to make a simple pasta salad. My recipe had two big advantages: it was easy, and it produced one of the few pasta dishes I'd ever made that tasted even better the next day than it did when it had just been cooked. It consisted of fettuccine tossed with shrimp, avocado, red onion, tomatoes, Calamata olives, fresh basil, balsamic vinegar, olive oil, and Parmesan cheese. Francie's ghost failed to materialize while I cooked, so I felt confident that I hadn't offended the dead. I set aside the shrimp and the pasta, which would be cooked just before the dish was served, and I mixed the other ingredients.

When Ade and Owen showed up at seven, one look at Adrianna told me that she was seriously annoyed with her husband-to-be.

"What's up? Why are you making that face?" I asked.

"You won't believe what Owen has done!" Ade turned to her fiancé. "If you think there's any chance that we're using those vows—"

"She's really overreacting," Owen protested before Adrianna could finish. "I just wanted to mix it up a bit. You know, do something untraditional. We don't want a formal, stuffy wedding ceremony, right? So I came up with something unique!" Owen handed me a folder that contained a sheet of paper with handwritten vows.

I eyed him suspiciously and braced myself. Owen's idea of untraditional or unique was most people's idea of crazy. I dragged a kitchen chair into my small living room and let Ade and Owen take the couch. Ade sat on one side of it with her head tilted and resting on her hand, while Owen sat at the opposite end of the couch with his hands solemnly folded. Despite the separation between the two of them, I could see that Adrianna was muffling a smile.

I skimmed through Owen's proposed vows. Oh no! "Seriously?"

Serious was exactly what my question was not. As if there were any possibility that I'd deliver these lines! Incredibly and ridiculously, Owen had composed wedding vows à la Dr. Seuss:

> *Do you take Ade as your bride?*
> *Will you stay loyal and filled with pride?*
> *Will you love her all your life?*
> *Even in times of marital strife?*
> *Will you take out the weekly trash,*
> *And provide for her some ready cash?*
> *Is it your wish that I proclaim,*
> *That she shall take your given last name?*

I couldn't bring myself actually to read the rest. Instead, I ran my protesting eyes down the sheet of paper. After catching sight of an especially hideous rhyme—something about a wedding ring, wanting to sing, and making Owen feel like a king—I gave up. Staring at Owen, I said, "I'm looking at you now, Owen, and you look like a perfectly normal human being, but it turns out that you are not." Owen, in fact, looked not only normal but even handsomer than usual. Maybe Ade's pregnancy glow had rubbed off on him. His cheeks had a rosy tint that brightened his fair complexion, and his black hair could've been primped by a *GQ* stylist. In case I'd failed to make my meaning plain on the first try, I said, "You're an idiot, Owen. I love you, but you're an idiot."

"Hallelujah!" Ade shouted and clapped her hands. "A voice of reason!"

"Come on, it's funny. Don't you think it's funny?" Owen pleaded.

"A wedding ceremony is not supposed to be funny," I instructed. "You don't have to use the traditional vows, but no way in hell am I reading this." I crumpled up the paper and flung it at his head.

"Yeah, and what was that business about giving me cash?" Ade demanded. "You don't talk about money in a ceremony. Or trash, for that matter."

"Okay, okay, I give in! But it's a happy occasion. I want everyone to have fun."

My voice suffused with the authority vested in me by the Commonwealth of Massachusetts, I said, "This is the first and probably only wedding at which I'm going to officiate, and I'm not going to make a freak out of myself by reciting a bunch of dumb rhymes." Fortunately, although I hadn't expected anything quite so preposterous as Owen's doggerel, I wasn't caught off guard. Suspecting that both Adrianna and Owen were more attached to the idea of writing their own vows than they'd be to the process of composing them, I'd done my wedding-vow homework and consequently was able to hand them copies of material I'd assembled from Web sites and written myself. "What about these?"

"I don't want that business about obeying the groom in there," Ade said as she reached for the papers.

Owen's face brightened. "Maybe we could put in a vow of *dis*obedience. I will never do anything Ade tells me to do!"

"You better watch it," Ade warned him. "Your frivolous attitude is making me worry. Did you get your tux yet? I swear, Owen, if you got some garish tuxedo in loud colors, I'll scream."

"I wouldn't do that." To my ear, Owen sounded all too serious. "I got the boring black one like you told me."

I'd have bet good money that Owen was lying, but Ade apparently believed him, and she didn't need to be more riled up than than she already was. As she read the vows I'd put together, Ade kept nodding, and even Owen agreed that although my suggestions didn't rhyme, they would work.

"Do you trust me to put together the service?" I asked them.

"Yeah, we do," Owen rubbed Ade's back. He looked at her and wiped the tears from her cheeks. "Babe, it's going to be a wonderful day."

I said, "Good. I'll do the whole wedding service, and all you'll have to do is repeat after me." Adrianna still looked stressed out, but at least she'd moved close to Owen and was leaning against him. "Relax," I said. "There's nothing to worry about. This is all fun stuff going on, okay?"

I cooked the pasta and the shrimp, and tossed them together with the vegetable mixture. As we ate dinner in the living room, we talked food.

"How's the menu coming?" Owen asked.

"Oh, I almost forgot! The food is going to be out of this world! Even though it's still August, I know you wanted a fall menu, so Josh is going to put out an amazing spread with that in mind."

"I know I'm a pain, but I always wanted to get married in the fall, and since that won't work out," she said, patting her belly, "we can at least eat like it's fall. I'm probably driving Josh crazy."

I brushed aside her worries. "Not a big deal. You know how Josh loves a challenge. He's going to do an extravagant pumpkin stew cooked in a pumpkin, a salad with dried cranberries and maple vinaigrette, tenderloin medallions, a roasted rack of lamb with grape-chili jam and goat cheese sauce. What else? I can't remember it all right now, but you'll love it."

"Sounds amazing," Owen said happily.

"Josh is off on Friday to prep all the food. I think he's coming here to do it. I'll actually get to spend some time with him, so it'll work out well for me."

I sounded more optimistic than I felt. When Josh was here, he'd be in his chef mode, and we'd have no real conversation. Still, it would be good to be together, and our shared focus on the wedding might restore our relationship.

I sent Ade and Owen off with the promise of a beautiful ceremony with vows that didn't rhyme. After cleaning up the kitchen, I spent an hour at the computer writing the service and quit only when I was so tired that my fingers started typing in Dr. Seuss style. I collapsed in bed with the intention of sleeping in the next morning. The prospect was shattered by the sound of feet pounding on my front door.

TWENTY

"CHLOE? Let me in!"

I glanced at the clock. What the heck was Josh doing here at eight a.m.?

I flung back the sheet and forced myself to stagger to the door. "Hi, honey," I managed sleepily. I rubbed my eyes and stared in confusion at Josh. My boyfriend had evidently kicked my door because his arms were full of trays and containers covered in plastic wrap. A small cardboard box was teetering off the top of the pile, and I grabbed a squirt bottle just as it began to fall. "What are you doing here? Oh, my God! Is today Friday?" I really was not awake yet. Panicking, I thought, *Oh, no! It's the day before the wedding!*

"No, no. It's Wednesday. I just got the rest of the week off, and I thought I'd start cooking for Saturday. I've got a ton to prep, and my kitchen is a wreck." In my opinion, the entire apartment that he shared with his sous-chef, Snacker, was a chronic disaster area, but I didn't say so. "The goddamn stove broke again, and Snacker left a huge mess in there. Seriously, there's no way I'm doing his dishes again, and he's working at Simmer while I'm off, so who knows when they'll get done. Can I use your kitchen?"

"Yeah. Of course." I plodded into the kitchen and set the squirt bottle box on the table. "Coffee. I need coffee."

I worked on brewing a pot of caffeine while Josh returned to his car for more food. I was psyched to have Josh here but totally surprised that Gavin had given him so much time off. Josh was lucky to get one day a week. Maybe Gavin had finally come to his senses and realized how badly he'd been treating his gifted and hardworking chef. Josh had had no vacation time whatsoever since he'd started at the restaurant last year, and Gavin must have realized that Josh was about to crack. Oddly enough, even though Josh would be cooking like a madman for the next few days, I knew that he was looking forward to catering the wedding. Chefs! For me, a vacation meant blue skies, burning sun, sterling ocean, fruity cocktails, and skimpy bathing suits, but Josh wasn't the type to lounge around on a beach and do nothing all day. What did he do when he finally had time off? Cook.

"Okay, I have to make the pasta and then marinate the vegetables for the strudels . . ." Josh said to himself as he checked off a mental list on his fingers.

"What kind of pasta are you doing?" My question was vital. I could probably live on pasta alone.

"A butter-poached lobster on tagliatelle with a yuzu pesto and mushrooms." Josh moved his eyebrows up and down and then winked at me. "You like the sound of that one?"

"Amazing," I said, echoing Owen. "Except, what on earth is yuzu?"

"Japanese citrus fruit. Sour. You'll love it."

"Strudels. What's in those?" I craned my head to get a look into my chef's containers.

"Grilled vegetables rolled in puff pastry. Fantastic." Josh clapped his hands. "All right! Outta my kitchen!" he ordered in a joking voice. "I've got a million vinaigrettes to mix up."

"Yes, sir."

"Oh, wait. Here. Can you charge my cell phone for me?" Josh handed me his cell and charger. "Thanks, babe."

I went into the bedroom, plugged in Josh's phone, and worked on Ade and Owen's ceremony. Who'd have guessed that writing a wedding service would be so difficult? At the end of two hours, when my script for the wedding was in pretty good shape, I decided to go snoop in my kitchen to see what Josh was up to.

"Yum. What's in that?" I sniffed a tray of vegetables that were marinating in an aromatic mixture.

"Not telling." Josh grinned. Then he snapped his fingers. "Oh, damn. I forgot to pick up the beef tenderloin and the duck breasts I ordered. That was dumb. I'm going to run and get them. Back in a few." Josh kissed me and ran out the door before I could even say good-bye.

I was proofing the ceremony when Josh's cell rang. In case the call had something to do with food for the wedding, I answered. "Hello?"

"Ah, yes, is Josh there?" The woman spoke with a heavy French accent.

"No, he should be back soon. Can I take a message for him?"

"Er, yes. Tell him Yvette called. He has my number."

"Sure. I'll tell him." I clapped the phone shut.

Who the hell was Yvette? On the night we'd been at the

emergency room, Josh had had a call from a woman. The other day when he'd been here, he'd again had a call from a woman. He'd certainly never mentioned Yvette to me. I hated the knots that were forming in my stomach. When Josh returned, I didn't give him the message. He was keeping some kind of secret from me, but I wasn't up for having it revealed right now.

Besides, I had my own secrets.

"Look at this beauty!" Josh gleefully held out the large beef tenderloin. "And the duck breasts are beautiful. I'm going to do those in a red wine and orange sauce. I'm on fire today!"

I had to agree. Josh was in the cooking zone I'd come to know so well: all of his creative juices were flowing, and he was reveling in an endorphin rush.

His phone rang again. I ran to my bedroom, grabbed it, checked caller ID, and returned to the kitchen. "It's Robin," I said. "You want to take it?"

"Sure." Josh wiped his hands on a dishcloth and took the call. "Hey, Robin. What's up?'

I shamelessly eavesdropped on the conversation. Without even hearing what Robin had to say, I could tell that she was slathering on the praise and making grand promises. "Really? Thanks so much . . . Good, good. I'm glad . . . Excellent news . . . You think? Wow!" Josh hung up and turned to me. "Guess what? Robin called to tell me that we're going to film the next episode on Tuesday. That's a relief."

Reluctantly, I said, "Josh, I found out something kind of strange."

"What?" Josh began finely chopping a pile of herbs.

"It turns out that Robin and Marlee are friends. Good friends. It seems pretty likely that this supposed competition is rigged so that Marlee will win." As much as I hated to dash Josh's hopes of winning his own TV show, I had to tell him.

Josh stopped his knife work and stared at me in confusion. "What?"

"Josh, I know. I understand. It's rotten. It's unfair. It's messed up. And not that anything would make it all right, but let me tell you that Marlee's kitchen is filthy, and her food sucks. And on top of all that, I think she's the one who killed Francie."

"Marlee? Mousy Marlee is a killer? You're crazy."

"Josh, Francie was the Mystery Diner." I let that sink in for a minute. "You should see what she wrote about Alloy."

I filled Josh in. In particular, I told him about the defaced review posted in Alloy's kitchen.

Josh was skeptical. "First of all, Chloe, even if Robin and Marlee are friends, it doesn't mean that she's necessarily going to win. It's up to the viewers who vote. And second, I don't think that anyone who was part of the show killed Francie. For a lousy review? Chefs are used to crummy reviews. It happens to all of us, and we don't all run out and kill the reviewer. If we did, there'd be a trail of evil-reviewer bodies spread out across the country. I still think it was one of Evan and Willie's stupid pranks that turned deadly."

In the spirit of full disclosure, I recounted the stories I'd heard at Ade's shower. In describing Evan and Willie's unfunny practical jokes to Josh, I again started to worry about their guilt.

"You see? That's what I'm talking about," Josh said. "Dropping rocks on someone's head? Sending their brother skateboarding toward a death trap? Owen is lucky he survived growing up in a house with those two."

"God, you don't think they'll do anything at the wedding, do you?"

"Well . . ." Josh spoke slowly. "I talked to Owen the other day when he dropped off Simmer's seafood order."

"And?" I said, panicking.

"He told me that Evan and Willie have been threatening to show up at the wedding with shotguns. You know? Shotgun wedding."

"What? They'd better do no such thing! The last thing those two nutballs need is to get their hands on shotguns. Does Ade know about this?"

"No, and you're not going to tell her. Owen said he'd convinced them not to do anything stupid like that on his wedding day. It'll be fine."

My lovingly crafted script for the wedding service made no provision for any such vile interruption. What if they made good on their threat? They'd catch hell from me, but I had no idea how I'd give them hell without ruining the wedding. As for Adrianna, she might just turn the shotguns on them.

By late afternoon, Josh, having finished the preparations he could do three days before the wedding, was crashed out asleep on the couch while *The Usual Suspects* DVD played on the television. To avoid awakening him, I went to the bedroom and spent an hour and a half on the phone confirming wedding arrangements. The white tent would be set up tomorrow, Thursday, and then the tables, chairs, linens, china, glasses, and silverware would be delivered on Friday. The order for champagne, wine, liquor, and ice was set, as was the delivery on the day of the wedding, when the floral decorations, bouquets, and boutonnieres would also arrive.

My fridge was brimming with gourmet food and fresh ingredients. I rooted through the produce, decided that Josh could spare a few items, and made a quick trip to the local seafood store to pick up a bag of mussels for a simple but aromatic mussel bouillabaisse. Josh was still snoozing when I returned. I thinly sliced green and red peppers, fennel, and onions, and then quartered a few tomatoes and began sautéeing the vegetables in butter. I added tomato paste, wine, and garlic, and let the mixture cook for ten minutes. The smell was already wonderful, and when I added clam juice, it got even better. I turned the heat down a bit to let the pot simmer. About an hour later, when Josh woke up, I tossed in the mussels and a pinch of saffron. An advantage of having a chef boyfriend who cooked in my kitchen was that Josh routinely left interesting spices and seasonings, including luxury items like saffron.

When the mussels opened, I dished out large bowlfuls for both of us and was pleased to get a compliment: "These mussels rock, babe." But when we'd finished eating, Josh fell back asleep on the couch, so I crawled into bed by myself.

On Thursday morning Josh continued with his wedding preparations, but my own wedding duties meant that I couldn't stay to smell his latest creations. When I was about to leave, the two cats sat poised on the small kitchen table, following Josh's every move in the hope that he'd drop a piece of meat.

"Inga, Gato, and I have this all under control. Don't you worry about us!" Josh was slightly manic today. Waving an oversized wooden spoon around, he announced, "Inga is in charge of cutting the pasta, and Gato will supervise her."

"That's reassuring. What are you working on this morning?"

Josh checked his prep list for the wedding. "Tabouleh, fruit chutney, celery root soup, butternut squash puree, fennel puree, and pickled peppers. That's just to start. Easy stuff, though."

Leaving Josh to cook and, evidently, to train cats as

sous-chefs, I went to a boutique in Brookline to pick up my dress and my mother's. Adrianna had wanted us to choose our own dresses, and she hadn't wanted us in traditional bridal-party wear, so we were saved from having to sport pastel satin with poofy sleeves. I was wearing an adorable silk taffeta sleeveless dress in a soft shade that the salesperson referred to as "chocolate." The dress had a fitted bodice, a scoop neck, and a pleated skirt. My mother had picked out a classically tailored suit in periwinkle blue with a beaded shell in a darker blue to go underneath. A wedding-party miracle: outfits we would wear again!

Instead of returning home, I decided to deliver our wedding finery to my parents' house. Otherwise, I'd have risked leaving our beautiful things behind on the wedding day. When I pulled up to my parents' house, the sight of the gigantic white tent being erected in their yard made the wedding vividly real: Adrianna honestly was getting married! Filled with excitement, I grabbed the garment bag from the car and practically skipped over to my mother, who was standing outside supervising the tent crew.

"Look at this!" I cried. "The tent is going to be fantastic!"

"The tent is fine. It's the yard that's the problem," my mother growled.

I glanced around, looking for dead shrubs or insect-infested plants. "What are you talking about? The yard looks great."

"No, it doesn't look great. It's late August, and almost everything is past its bloom time. I should have planted more late-blooming flowers when we decided to host the wedding here. Dammit!" My mother crossed her arms and continued to survey her garden with dissatisfaction. "Dammit!" she repeated.

"This event isn't actually a garden tour, Mom. It's a wedding. And we've got plenty of floral arrangements coming. It'll be fine."

"No, it won't be fine. Everything out here is shabby and blowsy."

My poor mother was funneling all of her anxiety about the wedding into unhappiness about her lovely yard. In a way, I couldn't blame her. None of us had thrown a wedding party before. "Well, we do have our outfits," I said. "I just picked them up. I'm going to put them in the house." I gave my mother a hug. "Please don't worry. This wedding is going to be perfect."

TWENTY-ONE

ON Friday, the day before the wedding, I awoke to a scene of devastation. Entering the kitchen in search of coffee, I stared in horror at the apparent evidence that the explosive force of a small bomb had hurled cooking implements and food items everywhere. The bomb had a name: Josh. My boyfriend, in full cooking mode, was preparing a salmon mousse while simultaneously parcooking large pieces of meat on the stove top.

"How's it going, Josh?"

"Good. Good, I think. Thank God your father is grilling dinner tonight."

"We'll see if you thank him later. Dad has the enthusiasm, if not the skill."

By braving the wreckage of the kitchen, I managed to make coffee. As soon as I'd had a cup of it, I got ready to leave for my parents' house, where Ade and I were going to spend the night. Ade had insisted that even though the word *traditional* described nothing about the wedding, she still wanted to spend the night apart from Owen. Furthermore, she was determined that on Saturday, he wouldn't see her before the ceremony.

I packed a bag with almost every one of the hundreds of beauty-supply items I owned as well as with my digital camera and with clothes for tonight's rehearsal and dinner. Later in the day, I would pick up Adrianna and return to my parents' house with her.

"Josh, are you going to be able to handle all of this yourself?" I wrinkled my brow as I watched oil splatter out of a Dutch oven.

"Trust me, babe," Josh said with a wink. "I'm in my element here. I guarantee everyone will be blown away. Besides, I'll have help tomorrow. Digger will be there to deal with the kitchen during the ceremony while I'm standing up there with Owen. And that Emilio kid'll be there, too, right? Your mother said he was going to do whatever we needed."

Emilio. Yum. I shook all thoughts of that hottie out of my head. "Okay, then. I'm off. I guess I'll see you tonight."

"Catch you later, hon." Josh didn't stop to give me a hug or a kiss.

I arrived at my parents' house just as a delivery truck was pulling in. The chairs, tables, dishes, and glasses were there right on time. The white tent was fully set up now, too, and looked incredibly elegant. Things were coming together! Even the weather was cooperating. Today was quite hot, but the forecast for tomorrow promised temperatures in the mid to low seventies and, thank heaven, clear skies.

"Mom?" I called as I entered the living room and dropped my bags on the couch.

"Chloe? Is that you?" Mom poked her head out of the kitchen. "We have an emergency."

Oh, no! By foolishly telling myself that everything was coming together, I'd jinxed the wedding. Grimly, I asked, "What's going on?"

"Come look at this." My mother's voice was shaking.

I followed Mom as she led the way through the house to the front door and across the lawn to the tent. At the entrance, she came to a dramatic halt. *"This,"* she said with disgust, "is where Adrianna will appear! *This* is where the bride will enter! Can you believe it?"

"What the heck are you talking about?"

"Chloe! It's dismal! And barren! We need plants. More plants. Lots of greenery! I need you to run down to the nursery and get . . . plants! Lots of them!" With the frantic air of someone boldly averting disaster, she gave me directions to the nursery, which emerged as the one owned by Emilio's family. "Take the van. It's here, fortunately, so that will save you some time. Charge whatever you get to our account there. And splurge! Go nuts! I want tons of plants."

"Mom, the flowers are arriving tomorrow—"

"I know that! But this tent is mammoth, and we're not going to have it look empty. Get plants with height! And lots of blooms! Hanging plants, too! Run!"

My mother was having a floral breakdown.

I was in no mood for an argument. Consequently, I refrained from challenging her insistence that the tent looked desolate and was thus in dire need of the help that plants would provide. Fortunately, the van parked at the end of the driveway was one of the new ones rather than the old gray rattletrap that had unhappy associations. Unfortunately, however, the nursery was only a few miles from the house; I'd have preferred a long respite from my mother's frenzy.

Nursery turned out to be a misleading term for Emilio's family's sprawling, impressive garden center, which had eight large greenhouses and a main building with a garden-supply store, as well as two or three big outdoor areas devoted to trees, shrubs, and small plants of all kinds. I found a wagon and began strolling the aisles of the first greenhouse in search of plants that would appease my mother—in other words, horticultural tranquilizers. Knowing my mother as I did, I avoided anything that would have to be planted in the ground. It would have been just like Mom to decide that the whole family had to spend the rest of the day and night digging holes and planting shrubs.

"Chloe?"

I whipped around to see Emilio before me. "Hi," I gasped. "I'm looking for plants," I added stupidly, as if there were thousands of other reasons for pushing a wagon through a greenhouse.

"Do you need any help?" Oh, those darn dimples.

I explained my mother's instructions, and Emilio nodded. "Sure. Why don't you come with me. I can help you."

Can you ever, Emilio.

He added, somewhat disappointingly, "We've got a bunch of new fall plants in terra-cotta containers."

Within minutes, we'd made so many selections that we needed a second cart. "I can't believe I've never been in here before," I said as I admired the many healthy plants. "This is a wonderful nursery."

"Thanks. Let's check over here, too. We've got tons of perennials and biennials that are seriously discounted because it's the end of the season. They're in pots. You won't have to sink them in the ground. Some of them are in bloom. Not all, but some."

"Let's take a look," I said. "My mother will have a fit if

I show up with yellow mums like the ones in the supermarkets."

I followed Emilio into another greenhouse where, just as he'd said, there were bargain-priced perennials and biennials, some flourishing, some rather battered. I browsed the aisles and stopped in front of a group of low, green plants with some tired-looking old leaves mixed with bright new growth. I didn't have to read the labels to recognize foxglove. Foxglove! Digitalis! Lots of it, all cheap, all readily available to absolutely anyone. Oh, and all deadly, of course. Well, so much for finding out who did and didn't have a garden. Anyone, including an apartment dweller, could have bought the plants that were the source of the poison that killed Francie.

"Emilio? Have you been selling a lot of this foxglove?"

"Probably not. Most foxgloves bloom in the spring. They're not at their best right now. Look at them. But I'm not sure. I'm not always here at the nursery. Why?" he asked with curiosity. "Bethany won't want them. Your mother wants a show. For the wedding tomorrow. Not something that'll bloom next year."

"I know," I said. "It's . . . there's just something I'm wondering about. Do you think we could find out from somebody else who works here?"

Emilio had been nowhere near Leo and Francie's house on the day of her murder, of course; he couldn't possibly have had anything to do with it and was obviously not a suspect. Even so, I couldn't bring myself to admit my reason for wanting to know who'd bought foxglove. I could barely imagine how I'd phrase my purpose. *Well, Emilio, I'm leading a secret life as social work's answer to Nancy Drew.*

Happily, he didn't demand an explanation. All he said was, "Yeah, I guess I could ask my cousins." Emilio waved to a young man across the greenhouse who then approached us. Emilio began speaking rapidly in Spanish. The only word I understood was the one repeatedly spoken in English: *foxglove*. The young man kept nodding his head. Then he smiled at me and left.

"He says that they've sold lots of foxglove to lots of Americans," Emilio reported with a smile. "I don't suppose that helps you."

"I wouldn't say it narrows the field, but thanks anyway." I'd run out of time to pursue my investigations. I had to get the plants back to the house, and I had to pick up Ade. "So my mother said I could just charge all this stuff to her account," I said.

"Of course. I'll write it up."

Many hundreds of dollars later, Emilio offered to help me load the plants into the van. As we worked, he said, "I guess I'll see you at the wedding tomorrow."

"Yeah, I hear you and your cousins are going to help out. That'll be great."

"Hey." Emilio placed a potted sedum in the van and then posed charmingly with one arm against the sliding door. "I was wondering if you might want to get together sometime. After the wedding, of course. I thought I could take you out to dinner. There's a new little French restaurant on Exeter Street. In the Back Bay, near my apartment."

Oh, God. I wished that my immediate thought were something other than what it was. I should have been thinking that there was no way on earth that I'd ever be interested in anyone but Josh. As it was, all I could think was that this was an adorable, smart, socially and environmentally conscious guy who worked regular hours and . . . Hold it! The weirdness between Josh and me certainly didn't mean that I should accept Emilio's offer. Or did it? No matter what,

I couldn't just keep standing there staring at him. Mustering up the courage to respond, I said, "I'm flattered. I really am. But I have a boyfriend. Josh. He's the one doing all the cooking tomorrow."

How could my mother have failed to mention Josh when she'd asked Emilio to help? A simple statement—"My daughter's boyfriend is catering the wedding"—would have been sufficient. When things got uncomfortable tomorrow, it would be my mother's fault.

"I'm sorry. I didn't know." Emilio shrugged. "I had to try. I just got out of a relationship, and I thought I should take a stab at dating again. Let me know if anything changes."

I drove away. I wished that Emilio hadn't asked me out, and I wished that I hadn't hesitated. I exhaled deeply. After checking my watch, I decided that instead of going directly to my parents' house, I should pick up Adrianna on the way. After four tries, I finally parallel parked the van on Ade's street. Climbing the stairs to her apartment, I wondered, as I had many times before, how a humongous pregnant lady made it up these steps every day. I let myself in only to be greeted by the unmelodious sound of Kitty's voice.

"Is that what you really want to wear tonight? All right. If you think that's appropriate, be my guest."

"Mom! I swear on my baby's life that if you don't shut your—"

"Hello?" I called cheerily, hoping to abate some of the tension. "Where is the bride-to-be?"

"Chloe. Thank God." Adrianna emerged from the bathroom with a major scowl planted on her face. She wore a clingy yellow top, a white knee-length skirt, and sandals with three-inch heels. I loved it that Ade hadn't spent her pregnancy shrouded in oversized outfits. Her clothes hugged her beautiful curves and celebrated her pregnancy. In my opinion, Kitty had no reason to criticize Ade.

"Hello, Chloe." Kitty's smile was forced. "Adrianna, I just think that you could find something less . . . revealing than that outfit. You are a bride, after all. You could be less obvious."

"Less obvious? You mean I'm supposed to make it less obvious that I got knocked up before I was married?" Adrianna sounded incredulous. "You think I can hide my pregnancy? You think I'd want to? Say it, Mom. Just say it! *You* want to pretend I'm not pregnant. *You* want me to play the part of some virginal bride, right? Well, tough."

"Adrianna Zane! How dare you!" Kitty had turned an alarming shade of red. Her lips were tightly pursed.

"How dare I what? How dare I say what you're thinking? You hate that I'm pregnant. You hate Owen, and you probably hate me." Despite her raised voice, Adrianna looked remarkably calm for someone who was duking it out with her mother. "I cannot deal with you right now. I can't change how you feel and how you treat me, but I don't have to put up with it."

Kitty stood frozen, aghast at her daughter's brutal frankness.

"Chloe, I'm packed and ready to go. Mother, you can let yourself out. I'll see you tomorrow if you can drag yourself to the wedding. But I want you to leave right afterward. I don't want you around after the wedding, and I don't want you around when I give birth. Come on, let's go."

I picked up Adrianna's bags, she carried her wedding dress, and we bolted. We said nothing until we were seated in the van.

Ade managed to buckle her seat belt and then took a

look around the plant-packed van. "This is not exactly the glamorous limo ride I was expecting, but thanks for getting me."

"No problem. I thought a limo might be too pretentious and clichéd. A van packed with greenery hit me as celebratory without being excessive or trite."

"Good thinking."

I did a forty-point turn to get us out of the tight parking space. "You okay?"

"Yup. I'm quite okay. Actually, I'm fantastic." Ade smiled broadly. "I'm ready to get married, Chloe. I'm really ready. Kitty can suck it!" she cheered.

"That's my girl!" I yelled happily. "Kitty can suck it!"

TWENTY-TWO

"LOOK at the tent!" Adrianna's eyes lit up with happiness as I pulled the van to the front walkway. "It's just beautiful, isn't it, Chloe?"

"It's gorgeous. The ceremony is going to be amazing. Let's go put our things in the guest bedroom, and then we'll look around."

When my father opened the front door for us, he was humming Wagner's "Bridal Chorus."

"Oh, here we go." I rolled my eyes.

"I love it. Keep up the music, Jack." Adrianna hugged my dad.

"Can you believe this weather?" he exclaimed. "I'm going to sit out on the deck tonight and do some meditation. Did Chloe tell you I've become addicted to yoga?"

"Dad, not now!" I said, exasperated.

Mom entered the living room. "Did you get everything we need? Oh, hello, Adrianna. Isn't this fantastic? Chloe, where are the plants? Did the nursery have what we need? Jack, start unloading the plants from the van. Bring them all into the tent."

While my father obediently headed for the van, I calmed my mother down by informing her that I had enough foliage to fill four tents. Ade stifled a yawn. I took the wedding gown from her arms and asked, "Do you want to lie down for a bit while we unload the plants?"

"I think I should. I feel like I'm ready to burst."

Mom put her arm on Ade's and fired off ten or twelve questions one right after the other, including: "What has your doctor said? Does she think you're getting close to delivering? Are you having Braxton Hicks?" My mother, I suspected, had consumed one espresso too many today.

"Um, actually, I skipped my appointment this week and rescheduled it for next week. Owen and I aren't going anywhere for a honeymoon, so he'll be around to go with me." Ade saw my mother's alarmed face. "Honestly, Bethany, I feel fine. I really do. I'm just tired, that's all."

"If you say so. Make yourself at home in the guest room, and come and join us when you've gotten some rest."

My parents and I spent the next few hours moving all the nursery purchases from one place to another in the tent. Astonishingly, my mother was eventually satisfied. The ceremony would take place on one side of the tent, where white folding chairs were set up for the guests. The other side of the tent already had some tables and chairs in place. Fifty or so people made for a fairly small wedding, but additional tables would have to be added once the ceremony was over. Long tables covered in white tablecloths were ready for Josh's food. Another table would serve as the bar.

Adrianna roused herself in the late afternoon. To my relief, she looked thoroughly refreshed and even energetic. Nodding at a monstrous blue box that she held in her hands, she announced, "Nail time, ladies!"

My mother and I let Ade paint our fingernails in a shade called Sheer Tutu Pink. Meanwhile, my father prepared the grill for tonight's dinner. I called Josh, who muttered something about "crazy lamb" and "stupid pot's too small." Otherwise, I got barely an intelligible word out of him except a promise to be at the house for the rehearsal.

Josh and Owen arrived in Owen's refrigerated fish truck, which held some of the food that needed to be stored at my parents' house. "Your fridge is filled to capacity, Chloe," Josh said, "and this stuff I won't need until tomorrow."

"How is everything coming?" I asked.

"We're in good shape. Risotto is ready, squash puree is done, soup is ready. Everything. It's all good. Dinner will be fantastic tomorrow."

At six thirty, the wedding party assembled in the tent. I stood at the front of the aisle, flanked by two empty white podiums. Tomorrow, they'd hold floral baskets. Owen, Ade, Mom, Josh, and my father all sat before me in the white chairs while I went over the ceremony.

"Tomorrow," I said, "the guests will mostly seat themselves, but Evan and Willie will be here to act as ushers if needed." Owen had refused to have either of his brothers in the wedding party; he'd maintained that the risk of their misbehaving was simply too great. "Owen, come stand right here. Don't fidget, pick your nose, touch your hair, or otherwise move unless I tell you. Stand there and watch the back of the tent for your bride. Mom and Josh, when the music starts, you will walk down the aisle together, followed by Adrianna and Dad. Let's do that now." The music would be provided by nothing fancier than my MP3 player hooked up to outdoor speakers.

The members of the wedding rushed to their places, and then Josh looped my mother's arm through his and escorted her down the aisle. "Now Adrianna and Dad . . . Good. Dad, you kiss Ade's cheek, pass her off to Owen, and sit down. Wait! Owen, *you* don't kiss her now!"

"Sorry, sorry." Owen beamed. "I couldn't help myself!"

I continued. "The music will stop, and I'll begin the ceremony. That part is a secret until tomorrow, so all you need to know is that at some point I will get to the vows and ask you both to repeat what I say. And, Owen, let me dash your hopes right now. There is no rhyming. Then I will pronounce you husband and wife. *That's* when you get to kiss. Then Mom and Josh walk back up the aisle, followed by the bride and groom. That's it."

I received a small round of applause for leading such a quick rehearsal, and all of us moved to the patio by the grill. Because tomorrow would be so busy, tonight's dinner was simple: Dad was grilling chicken, and Mom had made a big salad. Josh, I could tell, was having to struggle to restrain himself from taking over at the grill. Inevitably, Dad was singeing some of the chicken pieces.

I filled a paper plate for Adrianna, who was seated next to Owen. "You got your tux, right?" I asked.

Owen nodded. "All set. I picked up mine and Josh's today."

"Can I see them?" Ade spoke nonchalantly, but I knew that she wanted to make sure that Josh and Owen would, in fact, be dressed in black and not blue.

"They're back at the apartment. I didn't want to leave them in the fish truck and take the chance they'd smell like seafood."

Adrianna looked surprised and impressed that Owen had had the foresight to avoid smelling like fish during their wedding. I felt skeptical. I didn't expect him to go out of his way to stink of seafood, of course. Still, I didn't trust him to present himself appropriately and wouldn't trust him until tomorrow when—if—he was actually standing next to me fully outfitted in the conventionally handsome attire he'd sworn to wear for the wedding.

"I'd like to make a toast." Owen rose, helped Ade out of her chair, and lifted his glass of beer into the air. "To Jack and Bethany. Before we head into the inevitable chaos tomorrow, we both want to let you know how unbelievably grateful we are to you both. You are giving us exactly the kind of wedding we want."

Ade continued. "Owen and I didn't want a formal, stuffy reception, and this dinner-party style you've put together is really us. You both know that my father is out of the picture and that my mother is not exactly the mother I would have handpicked. You two have made us feel like part of your family, and we will never forget that. And Chloe? I couldn't ask for a more loyal, special friend. I love you."

Owen wiped his eyes and put his arm around Ade. "I'm so sorry about your mother," he whispered. She nodded and lifted her lemonade. "To the Carter family!"

We all clinked glasses and traded mushy hugs and kisses.

"There is one more treat for you two," I said as I handed Owen the envelope Nana Sally had slipped to me at the end of the shower.

"Whoo hoo!" Owen yelled. "We're going to the Ritz! Nana Sally is sending us there for our wedding night." The groom did a goofy little dance that involved weird hip thrusts and snapping fingers.

Ade giggled and then managed to settle him down. "God,

I've always wanted to go there. That's going to be fantastic! Oh, and Jack and Bethany, we have something for you."

The bride and groom handed my parents a gift-wrapped box. My father was busy burning chicken, so it was my mother who opened the package and lifted out a hand-blown glass vase.

"I know it's not much," Adrianna said, "but we thought you'd like it."

"It's simply beautiful. You shouldn't have," my mother said as she admired the vase.

"Chloe, we have something for you, too." Owen gave me a piece of paper that had been rolled up and tied with a pink ribbon.

I slid off the knot and unrolled what looked like an official invitation. I read the page and looked up at my dear friends. "Are you sure?"

Ade and Owen nodded. "Absolutely."

"What does it say?" my father asked.

I cleared my throat and grinned. "They want me to be their baby's godmother."

TWENTY-THREE

THE next morning, I turned over in one of the twin beds in the guest room and looked at Ade, who was still asleep in the other bed. The bride-to-be was curled on her side, her mouth open, drool making its way down her chin. Her hair had tangled itself into such a Medusa-like mess that I decided to force her into the shower the second she woke up; if she got a look at herself in a mirror, she'd start her wedding day by freaking out.

The ceremony was at four o'clock, and it was already nine thirty. How had we slept so late? I could hear dishes clattering downstairs, and I knew that the household must be bustling with wedding preparations.

Ade snorted and woke herself up. "I'm getting married today, aren't I?" she said, stretching her arms.

"That's the plan." I got up and sat on the edge of her bed.

She rubbed her belly. "Baby, how about you move that elbow off of my bladder, okay? It's quite annoying."

"Can I feel?"

Ade nodded. "Go ahead. The baby doesn't move around as much now because it's so squished in there, but you can feel a knee. Right here." She placed my hand on the side of her stomach, and I felt something hard against my hand. "At least I think it's a knee. Might be some other body part, but there is definitely something pushing on my bladder, too."

"I know this sounds ridiculous, but I cannot believe that there's a little person in there. Right there!" I leaned in and whispered to her stomach. "Baby, it's Auntie Chloe here. Please move around so that your mommy doesn't spend the day needing to pee. Okay?"

We waited silently, hoping that the baby might actually respond to the request. Ade shook her head. "Nothing. This kid isn't budging. Maybe after I get up and walk around. Help me up."

By rolling and pushing, I got Ade out of bed. Then I walked her to the bathroom and got her into the shower without giving her the opportunity to see herself in the mirror. "I'll go get you some breakfast, okay?"

"That would be great. After that, we should get started on our hair. That's top priority, so we don't run out of time later."

"Gotcha." I tossed on my overpriced but adorable Juicy hoodie and pants, pulled my hair into a ponytail, and headed downstairs to the kitchen to see what I could find to feed Adrianna. With all the wedding food in the house, I wondered whether there were any breakfast possibilities at all.

Josh was already in the kitchen. With him were the cousin of Emilio's I'd met yesterday at the nursery and another dark-haired guy who looked so much like the first that he had to be a relative. Both of Josh's assistants were busy slicing their way through a mountain of vegetables. Josh himself was buried in the fridge, pulling out one container after another. "Morning, beautiful!" he chirped.

"You're hard at work already, huh?"

"Yup. This is Alfonso and Héctor, Emilio's cousins, who are helping me with everything."

I waved at the two cousins, and both smiled warmly at me. I was glad that Josh spoke Spanish—or at least spoke what he called "kitchen Spanish," enough of the language to communicate his culinary needs. "I met one of them, Alfonso, when I was picking up all those plants for my mother, but I didn't get his name. So Emilio is here, too, I assume?" Not that I was itching to have Josh and Emilio in the same room.

"Apparently, but I haven't run into him yet. He might be out in the tent helping rearrange the six thousand plants and setting things up outside."

I grabbed a box of cereal, a gallon of milk, and some bowls and spoons and headed back upstairs to deliver breakfast to the bride.

"Chloe, you're up. Is Adrianna awake, too?" My mother stopped me as I was starting up the staircase.

"She's in the shower. She wants to do our hair as soon as possible. Sound good? Is everything going all right so far?"

"Mostly. I had to send Emilio to go pick up the flowers. The store messed things up. He should be back within an hour. Other than that, I think we're on track."

"Where's Dad?" By now, my mother must have put him to work.

"Oh . . . um . . ."

"Dad," I said. "My father. Your husband. Jack. The man who burns chicken."

"Chloe, I know who Jack is. He's around somewhere. Don't worry about him. Just tell me when Adrianna is ready for me."

Since Ade was still in the shower, I left the breakfast supplies on the dresser and made the beds. When I went back downstairs, Robin and Nelson were quarreling in the living room. "That film belongs to me, Nelson!" Robin was glaring at her cameraman. "You weren't supposed to make a copy of it. The police were the only ones who should've seen it." Robin's dark hair was yanked tightly off her face, and her beady eyes were bulging in anger.

"The camera belongs to me, and you don't need the film anyway," Nelson shot back. "It's not like the station is going to be airing the footage from that day, are they? Josh's *Chefly Yours* episode was scrapped, so who cares?"

"Listen to me," Robin snarled, "your job is to film the series. Since you filmed that episode for me, the film was and is mine, and since that footage obviously isn't going to become part of the series, you shouldn't have a copy."

"That's exactly why I have a copy, Ms. Director! It's not part of your rip-off show, so I can keep it!" Nelson's raised voice was echoing throughout the room.

The last thing Ade needed was to overhear a nasty argument. "Could you two keep it down, please?" I said sharply.

"Sorry," said Robin, looking appropriately ashamed. "Look, we'd love to film Adrianna while she's getting ready. Is she upstairs?"

"I really don't think she'll want you up there." I certainly didn't. On inspiration, I said, "Adrianna is a very private person. She's thrilled that you're going to film the wedding, but she'd rather you focus on food preparation than on . . . bride preparation. Why don't you go into the kitchen and tape Josh while he's cooking?"

"Perfect! Nelson, let's go."

Nelson raised his camera and aimed it at me. I sighed inwardly but said nothing to him as I led the pair back to the craziness of the kitchen. A glance told me that Nelson would practically be filming a crowd scene. Josh and Emilio's cousins were still at work, Digger had arrived and was scraping out pumpkins for the baked pumpkin stew, and my mother was rushing around pointlessly moving platters from counter to counter and probably driving Josh bonkers. I just had to get her out of his way soon. But what really hit was the presence of an uncomfortable number of people who'd been around on the day of Francie's murder: Josh and me, obviously, as well as Digger, Robin, and Nelson. And Willie and Evan would be here soon, too. How had Adrianna's wedding turned into a reunion of homicide suspects?

"Does everyone know each other?" my mother asked. Without waiting for a response, she began introductions, each of which included a short bio. "Digger is the executive chef at a delightful tapas restaurant. He's going to be Josh's right-hand man today."

Sweat glistened in Digger's curly hairline. He gave a gruff "Yo!" to the room as he set a stainless-steel tray on a counter.

"And Robin." My mother gestured to the cable-TV director, who was busy trying to get Nelson to move the camera off me. "Robin did a splendid piece on gardening a few years ago. She not only featured our landscaping business but also filmed part of that show at the nursery owned by Emilio's family, the one where these two assistants work." When Mom pointed at Emilio's cousins, I noticed that Héctor was staring intently at Robin.

My mother continued her spiel. "Next is Alfonso, currently in charge of inventory and ordering at one of my favorite nurseries. He doesn't speak English, so thank goodness we have Josh and Emilio here to translate. Where is Emilio, by the way? He should've been back by now."

As if on cue, Emilio entered the kitchen. "I'm here. Sorry that took so long." He was holding an open box filled with flowers. I couldn't wait to get a better look at the flowers. Ade had ordered deep orange roses for the bouquets. Even from across the kitchen, I could see how beautiful the color was.

"Oh, good," my mother said. "Everyone, this is Emilio. Emilio, this is Robin, Nelson, and Digger. Of course, your cousins and Chloe you already know."

When Emilio smiled at me, I did my best to remain cool as I smiled politely back. I wished Nelson would get that silly camera off me.

"And this is Josh Driscoll," my mother said, pointing to Josh, who finally set down the knife he'd been using to slice mushrooms.

Josh wiped his hands on his apron. He looked up, ready to greet Emilio, but all of a sudden, his face hardened.

Emilio looked momentarily confused and then started to speak. "Oh. It's you. We've, uh, we've actually met before—"

"That's right. We have met before, you goddamn bastard!" Without warning, Josh rammed his way through the mob of people in the kitchen, reached Emilio, came to an abrupt halt, drew back a fist, and punched Emilio squarely in the jaw. The first punch was powerful, but before Emilio had a chance to recover from the blow, my chef socked him again. Hard. Emilio spun sideways, and as he fell to the ground, he dropped the flower box and sent the bouquets and boutonnieres flying everywhere.

I was flabbergasted and furious. "Oh, my God! Josh, what are you doing?" I reached Josh and grabbed his arm before he could haul off and hit Emilio again. Somehow,

Josh must have discovered that Emilio had asked me out. Who would have told him? How on earth had he found out?

"You want to know who this is?" Josh looked at me with fury in his blue eyes. "This is the asshole I took Inga from. This is the creep who was going to throw that cat in the river."

Twenty-Four

"WHAT?" I yelled in disbelief. "What!"

Emilio had managed to rise to his feet, but I marched up to him, shoved both hands against his chest, and knocked him back down.

"You sicko!" I screamed. "You get out of here! Get out of here now, before I grab one these knives and cut your throat, you fiend! You were going to drown a poor, helpless little cat! *My* poor, helpless cat! Get of here right now before I knock you senseless and drag you to the bathtub and hold your head underwater and see how you—"

While I was in the midst of my tirade, Emilio scrambled to his feet. Clutching his jaw, he crushed Ade's flowers as he backed out of the kitchen. Everyone who remained was frozen in place, but poor Héctor and Alfonso looked more dazed than anyone else. As Josh began explaining the situation to them in Spanish, I explained in English.

"Good God!" my mother said, shaking her head. "Well, we simply can't have *him* here. Good riddance! What kind of monster would do that to a cat? And Emilio of all people! I never would have guessed. Never!" She paused and said, "And to think that he went to Princeton!"

Digger's muscular hands began forcefully yanking seeds from the pumpkin. "Seriously. What a scumbag!"

Robin remained silent but scurried to pick up the mass of flowers that had fallen to the floor.

I took a deep breath. I couldn't help but feel that the gods were conspiring to ruin what was supposed to be Adrianna's perfect day. But Inga, I reminded myself, was, after all, safe; Josh, my Josh, had snatched her from Emilio's clutches. "Okay," I said, "let's all just calm down. Adrianna is going to lose it if she finds out that there was an actual fistfight at her wedding. Or almost at her wedding. Although, I suppose it was more of a clobbering than anything else." I grinned at Josh, who winked at me. I mentally kicked myself for having given Emilio a second thought.

"Yeah, and I got it all on film!" Nelson whispered excitedly.

I didn't have time for Nelson and his obsession with so-called reality. "Mom, let's get out of the way and get upstairs so Adrianna can start on our hair."

We were on our way to the stairs when I heard my name called. Turning around, I saw Héctor walking toward me.

"Chloe," he said in a heavily accented voice.

"Yes? Héctor?" Despite all the time I'd spent trying to teach myself the language from online sites, my Spanish was pretty bad. "Mom, I'll meet you up there."

Héctor began speaking so rapidly that I couldn't even begin to guess what he was trying to tell me. What's more, I really had to get upstairs to be with the bride. "I'm sorry, I'm sorry," I apologized. "Josh. Go see Josh. He'll understand. I have to go."

My mother and I found Adrianna in front of the full-length mirror on the inside of the closet door in the guest room. She was wearing a robe and had her hair bound up in large rollers.

"My matron of honor! And my solemnizer! Is that even a word?" Even with a crazy mountain of curlers on her head, Ade was all glowy and adorable.

With tremendous formality, I announced, "We are here and at your command. Who's first?"

"You are, Chloe. Go shower, and I'll get you started. And then Bethany."

By the time our hair was done, it was midafternoon. Mom's hair had been parted on the side and flatironed straight. My highlighted red hair had been slathered in serums and styling creams to prevent any dreaded frizziness; I now had a gorgeously soft and smooth mane that Ade had blown dry with a gigantic round brush that gave me plenty of height at the roots and curl at the ends. I really needed to practice my blow-drying skills so I could duplicate this result myself. Ade's blonde hair fell in soft curls down her back, and the front was pulled away from her face by the veil I'd worn while prancing around her apartment. My mother and I had on our wedding outfits, but Adrianna hadn't yet put on her gown.

"I have to go check on your father and make sure he got out the, uh, well . . . nothing! I'll be back in time for the ceremony, Adrianna. Don't worry!" Mom rushed out of the room.

"I haven't seen Jack all day, have you?" Ade asked with a

hint of concern. "I hope your dad will appear in time to walk me down the aisle."

"He wouldn't miss it. Not a chance. I'm sure everything is fine." I watched while Adrianna did her makeup. "Are you nervous yet, Ade?" I took some pictures of her with my digital camera while she peered at herself in the mirror.

"Not at all. Especially because my mother knows she isn't allowed to see me until the ceremony. The last person I wanted to spend time with today was her. I'm just so glad I have you and your mother with me while I get ready. There! My makeup is done." She turned to me, and her eyes lit up. "I think I should put on my dress."

We unzipped the white gown from the garment bag, and I helped Adrianna to step into the dress. When I zipped up the back, I was quite relieved to find that the fit was perfect. "Let me look at you."

I stood in front of my best friend and clasped my hands to my mouth to stifle my choked gasps. The crisp white material was fitted over her chest and tied halter-style at the nape of her neck. Adrianna had altered the dress so that it fell softly against her belly and accentuated the beautiful shape of her late-pregnancy body. Gentle gathers of fabric made up the skirt. Her wedding dress was simple, with no lace or huge bows: just clean, flowing lines. I felt overwhelmingly happy that Kitty wasn't here to make snide comments about Adrianna's decision to wear virginal white.

I grabbed a tissue and dabbed my eyes. "You're breathtaking, Ade. You really are." I started maniacally snapping pictures. I looked at my watch. "It's getting close. Oh, we almost forgot the flowers! I'll go find the bouquets. And then I have to get all my papers for the ceremony."

"Okay. I'll just be here."

I couldn't leave Ade by herself. My dad was going to

walk her down the aisle, but she needed a woman to wait with her. "Don't worry. I'll send someone up to sit with you. Give me a hug."

"Watch the dress." Ade shrieked as I leaned in. We hugged gently, not wanting to crinkle our dresses or ruin our makeup.

"I'll see you on the aisle." I opened the guest room door and stepped into the hall.

"Oh, screw it. Give me a real hug." Ade held her arms out. I raced to my friend and squeezed her tightly. "This is it."

TWENTY-FIVE

I had to find someone to stay with Adrianna while we dealt with last-minute details. In so many ways, Ade really was alone: she had almost no women friends, her father had disappeared, and her hostile mother was worse than none. If she waited by herself, she was bound to feel painfully solitary. My mother was her matron of honor, but this was Mom's house, and she was mobbed right now. I looked out the front door and spotted my sister. No, Heather wouldn't do; she couldn't open her mouth without criticizing someone or something. Although Heather wouldn't intentionally hurt Adrianna, she might blurt out something thoughtless and stinging. Besides, she and her husband, Ben, were busy trying to keep their kids from ruining their fancy outfits. And they did look adorable; one-year-old Lucy was wearing a poofy pink dress and white Mary Jane shoes, and five-year-old Walker had on a navy suit. I had visions of them serving as flower girl and ring bearer at my own wedding. Romantic visions of Josh and me riding off into the sunset momentarily distracted me. I shook off my fantasies and continued looking for an appropriate person to stay with Adrianna.

Owen's relatives were impossibly difficult, and Kitty was obviously out, too. Then I saw Naomi and her boyfriend, Eliot, on the front lawn, admiring the tent. Aha! Naomi was, well, Naomi. New Age, corny, touchy-feely, yes, but Naomi was absolutely genuine, and she was sweet, supportive, and reliably kind. "Naomi!" I waved her over. "I need a favor."

For the wedding, Naomi had fastened her dozens of braids with turquoise beads that matched her long garment, which appeared to be an actual sari draped in some non-Indian manner. On her feet were what I recognized as brand-new tan suede Birkenstocks. On the positive side, Naomi said that she'd be more than happy to stay with Adrianna until my mother could officially begin her matron-of-honor duties. "Chloe," she said with her usual enthusiasm, "I brought a copy of the letter of reference I wrote for you. The one I sent to the secretary of state's office. I thought Adrianna might like a copy for her wedding album. Here, I'll read it to you."

Keeping one eye on Naomi, I used the other to look out the front door for arriving guests.

"This is my favorite part," Naomi said happily. "'Chloe Carter has a remarkable soul, and I offer up my sincerest hope that she be allowed to unite her two friends—'"

"Son of a bitch!" I screamed.

"Well, that's not very nice, Chloe." Naomi crinkled her nose at me.

"Not you, Naomi. Owen." I pointed to the groom, who stood outside talking to Josh.

Josh looked positively dashing. More than dashing. Regal. As Adrianna had requested, he wore a black tuxedo. Owen was another story. His neon purple tuxedo and matching top hat were, in all probability, visible from outer space.

I stomped over to the groom. "I swear that you'd better be kidding, Owen."

The petrified-looking Owen was on the verge of tears. "I don't know what to do, Chloe. I rented this one and a black one. This was the joke one, and I was just going to wear it for a while before the ceremony. But the rental place didn't get me my black tux. They sent Josh's, and when I looked in the bag yesterday, I saw the black and figured everything was in there. Ade is going to kill me!"

"We could just spray paint you," Josh suggested flippantly.

Oh, my God! This had to happen now, at the last minute! I moved to the entrance to the tent, looked in, and saw that many of the guests had already arrived. Ade would flip out if we ran late. Since Dad wore jeans almost everywhere, the only suit he owned was the one he was wearing. Besides, he was smaller than either Josh or Owen. One of the guests? I could hardly charge up to one of the men and demand that he immediately exchange his suit for a purple tuxedo.

"You are a stupid, stupid man, Owen!" I put my hands on my hips. "Switch. You'll have to switch. Josh, put on that horrible purple thing and give Owen your tux."

The boys started to protest, but I held up my hand. "We have twenty-five minutes until the ceremony. There is nothing else to do." I yanked the horrible top hat off Owen's head. "But nobody is wearing this."

As I stormed off to locate the flowers that Emilio had dropped when Josh punched him, I realized that Nelson had been filming the entire tuxedo fiasco. Remembering Robin's quarrel with Nelson, I resolved to participate in the editing of this film and to get my hands on any copies that Nelson might make. Adrianna was damned well not going to be exposed to Nelson's vision of so-called reality.

I brushed past the cameraman and was heading toward the kitchen when I caught a glimpse of my father, whom I hadn't seen all day. He was scurrying through the living room. On his head was a baseball cap, of all things. "Dad! Dad! Where have you been?" Then his appearance registered on me. "What on earth happened to you? What is that black stuff all over your face?" I pulled off the baseball cap. "And your hair? And your hands? Dad!"

"It, um, well, it seems to be tar. Tar. In fact, that's what it is. Tar."

I stared helplessly at my father. Struggling to control my voice, I said, one word at a time, "Tell. Me. What. Happened."

"Well, after everyone went to bed last night, I thought I'd take a scotch up to the second-floor deck and relax. You know, look at the stars, be one with the earth. My yoga teacher suggested we meditate outdoors. I thought it would be great. I wanted to commune with nature, so I lay down on the deck. Then when I tried to get up, I realized I was stuck."

I shut my eyes. This supposed deck above the living room of my parents' Spanish colonial revival house was, in fact, a roof, a large, flat area surrounded by a stucco wall. No one really used the roof, which had leaked badly and stained the living room ceiling until my parents had finally had it coated with tar.

I glared at Dad. "And it was hot yesterday, so the tar heated up and started to melt. And now you are covered in it."

Dad nodded and suppressed a laugh. "I think I took off all the hair on my body when I finally got myself up."

"You were naked?" I hissed.

"Yeah. That's the best way to meditate. At first I thought I was glued to the deck, and when I managed to get loose, I crawled into bed, and now the sheets are ruined. Your mother is pissed, let me tell you. She tried pouring olive oil on me to get it out, and that helped a little bit. There was a lot of tar in my hair, but I fixed that. I took a pair of scissors and cut it out."

"That would explain the jagged spikes jutting out of your head." Had all the men around here gone crazy? In desperation, I slapped Owen's purple top hat onto my father's head. "Here. Wear this. I don't know what to say to you except that you are a big dope. Go put on your suit and be ready to walk Adrianna down the aisle in a few minutes. I have to go find the flowers."

On the dining room table sat the box of flowers. Because of Robin's efforts, some of the blooms had survived the Josh versus Emilio outbreak. If you looked closely, you could see that some stems were crumpled and that there were fewer orange roses than there should have been, but it was far too late to buy new flowers. I caught Naomi just as she was coming down the stairs in search of Adrianna's and my mother's bouquets. "Whatever you do, don't say anything to Adrianna about what Owen is wearing. Or *was* wearing. Or what . . . Just please keep her calm and happy."

I couldn't help noticing that Naomi herself was a lot calmer than I was. All of her yoga, herbal remedies, acupuncture, and other alternative practices and preparations were apparently more effective than I'd ever imagined. "Don't worry about a thing, Chloe," she said with a beatific smile. "Adrianna and I are having a significant bonding experience."

I hurried to the kitchen to retrieve my script for the ceremony from my purse. Digger was now in charge, and under his supervision, Alfonso and Héctor were beginning to plate appetizers on serving trays. I retrieved the typed pages and nearly collided with Nelson, who was evidently trailing me again. Well, if he was filming me, he'd inevitably capture Ade and Owen as they said their vows. In any case, I had no time to argue with him now.

"Chloe. Chloe." Héctor tapped my shoulder.

"Yes. What is it, Héctor?"

Again he started speaking in Spanish that I couldn't follow. I shook my head in confusion. Then I caught the word *foxglove*.

"Wait! Say it again. I don't understand. I'm sorry."

"He's saying something about Americans buying flowers," Digger explained. Digger and Héctor exchanged words for a moment. "Oh, okay. He wants you to know that one of the Americans who bought foxglove plants is here today. She has brown hair in a ponytail. The woman with him." Digger pointed to Nelson. "He means the director. Robin."

Robin, who had been to the nursery while making the gardening film that had involved my parents. Robin, who lived in an apartment without access to a garden or balcony and who'd said that she had no interest in plants. Robin, who'd thus had no horticultural reason to buy foxglove. Robin, who had been present throughout the filming of the reality TV episode, including the entire time in the kitchen. Well, this was the worst possible moment to take in the implications of this new information, never mind to act on it. For Pete's sake, I had a wedding ceremony to perform!

"Foxglove," Digger said. "Isn't that—"

"Yes, but never mind," I said. "Not now!"

As I was hurrying through the dining room on my way to the tent, I ran into my mother as she headed upstairs. "Mom?"

"What is it, Chloe? I've got to get your father so we can start the ceremony."

"I know. Quick question. One second. When Robin did the gardening film, were there any references to poisonous plants? In particular, did you talk about foxglove?"

Mom shot me a look of exasperation. "I don't know why you want to discuss this now, but, yes, as a matter of fact. The film was mainly about flower borders and included talk about the toxicity of many common ornamentals, including foxglove. What a thing to ask when you're supposed to . . . Chloe, get going!" My mother hurried up the stairs and called over her shoulder. "Take your place, Chloe. The music is playing already, but Josh has the remote, and he's going to start the processional when you're ready."

I exhaled deeply and made my way out the front door and toward the tent. Josh, in ghastly purple, stood just outside the entrance with Owen, who looked even handsomer than usual and was dressed exactly as Adrianna would want. As I took my first step past the masses of potted plants I'd bought at the nursery and into the tent itself, Josh, right on cue, changed the music. Flanked on either side by wedding guests, I felt suddenly awed by the responsibility that the Commonwealth of Massachusetts had granted me, and as I walked down the aisle, my knees shook. Flashes from cameras blinded me, and I was afraid that I'd trip over Nelson, who was a few feet in front of me as he walked backward down the aisle, his camera trained on me. When I finally stood before the guests, my stomach lurched. Owen's father was seated in the front row with Phoebe and a few other cousins. Two chairs in that row had been left empty for the mother of the bride and the mother of the groom, Kitty and Eileen, who would be ushered in by Willie and Evan. The prospect of facing Kitty did nothing to calm me. I cursed myself for ever having agreed to perform this ceremony. Who did I think I was? Why had the Commonwealth of Massachusetts ever agreed to give me such power? But by then, Josh and Owen had joined me. They were standing to my left, facing the side of the tent.

Nelson had now moved toward my right, his camera still fixed on me, but at least he was not blocking my view of the aisle and the entrance. Eager to get the ceremony under way—desperate to get it over!—I stared at the opening of the tent, through which Eileen and Kitty should now be entering with their escorts. My hands were shaking so hard that the papers I was clutching rattled loudly.

Instead of escorting in Eileen and Kitty, Willie and Evan abruptly stepped into the tent by themselves. Staring at them in horror, I nearly dropped my papers. Those two idiots had actually brought shotguns! Monsters! They were doing what they'd threatened, supposedly in jest. No! Absolutely, positively not! In an emotional turnabout, I suddenly felt entitled to the central role I was playing today. I was, after all, the minister-priest-rabbi-justice-of-the-peace figure here. It was I who possessed a Certificate of Solemnization issued by the Commonwealth of Massachusetts. Therefore, I, Chloe Carter, was in charge!

In my most swift yet dignified manner, I marched to the tent entrance, faced the miscreants, and backed them out of the tent. "No way!" I growled at Evan and Willie. "If you do not get rid of those guns this second, I'll shoot you myself!"

TWENTY-SIX

MY muted voice must have rung with the authority of the governor, the secretary of state, the attorney general, the head of the state police, and every other Power—with a capital *P*—in the Commonwealth of Massachusetts, because the brothers immediately obeyed me. Pointing at the potted plants, I whispered, "In there!" Mercifully, there was enough foliage to conceal the weapons. Lurking a couple of yards behind Willie and Evan were Eileen and Kitty, who had clearly been enablers, if not actual coconspirators. With a little smirk on her face, Eileen said, "Now, Chloe, the boys were only—"

"It is no joke," I whispered. With that, I pivoted around and tried to stroll casually back to my spot before the guests. I smiled and then nodded to Evan and Willie, who, deprived of their shotguns, escorted Eileen and Kitty to their seats and then took their own. My mother was the next to make her way down the aisle. By comparison with Eileen and Kitty, she seemed like an angel, and as Nelson recorded her progress, I was pleased that he was managing to point the camera at someone other than me.

My father and Adrianna appeared at the entrance, he with the ludicrous purple top hat balanced on his head, she the ultimate beautiful bride. Glancing at Owen, I saw that he was frozen in awe. I'd been dreading the moment when Adrianna caught sight of Josh's outfit, but I'd underestimated her: she took one look at him, a vision in purple, and giggled the entire way down the aisle. My father's coordinating hat must have prepared her for subsequent silliness. Dad led her to our little group and sat down.

Adrianna and Owen turned to face me. I locked eyes with my best friend. She tipped her head toward Josh, then toward my father, then down at her slightly battered bouquet, and rolled her eyes. We grinned at each other, and I relaxed.

"I want to welcome you all. We are gathered here to celebrate one of life's great moments and to add our loving wishes to the words that will unite Owen and Adrianna in marriage." My hands did not shake, and neither did my voice. By the time my mother and Owen's father read poems, I was thoroughly enjoying myself.

Then I began the exchange of vows. "Owen, repeat after me. I, Owen, take you, Adrianna, to be my wife, my constant friend, my faithful partner in life, and my one true love."

When Adrianna slipped the simple silver ring on Owen's finger, I got choked up and had to pause before the pronouncement. Adrianna and Owen held hands tightly and waited for me.

"By the authority vested in me by the Commonwealth of Massachusetts, witnessed by your friends and family, I have the pleasure to pronounce you husband and wife. You may now seal your vows with a kiss."

And did they ever. Their kiss went on for so long that the guests had to begin a second round of applause. The newly married couple finally parted lips and made their way back down the aisle.

Because this was a small and informal wedding, Adrianna and Owen had decided to forgo the traditional receiving line. They didn't vanish for professional photographs, of course. Rather, a lot of guests surrounded the couple and snapped pictures outside the tent. Josh wrapped me in his arms, whispered, "Great job, babe," and then ran off to the kitchen to help Digger and Emilio's cousins with the food. I had my picture taken with Adrianna and Owen and accepted compliments from guests about the ceremony.

Héctor and Alfonso arrived with trays of hors d'oeuvres, and champagne began to flow. The chairs that had been in rows for the ceremony were moved to make room for extra tables, and within minutes, guests were mingling merrily in the tent and munching on delicious food. I sampled a baby creamer potato with salt cod brandade and Osetra caviar, and then tried Maine lobster with shaved daikon, Thai basil, and pink peppercorn vinaigrette. Outstanding!

I dragged Adrianna away from the crowd for a moment to explore the buffet table, where more appetizers awaited us. "You must be starving."

Adrianna nodded vigorously. "Famished. God, look at all this! I can't believe Josh pulled it off."

I took a small plate and filled it with butternut squash puree topped with shrimp, arugula, and radish, and drizzled with a brown-butter vinaigrette. I took a taste and groaned happily. Individual servings of celery root soup were topped with small pieces of seared foie gras, pickled apples, celery leaf, and truffle honey. The soup was indescribably delicious. Next I tasted grilled tuna served with couscous tabbouleh and tropical fruit chutney with mint tarragon dressing. I was able to identify mangoes, pineapple, tomatoes, and red onion in the delectable fruit chutney but couldn't figure out what else was in this creation. I'd have to ask Josh. When I heard guests raving about the food, I swelled with pride at my boyfriend's accomplishments. Ade and I scarfed down food and then got whisked off to have more pictures taken. Every member of Owen's family had a camera, and every single person insisted on taking plenty of shots.

I barely had a moment to ponder what I had learned about Robin and her knowledge of the lethal foxglove. Just when I thought that I finally had a minute to devote to working out what had happened, large chafing dishes with piping hot entrées began to appear on the tables. Ade and Owen served themselves, and I followed, piling my plate with medallions of beef with cognac; duck in a red wine and orange sauce; vegetable strudels; and a green salad with maple syrup dressing and dried cranberries. I eyed the lamb with grape-chili jam and goat cheese, and the incredible pumpkins that had been roasted with Gruyère cheese, mushrooms, crème fraîche, and bacon. A large chafing dish held a tempting tagliatelle with lobster, yuzu pesto, and exotic mushrooms. Another dish featured a whole snapper with pickled peppers, chorizo, and fennel puree. I knew I'd be back within a few minutes to refill my plate.

I sat down next to Adrianna. "Are you happy with everything, Ade? I can't believe you haven't strangled Josh or my father for wearing those crazy clothes."

Adrianna chuckled. "Well, I was a bit taken aback when I saw Jack and that flipping ugly hat, but he pulled it off and showed me a head of hair full of black goo. He looked so pathetically sorry that I couldn't be mad at him. As for Josh? Well, I'm pretty sure Owen is responsible, but I can't be mad at him today, can I."

"He did try, Ade. I swear! I guess there was a mix-up—"

"I'm not worried about it. I'm having a wonderful time. You were amazing up there, Chloe, and the ceremony was beautiful." Ade wrapped an arm around me and squeezed. "Another wonderful thing is that my mother has yet to speak to me today. I couldn't be happier!"

Josh, having freed himself from the kitchen for long enough to sit down, took the chair next to Owen's. "The food is coming out awesome, huh? Everything good for the happy couple?"

Adrianna and Owen both nodded enthusiastically.

Throughout dinner, people clinked their glasses with silverware, thus prompting Owen and Ade to kiss repeatedly. Naomi, her boyfriend, Eliot, and my sister, Heather, joined us at the table.

Heather happily dug into her plate of food. "Ben is chasing the kids around, so I get a few minutes to actually sit down and eat. Will wonders never cease?"

Heather and Naomi began a debate about natural childbirth. "Listen, Naomi, I know you are trying to help Adrianna, but I have two kids. Drugs are a godsend."

"I'm sure Adrianna will do what's best for her and the baby." Naomi winked at Adrianna as though the two were pulling one over on Heather. "Speaking of which!" Naomi rose from her chair and, raising her glass, accidentally submerged one of her long braids in her champagne. "I'd like to make a toast. To Adrianna and Owen, on the impending arrival of the fruit of their union!" Naomi removed her hair from her glass and took a long drink.

My parents and Josh made loving toasts, as did Owen's

father and Nana Sally, both of whom welcomed Adrianna to the family. Kitty made the best toast of which she was capable: none at all. I watched to make sure that Nelson was filming all of the speeches, as he was, probably because Robin stayed right by his side and kept muttering directions and scolding him for not following all of her orders. At one point, their bickering began to escalate, but Robin had the sense to shoo Nelson out of the tent to finish the spat.

I went back to the buffet table to help myself to the lamb. Then I set my plate down and filled a small bowl with the incredible roasted pumpkin stew. I took a spoonful of the stew. Heaven! Rich, gooey, and cheesy. As I ate, I walked slowly along the edge of the tent to survey the scene and fix it in my memory. As I was wondering whether Robin and Nelson would be able to resolve their differences for long enough to finish filming the wedding, I heard Nelson's voice and then Robin's. The two were no distance from me; only the fabric of the tent separated us.

"You're getting the angles all wrong, Nelson, and—"

"I swear on my mother's life, Robin, if you don't shut up and let me record this thing how I want, I'll blow your dirty little secret. How'd you like that, huh?"

"What are you talking about? You don't know anything." Robin was seething.

"Oh, yeah? I know about you and Leo Loverboy. So, now what do you have to say for yourself, Ms. Director? I bet a lot of people would be interested in that. You two have been going at it for months. And having him be the chosen shopper for the show was no accident. You set that whole thing up. So shut your trap about what I film."

TWENTY-SEVEN

WHOA! The conversation stopped me in my tracks.

Robin and Nelson reappeared in the wedding tent, but I lingered at periphery of the crowd. Robin had been having an affair with Leo. Even though she had no garden, she had bought foxglove, which was not a houseplant. Because of the gardening film she'd made with my parents, she'd known of the nursery where she'd bought the plants and known of their toxicity. It was she who'd chosen Leo as the featured shopper; she'd engineered his participation and thus, of course, Francie's. Once in the house with Francie, she'd poisoned food that Francie but not Leo would eat. Robin must have prepared the plants in a way that made it easy to slip the poison into the food that Josh had served to Francie. According to what I'd read about foxglove, every part of the plant was so toxic that the preparation would have required no skill. And if others, too, were poisoned? Robin hadn't cared. If others got sick, or even if they died, so much the better! Francie's death, instead of appearing to be a deliberate murder with Francie as the victim, would pass as an accident—in other words, exactly what the police officer saw it as when he arrived at the house. What's more, after Francie's death, it had been Robin who'd arranged to have me remove Francie's clothing from the house; Robin had used me to eradicate the traces of her lover's ex-wife.

Had Leo known of Robin's plan? Had he known that he'd be the *Chefly Yours* shopper and that Robin was going to poison his wife during the filming? Or had he realized only after Francie's death that his lover had murdered his wife? Suddenly, my focus shifted to my own safety. As soon as Robin saw the wedding footage, she'd see and hear the exchange between Héctor and me that Digger had translated. She'd learn that I'd been interested in the purchase of foxglove and that Emilio's cousin had identified her as the buyer. She'd immediately conclude that I was piecing together the elements of the murder.

But I couldn't spoil Adrianna's wedding reception. Despite Josh's eccentric tuxedo, my father's tar fiasco, Josh's fistfight with Emilio, the consequent damage to the flowers, and Evan and Willie's attempted shotgun prank, we had avoided ruinous catastrophes; the ceremony had been beautiful; Adrianna and Owen were now, in fact, married; the food was even more delicious than I'd expected; and the reception was lively and joyous. I would simply have to wait until the bride and groom had left for the evening before I called the police and told the entire story to a detective. Robin hadn't yet seen the film and couldn't watch it while

Nelson was still shooting. Therefore, no one was in immediate danger. I retrieved my plate and returned to the table to finish dinner. Josh had vanished. In his place sat Kitty.

"You know, darling," Kitty began, leaning in to speak to her daughter, "I talked to my friend Rhonda the other day. She wants a divorce, the poor thing. Horrid man she married, really, and I can't blame her. But she says she'll never leave him because he's got all the money, and they don't have a prenup. I guess you two won't have that problem. You know, fighting over money. No need for a prenuptial agreement if there's nothing to fight over!"

"Kitty, would you like anything else to eat?" I said in a panic.

"No, thank you, dear. I'm not even sure what half of the food is."

Bringing up divorce and money at her daughter's wedding was bad enough, but insulting Josh's food? Now she had really crossed the line! I saw Ade inhale and exhale through her nose and will herself to ignore her mother.

As dinner wound down, coffee and dessert plates arrived on the buffet tables. Digger and Alfonso lined up row after row of martini glasses filled with a mixture of crumbled ladyfingers, limoncello, and mascarpone, and topped with fresh raspberries. The bright yellow of the lemon liqueur and the red of the berries looked cheerful and celebratory. As for the ladyfingers, I could eat those spongy delicacies by the dozen. In other words, the dessert was bound to be right up my gastronomic alley. A tray of figs poached in champagne, vanilla, cinnamon, and lemon zest arrived with a pitcher of cream. How was I going to make room for everything? Somehow or other, I'd find space.

"Oh, Chloe, look! Here come the cupcakes!" Adrianna pointed to one of the buffet tables.

Ade had decided that what she wanted instead of a typical wedding cake was a cupcake tower fashioned from Sprinkles brand cupcakes. Josh had ordered mixes in red velvet, dark chocolate, and vanilla and had baked a hundred and fifty cupcakes that he'd iced this morning and arranged in a tower. Josh and Héctor entered the tent, both supporting the tray of tiered cupcakes.

"How fun is this!" Ade said happily.

"This was the coolest idea, hon." Owen rubbed his hands together. "Let's go cut the cupcake, my blushing bride."

"Cupcakes," snorted Kitty. "Whoever heard of such a thing! Childish, I call it. How are they going to cut a cupcake?"

I rose from my chair. "With a knife."

Nelson and Robin followed the couple to the buffet table. I kept a keen eye on Robin to make sure that she didn't get close enough to sprinkle the Sprinkles with poison. The bride and groom choose one cupcake from the top of the tower and held the knife together as they split the cake in two. I cheered as Ade frosted Owen's nose with her half and then *awwwed* as they shared a gooey kiss. I caught Robin forcing Nelson's camera away from me and back onto Ade and Owen.

When the couple took their seats, Robin threw her hands on her hips. "Nelson, I've had it. You are totally incompetent! Give me the damn camera, Nelson! I mean it!"

"Yeah, right." In showy defiance of Robin, Nelson slowly played the camera back and forth over the crowd.

I felt certain that this time, Robin and Nelson wouldn't take their fight outside, and I was equally sure that they wouldn't make peace on their own. To prevent an ugly scene, I stepped in. "Stop it!" I ordered in an undertone. "Both of you! Come over here." I herded the pair out of the tent and stopped just outside the entrance. I didn't relish having to chat it up with Robin, but I had no choice; I couldn't allow the two of them to make a spectacle of themselves at the reception. "What the heck is the problem now?"

Ignoring me, Robin resumed her attack on Nelson. "Get this straight. I am making this film. Me! I am in charge. It's not about whatever pretty girl you happen to feel like looking at. I'm the producer and director. You're just the cameraman. I'm the brain, you're the eyes, and that's all you are. You shoot what I tell you to. Got it?"

Nelson leaned forward. "Maybe the film *was* yours, but it's mine now. And my film is much more interesting than yours would have been. I'm an artist, and you're nothing but a third-rate, unoriginal, imitative, small-time hack!"

Robin laughed condescendingly. "You're nothing but a technician. If you think that you are *ever* going to be a filmmaker, you're dreaming. You don't have the talent. As a cameraman, you're barely adequate!"

"Oh, Robin." Nelson spoke all too calmly. "I warned you. You have no idea what I have on film. I have so much! A great shot of you buying foxglove not too long ago. I bet you'd love that little sequence, my dear. It's all right here, baby." Nelson sneered and patted the camera that he held at his side. I had to wonder about his claim. Wouldn't he have downloaded that footage?

But Robin failed to share my doubt. She made a mad grab for Nelson's camera. He, however, held it in a firm grip. I was furious! Josh had been more than justified in punching Emilio, and he'd done it in the kitchen before the wedding, not just outside the tent during the reception. Now, I wasn't about to tolerate a physical altercation

"Cut it out!" I demanded.

Robin drew her leg in and then swiftly kicked Nelson

smack on the kneecap. Nelson yelled out in pain, and as he fell to the ground, Robin wrestled the camera from his hands. While Nelson was clutching his knee and swearing, Robin jabbed at the camera in what seemed to be an inept effort to locate the part that held the recording.

"You two are totally out of control!" I whispered angrily. "And don't you dare ruin the wedding footage," I warned.

"Stay out of this, Chloe. It has nothing to do with you." Robin turned the camera upside down and began trying to pry out its innards.

Nelson snorted. "Actually, it has a lot to do with Chloe. Chloe was asking questions about—"

I cut him off. "There has to be a way to work this out."

"Leave me alone!" Robin raised her voice. "Mind your own business, Chloe. And your boyfriend's, too. I happen to know a lot more about Josh than you do, so maybe you should pay a little more attention to him and less to me."

"What are you talking about?" I asked, completely confused and momentarily distracted. "What do you know about Josh?"

Robin halted her fiddling with the camera and looked smugly at me. "I know he's not the chef at Simmer any longer. He quit. The new chef there is his supposed friend, Digger. Digger starts tomorrow. Marlee told me. You know how quickly restaurant gossip flies around."

Robin had to be out of her mind. "You don't know what you're talking about, Robin. Josh would have told me if he'd left Simmer. And there is no way Digger would take Josh's job. It's an unwritten rule that you don't take your friend's job, no matter what the restaurant."

"How dumb can you be? You know these chefs. They all want to be stars. Digger wouldn't hesitate to take a job on

Newbury Street, even if it ticked off his good buddy. God, Chloe, you don't know anything." Robin laughed heartily.

Nelson stood up, his knee apparently not permanently damaged. "On the contrary. Chloe knows quite a bit. In fact, she knows everything she needs to about you, Robin. She knows about Francie. And the foxglove. She must be waiting for this wedding to be over to call the police. Isn't that right, Chloe? Just wait until my movie hits the Internet."

Robin's face blanched.

I'd underestimated Nelson. All along, he'd known that Robin had killed Francie, whose agonizing death had registered on him as nothing more than a sort of twisted docudrama. As I was staring at Nelson, Robin, camera in hand, bolted toward the street and her car. Dammit! She was welcome to whatever evidence the camera held, which was not the only evidence of her guilt. Among other things, Héctor, Nelson, and I could testify. But that camera was valuable: it held the only recording of Adrianna's wedding! And I was not about to let Robin destroy irreplaceable images so precious to my best friend. I took a few steps back and grabbed one of the shotguns that Evan and Willie had stashed in the plants by the entrance to the tent. I knew that those shotguns weren't loaded, of course. But Robin didn't share my knowledge.

I assumed my best gun-toting stance, or what I imagined that a gun-toting stance should be, and hollered at Robin. "Stop or I'll shoot!" Those words from my mouth? Whoever would have thought?

A second later, I heard a shot and saw Robin fall to the ground, facedown. Blood quickly stained the back of her shirt. She lay still.

But I hadn't fired the gun. I hadn't so much as brushed the trigger with my finger.

I whipped around and saw Nelson with the second shot-gun still aimed at the immobile Robin. Thank God I hadn't accidentally pulled the trigger myself. Why were these guns loaded? Willie and Evan, I realized, hadn't just intended to march in with the shotguns. They'd planned to discharge the weapons!

Guests began pouring out of the tent. "Call an ambu-lance!" someone shouted. "I'm an EMT. Get out of the way."

A young man, a friend of Owen's family, pushed his way through the crowd and knelt down next to Robin. I turned and stepped away. Almost everyone at the reception took out a cell phone and dialed for help.

"Baby?" My chef had materialized next to me. I almost drove my head into his chest.

"Josh. Where is Ade? More importantly right now, where the hell are Evan and Willie?" I was beyond furious; I was livid.

"They're over there." Josh gestured behind him. "What happened?"

As we wove our way through shocked guests, I did my best to explain how Robin had ended up with a bullet in her back. At the same second when I located Owen's brothers, ambulances, fire trucks, and police cruisers began to arrive. I paid no attention to the emergency vehicles; rather, I con-centrated on Evan and Willie, who at least had the minimal decency to look appalled at the consequence of their aborted and unfunny prank.

"What were you thinking?" I demanded. "Arriving at this wedding with shotguns was bad enough, but *loaded* shotguns? What if Heather's kids had found them?"

Evan was the first to brave my wrath. "We were planning on firing a resounding volley into the air at the end of the wedding ceremony. It was going to be very dramatic."

"Dramatic? You were going to shoot off guns in the tent? Endangering our lives? Not to mention puncturing the tent! You two are the stupidest, most—"

"Chloe, I need your help." The voice was Adrianna's.

I felt terrible. Poor Adrianna must be a wreck. This was supposed to have been the perfect day she'd dreamed of. And now this! To my surprise, however, Adrianna looked remarkably happy for someone whose wedding had just become a crime scene.

I put a hand on her arm and said, "I'm so sorry about this. About everything! What can I do to help you? This is just terrible. First Josh punched Emilio, and then the flowers got wrecked, and then . . . Well, it goes on and on."

Adrianna spoke with unusual force. "Chloe, I need you to focus." She grabbed my shoulders and squared me in front of her. "Chloe, my water broke."

TWENTY-EIGHT

I stared at Ade. "Your what did what?"

The exasperated bride put her hands on my cheeks and pulled my face an inch away from hers. "My water broke. Meaning, my water broke, and I'm going into labor!"

"What?" I practically hollered. "The baby is coming now? Oh, my God. Oh, my God." I frantically looked around for I didn't know what. Something! Should I find Ade's hospital bag? Rush her to the hospital? And there was that pesky matter of the swarm of policemen roaming the grounds . . .

"Chloe, get me out of this dress before it's ruined. And then you can go find Owen. Crap, I wanted to go to the Ritz tonight." She scolded her belly. "You couldn't have waited another twenty-four hours?"

I rushed Adrianna upstairs to the bathroom and helped her remove her dress before any icky things got on it. "Okay, you get changed. I'll go grab one of those EMTs downstairs and find Owen." I hung the wedding dress back in its garment bag and zipped it shut.

"You will do no such thing!" Ade glared at me. "If you tell those guys, they'll send me to whatever hospital they want, and I want to go to Brigham and Women's like I planned and have my own doctor. I know that I have to go soon since my water broke, but I doubt this baby is going to fall out of me in the next few minutes. Oh, and for Christ's sake, don't let my mother know what's going on!"

"Gotcha!" I said. "I'm on it. Are you in pain? Do you need anything?"

"No, I'm okay for now, but I don't expect that to last, so you better find Owen. And one more thing," Ade started as she yanked a shirt over her head. "Care to explain the gunshots, screaming, and sirens downstairs?"

"Um, not really. Don't worry about anything! It's all under control. Gotta run!" I dashed out of the bathroom in search of Adrianna's new husband.

I found Owen in the chaotic crowd outside. The groom was still tearing into his abashed-looking brothers for their outrageous behavior at his wedding. "Shotguns? I mean, come on!"

"Owen!" I yanked him out of the crowd before someone tried to question me about the shooting. "Adrianna is having the baby."

"I know she's having the baby. I can't very well do it, can I?" Owen looked irritated with the shambles left of his wedding reception.

"No, dummy. She is having the baby now! Come on. You two have to get out of here and get to the hospital."

Owen's face blanched. "Now? What about the Ritz?"

"Your wife said the same thing. Come on."

I had taken two steps with the stunned Owen behind me when Naomi materialized in front of me. "The baby is coming now! Wonderful! Let me help. I know I can be of assistance in this impending event!"

"Actually, you can help. Go find Adrianna's mother, Kitty, and engage her in conversation. Anything will do, but just don't let her know that her daughter is in labor. Adrianna wants her out of the picture."

Naomi nodded in understanding. "Yes, that woman's aura is filled with negative energy, and she should not come near a woman on the verge of bringing new life into the world."

"Stay with her for about ten minutes and then sneak around to the side of the house and take my car. You can drive Owen and Ade to the hospital, and I'll be there as soon as I can. My keys are in my purse in the kitchen."

"Of course. Tell Adrianna to picture a delicate blue iris. Trust me, these imagery techniques work wonders in managing pain." Naomi rushed off into the crowd calling, "Kitty? Kitty? There you are! Let's talk about the experiences you'll have as a mother-in-law and grandmother."

"Okay, Owen, Ade is upstairs in the bathroom. I better go talk to the police officers, so just run, and I'll see you two as soon as I can get out of here."

"You want me to go up there alone?" Owen looked petrified.

"Yes! Stop looking so freaked out! You're not the one facing hours of painful contractions, so just get yourself together. Go!" I shoved Owen toward the house and approached the group of officers who were busy sorting out who in the hysterical mob knew anything of importance. I located Josh with one of the uniformed cops, a paunchy, mustached man who looked happily surprised to be working on a night when

something dramatic had happened in the typically dull suburb of Newton.

"Here," Josh said to the officer. "This is Chloe Carter, and
I think she has some information." Josh swung an arm
around my shoulder and pulled me in. "Evan and Willie are
under arrest, and their parents are already headed down to
the station. Can you fill this officer in on what you know
about Robin and Nelson? Can you believe that dopey Nelson shot her?" Josh shook his head and pointed to the street.
I saw Nelson handcuffed and being led to a cruiser.

Despite my desire to come off as an insightful crime
fighter in my own right, I gave an uncharacteristically terse
and abbreviated version of what I knew and what I had over-
heard. Robin and Leo had staged the shopping trip so that
he would be the chosen shopper, and Robin would have an
opportunity to poison Francie. I didn't know whether Leo
had known about the murderous part of the plan or not, but
I did know that he had failed to mention to anyone that he'd
been having an affair with Robin.

"Is Robin dead?" I asked hesitantly.

"Nope," the officer said, running his hand over his mustache. "Not yet. Can't tell what kind of shape she's in. Now,
miss, let's go over everything you saw again."

Argh! I just wanted to get out of there and get to the
hospital. I reminded myself that there was no way I would
actually miss the birth, since Ade would presumably be in
labor for many hours. But I did want to be there for her during her labor, so I decided the best thing to do was to reiter-
ate my story as thoroughly and patiently as possible and
avoid further questions.

Josh stayed with me until I was done. Then I hurried
him into the kitchen. I didn't want to waste time talking
with my family or anyone else right now. "Ade is in labor, so

I have to leave in a few minutes. Can you cover for me? They don't want anyone to know right now since Kitty is a horrid pill, and Owen's family is a bit busy trying to bail their other two sons out of jail."

"Absolutely. How exciting! I bet Ade and Owen are disappointed about not going to the Ritz tonight, though—"

"Would everyone stop saying that?" Honestly, who gave a rat's ass about the Ritz when a baby was on the way? "Listen." I took Josh's hand. "Robin was seriously unbalanced."

"Obviously. I'm just glad no one else got hurt tonight."

"Yes," I agreed. "She's deranged. And she told some horrible lies. Not just to cover up that she had poisoned Francie. Robin even tried to get me to believe things about you."

Josh looked quizzically at me.

I continued. "She had the audacity to try to convince me that you quit your job at Simmer and that Digger was taking over for you."

There was an uncomfortably long pause. Robin, I realized, had been telling me the truth.

"Josh?"

He sighed and looked around the room. "Yeah, it's true. That's why I've had so much time off in the past few days. It just got to be too much, Chloe. Gavin is off his rocker, and he's impossible to work for. I told Digger the job was his if he actually wanted it. I've been looking around for other jobs. I have a headhunter named Yvette." That explained all the phone calls Josh had been getting from a woman. "She actually found me a great job. In Hawaii. A private chef for a family there, Chloe. Great pay and free housing in their guesthouse. And they travel all the time. They said you could come with me, too." Josh finally looked at me. "I'm flying out of Boston in a few days. What do you say, Chloe? Do you want to move to Hawaii with me? Do you?"

TWENTY-NINE

"THIS simply must be the most gorgeous baby in the world." I gazed down at the newborn I held tightly in my arms. A blanket swaddled the tiny baby, and I could not stop staring at the little one's perfect features and healthy pink glow. "Patrick, huh? It's a great name."

"Isn't he perfect?" Adrianna beamed from her hospital bed. "I'd read so many stories about babies coming out with misshapen heads and blotchy faces, so I'd prepared myself that my kid might look awful for the first few days, but Baby Trick is too handsome for words."

"Baby Trick?" I giggled.

"Yeah. Isn't that cute?" Adrianna's hair was pulled off her face in a high ponytail. She'd changed out of the unflattering hospital gown into a pair of yellow silk pajamas. Considering that she'd given birth only forty-eight hours ago, she looked spectacular enough to remind me of the celebrities who appeared on the cover of *People* magazine showing off their newborns.

By the time I'd finished giving my umpteenth rendition of events to the police officers and detectives on the night of the reception, I'd arrived at the hospital to find Adrianna in full-blown labor. Naomi had stayed with Ade and Owen until I got there and had refrained from scowling when the anesthesiologist had stuck a needle in Ade's spine to deliver a good dose of medicine. Owen and I had held Adrianna's hands as she pushed; Owen had managed not to faint, and I had managed not to cry (too much) as baby Patrick entered the world.

"Thanks for spending so much time with me in the hospital. I can't wait to get out of here. Owen slept at home last night, but he should be back here in an hour or so to pack us up and take us home. I can't wait to get Patrick into his new house." Ade adjusted her pillows and winced, still sore all over from the delivery. "So fill me in on the rest of my reception. I missed all the drama with that nutball, Robin." Ade stifled a yawn.

"Robin is still in the hospital. I guess the bullet missed any major organs, and she'll be facing murder charges when she recovers. Nelson is being charged as an accessory after the fact. It seems that the night of the murder, while we were all on the way to the hospital, he made a copy of the video footage from that day's filming. All the footage was on a hard drive on his camera, and he transferred a copy to his laptop and was planning on cutting it to make his own reality episode with the more grisly scenes. And I'm sure he could have sold it for a ton of money, too. With all these weird TV shows and Internet video sites, he might have become a big deal." I shook my head in disgust. "Speaking of the reality show, that chef who runs Alloy? Marlee? Her restaurant was shut down by the health department late yesterday. One of her employees ratted her out about some serious violations, and the health inspector came out and closed the restaurant for repeated failures to correct critical violations of the State Sanitary Code."

Ade wrinkled her face. "Ick. I told you not to eat at that restaurant!"

"I don't think anybody will be eating there again."

"Speaking of closings," Adrianna started tentatively, "Owen said Simmer is closed. He called the guy who is covering his deliveries this morning and heard that the doors are locked, the lights are out, and no one is returning calls. What's going on?"

"Oh. Well . . . it seems that Gavin has a major cocaine problem. Really major. Not only was he using money from the restaurant to fund his habit, but he had become a real ass to work for. A few of the employees staged an intervention, and Gavin is now in rehab. He had to close the restaurant and is selling the business to try to salvage whatever he can financially." Obviously Digger wasn't going to be taking over as the executive chef there.

"What?" Ade's exhausted eyes widened in shock. "What about Josh? What's he going to do? Maybe he can get a job with better hours, and you two will get to have a normal relationship. Maybe this will be for the best, Chloe."

"Hmm, maybe." I felt my eyes start to well up. I did not want to have this conversation now. "So, Baby Trick it is." I gently rubbed Patrick's soft cheek with my thumb. "I'm in love."

"You're already in love with Josh. But I guess he won't mind sharing you with my little guy." Ade rolled over in bed and lay on her side, staring at her child in my arms, her eyes heavy with exhaustion.

"No, I don't think Josh will mind. Especially since he's not here."

"I'm sure he'll come by later."

"No, actually. He won't. He went to Hawaii." I cleared my throat. "Moved to Hawaii, I should say."

Josh's invitation to move with him had confused me. Adrianna, Owen, and Patrick needed me, and I needed them. And I had my second year of social work school upon me, and I was finally starting to feel connected to the work I was doing. But Hawaii with Josh would be . . . well, Hawaii with Josh. Paradise. Double paradise.

"Chloe, what are you talking about? What do you mean he—"

"Ade, I need to talk to you." My voice shook as I spoke. Patrick's face became blurry through my tears. "Ade, I don't know what to do. I just don't know what to do."

RECISPES

Roasted Rack of Lamb with Grape-Chili
Jam and Chèvre Sauce

Angela McKeller, Cookbook Author and Show Host

Atlanta, Georgia

www.kickbackkook.com

Serves 4

    1   rack of lamb, 8 chops
    ½   cup grape jam
    2   serrano peppers, seeds removed and chopped
    ¼   cup red wine vinegar
    ⅛   cup chèvre (goat cheese)
    ⅓   cup sour cream

Preheat oven to 450°.

Score the fat on top of lamb meat, making shallow crisscross knife slashes, but do not cut into the meat of the lamb. Cover the ends of the bones with foil to prevent charring. Sear the lamb by placing the rack of lamb in the oven, fat side down, in a shallow baking pan for 10 minutes. Then reduce heat to 325° and roast according to your preference using the following chart:

- An additional 15 minutes per pound for medium-rare; meat thermometer should read 145° after resting.

- An additional 20 minutes per pound for medium; meat thermometer should read 160° after resting.

- An additional 25 minutes per pound for well-done; meat thermometer should read 170° after resting.

Remove lamb rack from oven and tent pan with foil to rest for 10 minutes.

While lamb is resting, combine jam, peppers, and vinegar in a blender and blend well. Transfer jam mixture to a saucepan and warm the sauce over medium-low heat. Do not boil! (That would render a sauce too thick for use.) When sauce begins to produce a light steam, remove from heat.

In another saucepan, combine chèvre and sour cream over medium heat. Stir well until smooth and then remove from heat.

Remove the foil from the lamb, place meat on a cutting board, and cut between each chop so that you have 8 individual chops. Place two chops on each plate and top with 3 tablespoons of the grape-chili jam. Drizzle lightly with the chèvre sauce; using a squeeze bottle of some type gives a lovely presentation. Serve with your favorite sides.

Spinach and Artichoke Eggs Benedict with Spicy Hollandaise Served with Rosemary, Garlic, and Onion Breakfast Potatoes

Angela McKeller

Serves 8

Eggs Benedict

1 8-oz. pkg. frozen, chopped spinach, thawed and well-drained
1 14-oz. can quartered artichoke hearts, drained and chopped
½ tbsp. minced garlic
2 cups mozzarella cheese, grated
1 cup Parmesan cheese, grated
1 cup sour cream
⅛ cup mayonnaise
8 large croissants, halved and toasted
16 poached eggs

Preheat oven to 350°.

Combine first 7 ingredients. Bake in a ceramic or glass oven-safe dish until completely melted into the consistency of a dip. Spread each half of croissant with a heaping tablespoon of spread. Top each croissant half with a poached egg and top with 2 tablespoons hollandaise sauce (recipe follows).

Hollandaise Sauce

    12   egg yolks
    4   tbsp. butter
    1½   tsp. lemon juice
         Tabasco or Crystal Hot Sauce

Beat egg yolks together. Melt butter in a double boiler (water softly boiling) with lemon juice. When melted, slowly add egg yolks (equivalent of about one yolk at a time) so as not to scramble the eggs. Stir constantly until very hot and serve. Add salt to taste if needed. Give a quick dash of hot sauce on the finished dish for visual presentation and a bit of a kick.

Breakfast Potatoes

    1½   lbs. red-skinned potatoes, well-rinsed, cubed with
         skin on, and placed in a zipper baggie
    2–3 tbsp. olive oil (more if needed)
    3   tbsp. chopped fresh rosemary
    1   tsp. minced garlic
    1   sweet yellow onion, finely chopped

Preheat oven to 400°.

Place all of the ingredients in the baggie with the potatoes. Shake *very* well to coat potatoes with the other ingredients. Place on large cookie sheet sprayed with cooking spray. Do not layer or pile the potatoes; have one even layer. Bake for 45 minutes or until brown and crispy on the outside and tender on the inside. If they don't brown enough during baking, use a kitchen torch for a few seconds over the potatoes just until they are crispy and browned, and serve with Benedict.

Pumpkin Stew in a Pumpkin
Anne and Michel Devrient
Semur-en-Auxois, France

Serves 4–6

1   medium sugar pumpkin
1   large onion, diced
3   tbsp. unsalted butter
2   cups fresh bread cubes, cut into 1" cubes from
    a French loaf
2   garlic cloves, minced
3   cups mixed fresh mushrooms (button, portobello,
    chanterelle, oyster) cleaned, stems removed, sliced ¼"
    thick
    Salt and pepper to taste
3   cups Gruyère cheese, grated
4   strips cooked bacon, crumbled
1   container (7–8 oz.) crème fraîche or ½ pint
    heavy cream

Preheat oven to 200°.

Cut the top off of the pumpkin as you would if you were going to carve it for Halloween. Scrape out the seeds and loose pulp, being careful not to remove the pumpkin flesh itself, since pumpkin is the basic flavoring of this dish. Save the top of the pumpkin, which will be placed back on during cooking.

In a large skillet, sauté the onions and 2 tablespoons of the butter over medium heat for a few minutes, and then add the fresh croutons and toss. Stir and cook the croutons for another few minutes and then add the garlic. Toss the mixture and cook until the croutons begin to brown. Add more butter as needed to keep the mixture from drying out. Set aside.

In a separate pan, sauté 1 tablespoon of butter with the mushrooms. Cook until the mushrooms have released their juices and begun to reabsorb them. Season with salt and pepper. Set aside.

To assemble the pumpkin for cooking, put in layers of the bread mixture followed by a dash of salt and pepper, then a layer of the grated cheese, a layer of mushrooms, a bit of the crumbled bacon, and a thin layer of crème fraîche or heavy cream. Keep layering until the pumpkin is filled. End with a layer of cheese.

Put the pumpkin lid back on. Set the filled pumpkin in a casserole dish that will support its sides. Fill a roasting pan with 2 inches of water, and place the pumpkin, in its casserole dish, in the water. Bake for about 3 hours, checking from time to time, until the pumpkin pulp is getting soft enough to spoon up.

To serve, gently remove the pumpkin from the water bath and place on a large platter. Scrape out some of the pumpkin flesh with a large, sturdy spoon as you dish out each bowl.

Salad with Maple Syrup Vinaigrette

Meg Travis

Ipswich, Massachusetts

Serves 4–6

Salad

> Salad greens, approximately 1 head of lettuce for
> every 3 people
> 1 small log of goat cheese, crumbled (Make sure you
> buy goat cheese that's been salted. My favorite is from
> Vermont Butter & Cheese Company)
> 1 package of dried cranberries or Craisins
> ½ cup pecans, toasted and chopped

Mix together and toss with the maple syrup vinaigrette.

Maple Syrup Vinaigrette

> Sea salt and freshly ground black pepper to taste
> 2 tbsp. balsamic vinegar
> 1 tbsp. Dijon mustard
> 2 tbsp. grade B maple syrup
> 1 tsp. dried sweet basil
> ½ cup olive oil

Whisk together the salt, pepper, and balsamic vinegar
until the salt dissolves. Stir in mustard, syrup, and basil.
Whisk constantly while drizzling in oil: the dressing will
form an emulsion and thicken. Refrigerate until ready to
use. Bring up to room temperature before serving, since the
olive oil will harden in the fridge. Makes roughly ¾ cup.

Polpette (Tuscan Meatballs)

Josh Ziskin, Executive Chef at La Morra

Brookline, Massachusetts

www.lamorra.com

Serves 8–10 as appetizer

½   loaf bread, cut into large cubes

3   cups milk

1½   cups dried porcini mushrooms

5   lbs. ground beef

2   cups Parmesan cheese

¼   lb. prosciutto, thickly sliced and diced

4   eggs

3   cups flour

3   cups white wine

Soak bread in milk until it is fully absorbed. Soak porcini mushrooms in water until hydrated and clean. Remove and chop. Mix the next 4 ingredients, and then add mushrooms and bread. Mix well. Roll into desired-size balls. Flour each ball, and shake off the extra flour. Sear in a pan on all sides until light brown. Add wine until it comes halfway up the side of the meatballs. Put in oven and bake at 400° until cooked through, approximately 15 minutes.

Arancini (Fried Stuffed Risotto)
Josh Ziskin

Serves 8–10 as an appetizer

1	yellow onion, diced fine
4	tbsp. cooking oil
1	pound Arborio rice
½	cup white wine
1	quart water or chicken stock, warm
4	tbsp. butter
½–¾	cup grated Parmesan cheese
	Salt to taste
2	oz. Italian meat (salami, capicola, etc.)
6	oz. smoked mozzarella or Fontina cheese
2	eggs
	Flour for dredging
2	cups bread crumbs
	Oil for frying

Sauté onion in oil until translucent. Add rice and cook for 3 minutes until rice is coated in oil. Add wine and stir until absorbed. Add warm water or chicken stock, 2 cups at a time. Rice should absorb liquid each time before the next amount is added. Repeat until rice is fully cooked through. Add butter, Parmesan cheese, and salt. Stir until fully incorporated.

Lay mixture flat on a sheet pan until fully cooled. While rice mixture is cooling, dice Italian meat and cheese into ¼" dice. Beat eggs and place in a bowl. Place flour in a separate bowl. Place bread crumbs in another bowl.

When rice mixture is cooled, moisten hands. Pick up about 2 ounces of rice and create a cup shape in your hands. Add meat and cheese mixture inside cup, and close rice around mixture to form a ball. Once all aroncini are formed, roll each aroncini in flour, then egg, and then bread crumbs. Refrigerate for ½ hour. Deep-fry aroncini in oil until golden brown and warm through.

Warm Pasta Salad

Jessica Conant-Park
Manchester, New Hampshire

Serves 4

1	lb. pasta, preferably fettuccine
½	small red onion, thinly sliced
1	avocado, cut into ½" bites
1	container grape or cherry tomatoes, or 2 plum tomatoes, cut up
½	cup (or a good handful) Calamata olives, pitted and roughly chopped
1	bunch fresh basil, roughly chopped
½–¾	cup good-quality olive oil
¼	cup balsamic vinegar
1	big squeeze lemon juice
	Salt and pepper to taste
16–20	large frozen or fresh shrimp, peeled and deveined or 1 lb. chicken cutlets
	Other: olive oil, salt, pepper, sugar, and Parmesan cheese

Start cooking the pasta while you prepare the vegetables.

Mix all the vegetables and basil with the olive oil, balsamic vinegar, and a big squeeze of the lemon. Toss in a good pinch of salt and pepper. When the pasta is ready, mix it with the vegetables and dressing.

Heat a sauté pan with a splash of olive oil over medium-high heat. When the pan is nicely heated, add the shrimp or chicken. If using shrimp, cook for about 45 seconds to 1 minute per side until perfectly pink and cooked through. If using chicken, season both sides of the cutlets with a generous sprinkling of salt, pepper, and sugar. Sear on each side until golden brown. Don't move the cutlet around too much while it is cooking, because you want the sugar to give a wonderful caramelized crust.

Toss the shrimp or chicken in with the pasta salad and serve with Parmesan cheese. I prefer this dish with lots of dressing, so add more olive oil or balsamic vinegar if you like.

Medallions of Beef with Cognac Wine Sauce

Nancy R. Landman, President and CEO
Great Cooks & Company and Great Cooks at Home
Indianapolis, Indiana
www.greatcooks.biz

Serves 8

Tenderloin

2 tbsp. butter
2 tbsp. olive oil
1 beef tenderloin, trimmed
Salt
Fresh pepper
1 cup beef or veal stock

In a skillet, heat the butter and oil until butter sizzles. Sauté the tenderloin on all sides; if the fats aren't hot enough, the meat won't sear. Season the beef with salt and pepper. Finish cooking the meat in a 350° oven until desired doneness, approximately 20 to 25 minutes.

Deglaze the skillet with beef or veal stock. Reserve these drippings for sauce.

Cognac Wine Sauce

2 tbsp. butter
1 tsp. chopped shallot
1 cup red wine
2 tbsp. Cognac
1 cup beef or veal stock
Herbs and spices to taste (salt, pepper, thyme, bay leaf)

In a saucepan or skillet, heat 1 tablespoon butter. When hot, add chopped shallot, and sauté. Add red wine, Cognac, stock, herbs, and spices. Reduce mixture to ¼ cup and check seasonings. Add deglazed drippings from tenderloin. Add remaining 1 tablespoon butter bit by bit to finish sauce, whisking continuously.

Turned Vegetables

12	large Idaho potatoes, cut in half crosswise
12	large fresh carrots, cut in half crosswise
¾	cup clarified butter
½–¾	tsp. crushed dried rosemary
	Salt and fresh pepper to taste

Prepare turned vegetables: Carve or "turn" the vegetables into 7-sided ovals. Steam the vegetables until three-quarters done. Heat clarified butter with rosemary. Sauté vegetables until done. Finish with salt and pepper.

To serve: Slice beef and serve on warmed plates or platter on top of sauce. Garnish with sprigs of fresh herbs and turned carrots and potatoes.

Champagne-Poached Figs with Heavy Cream
Nancy R. Landman

Serves 8

1	bottle dry champagne or sparkling white wine
	Zest of 1 lemon
1	cup sugar

½   *vanilla bean*
4   *3-inch cinnamon sticks*
24–32 *ripe, fresh figs, preferably purple*
        Heavy cream for serving
        Fig leaves for garnish, optional

In a large saucepan, combine champagne or wine, lemon zest, sugar, vanilla bean, and cinnamon sticks. Bring to a boil and cook for 5 minutes. Reduce heat.

Add figs and poach over low heat until tender but not shapeless, 20–30 minutes. Transfer the figs to a serving dish.

Reduce poaching liquid to 1½ cups. Remove vanilla bean and cinnamon sticks. Pour sauce over figs. Serve at room temperature with heavy cream. Garnish with fig leaves if desired.

Magret de Canard Barbara

Barbara Seagle
Brookline, Massachusetts

Serves 4

⅓   *cup water*
2   *tbsp. sugar*
2–3   *navel oranges, sliced*
        Unsalted butter
        Four boneless duck breasts, skin and fat layer intact
        Salt and pepper to taste
⅓   *cup red wine*

Combine the water and sugar in a sauté pan and cook over medium heat until the sugar dissolves and the liquid comes to a simmer. Add the orange slices and cook over medium-high heat until the oranges are soft and caramelized to a deep brown color. Swirl in the butter at the end of the cooking. Set aside.

Score the fat side of the duck breasts in a crisscross (diamond) pattern right through the fat layer, but not cutting the meat. Salt and pepper the breasts lightly on both sides. Heat a sauté pan over a medium-hot fire and add the duck breasts fat side down. They will sizzle and smoke. An amazing amount of fat will be rendered off. Cook on the first side for about 10–12 minutes. Most of the fat layer will be gone, but some should be left. Turn the breasts and cook another 10 minutes. Timing will vary depending on the size of the breasts, but they should be a nice deep rosy pink. Do not overcook. Remove to a serving platter or plate.

Pour off all the fat from the pan and add the orange mixture and red wine. Cook this mixture down until slightly syrupy. Add the duck breasts and heat through, basting with the sauce.

Slice the breasts across the grain at an angle into thin slices and arrange in a fan on each plate. Place an orange slice or two beside the breast and top with a dribbling of sauce. Voilá!

Mussels Bouillabaisse

Raymond Ost, Chef and Co-owner of Sandrine's
Cambridge, Massachusetts
www.sandrines.com

Serves 6

6 *large tomatoes, quartered*
2 *green peppers, julienned*
2 *red peppers, julienned*
2 *fennel bulbs, julienned*
2 *Spanish onions, julienned*
½ *lb. butter*
4 *cloves garlic, crushed*
2 *cups tomato paste*
4 *cups white wine*
1 *gallon fish stock or clam juice*
3 *lbs. PEI mussels*
1 *pinch saffron*
   Salt and pepper to taste

Sauté the tomatoes, peppers, fennel, and onions in the butter until tender. Add the garlic, tomato paste, and white wine, and cook for 10 minutes. Add the fish stock or clam juice and simmer for 1 hour. Add the mussels and saffron, and simmer until the mussels open. Add salt and pepper to taste.

Grilled Tuna Served with Couscous Tabbouleh, Tropical Fruit Chutney, and Mint Tarragon Dressing

Raymond Ost

Serves 6

Tuna

> 6 6-oz. center-cut tuna steaks
> Olive oil
> Sea salt
> Black pepper

Brush tuna with olive oil and season with sea salt and pepper. Grill for 2 minutes on each side over medium-high heat for medium-rare doneness.

Tabbouleh

> 1 box couscous (small grain)
> 3 plum tomatoes, chopped
> 2 bunches flat parsley, chopped (not too fine)
> 1 red onion, chopped
> ½ bunch scallions, chopped
> Juice of 1 lemon
> ½ cup olive oil
> 6 sprigs lemon verbena (optional) for garnish
> Salt and pepper to taste

Cook couscous as directed on box. Cool completely. Add the rest of the ingredients and mix well. Season with salt and pepper to your liking.

RECIPES

Dressing

1   cup olive oil
    Juice of 2 lemons
1   tbsp. Dijon mustard
4   cloves garlic, chopped
½   bunch mint, chopped
1   bunch tarragon, leaves only
2   roasted red peppers (seeded and skinned)

Whisk ingredients together and set aside.

Tropical Fruit Chutney

1   pineapple, peeled, cored, and diced
2   mangoes, diced
1   red onion, diced
2   tomatoes, diced
½   bunch mint, chopped
½   bunch chopped parsley
      Juice of 2 lemons
2   tbsp. honey
4   cloves of garlic, chopped
½–1   small habanero pepper, chopped (Note: These
      peppers are extremely hot. Please wear gloves when
      handling. Use pepper sparingly.)

Mix all ingredients together and macerate for 24 hours.

To Serve

Make a bed of tabbouleh, place a tuna steak on that, and top with a few tablespoons of the fruit chutney.

Drizzle the dish with dressing and add lemon verbena for garnish, if you like.

Celery Root Soup with Foie Gras, Truffle Honey, and Pickled Honeycrisp Apples

Chef Erik Battes, Chef de Cuisine at Perry Street
New York, New York

Serves 6–8

Celery Root Soup

    2   large celery roots
    6   tbsp. butter
    2   shallots, sliced thin
    12 oz. chicken stock
        Salt, to taste

Peel and cut celery root in even, large dice. Melt the butter in a pot over medium heat and sweat the shallots until tender. Add the celery root and the chicken stock and cook until the celery root is completely tender. Puree in a blender and season to taste with salt.

Pickled Honeycrisp Apples

    1   cup champagne vinegar (or white wine vinegar)
    ½   cup sugar
    2   Honeycrisp apples (or other crisp, juicy apples), peeled
        and cut into small dice

Combine the champagne vinegar and sugar in a pot. Bring to a boil and then cool down. Cover the diced apples with the vinegar and sugar mixture (pickling solution) and let sit for at least 30 minutes. The pickled apples should hold for about 2 hours.

Glazed Celery Root

¾   cup butter
3   tbsp. water
     Salt, to taste
1   celery root, small dice

Combine butter and water in a pot and cook over high heat until the liquid becomes homogenous and creamy. Season the butter and water with salt to taste. Add the celery root and simmer gently until tender. Remove from heat and reserve.

Seared Foie Gras

Foie gras, 1-oz. piece per serving
Sea salt, coarse
Black pepper, coarsely ground

Heat a dry pan until aggressively hot. Place the foie gras in the pan and cook on one side until it is 85 percent cooked. Then flip the foie gras, cook for 15 seconds, and then remove from the pan. Season immediately with the coarse sea salt and black pepper.

To Serve

Celery leaves, picked from the center of the head
Truffle honey or regular honey*

Place a spoonful of the glazed celery root into the center of a bowl. Then top with a seared piece of foie gras. Top the seared foie gras with the pickled apples and some celery leaf. Drizzle the truffle honey all around the bowl. Pour the soup into the bowl table side.

Seared Shrimp with Butternut Squash, Brown Butter Ginger Vinaigrette, and Rocket Arugula

Erik Battes

Serves 4–6

Shrimp

20–30	*extra-large shrimp (5 shrimp per person)*	
1	*tsp. chili flakes, ground*	
5	*tsp. star anise, ground*	
5	*tsp. salt*	
	Olive oil	

Season the shrimp with the chili flakes, star anise, and salt. Sauté in a smoking-hot pan with a small amount of olive oil until just cooked.

---

* You may also use an herb-flavored honey (rosemary or thyme) or you can drizzle a bit of truffle oil on regular honey.

RECIPES

Brown Butter Ginger Vinaigrette

- ¼ cup butter
- 1 tbsp. ginger, brunoise (small dice)
- 2 tbsp. shallots, brunoise (small dice)
- 1 tbsp. rice wine vinegar
- 1 tbsp. lime juice
- 2 tbsp. soy sauce

Cook butter in a pot until the milk solids turn dark brown. Combine all of the other ingredients in a bowl and whisk in the cooked butter. Be sure to include all of the milk solids with the butter. Reserve warm.

Butternut Squash Puree

- Butternut squash, halved and seeded
- Salt
- White pepper
- Olive oil
- 2 tbsp. butter

Rub the butternut squash with salt, pepper, and olive oil. Cover with foil and roast on a sheet tray at 350° until tender. Scoop out the cooked squash. While hot, puree the squash in a blender until completely smooth. When ready to serve, combine 1 cup of the butternut squash puree with the butter. Work with a rubber spatula in a pot until combined. Adjust seasoning with salt.

To Serve

- Arugula, wild lettuce mix, or both
- Red radish, julienne

Lay down a line of butternut squash puree on a plate, and then set the seared shrimp on top. Combine the arugula or lettuce with a small amount of radish julienne, lightly dress with the warm brown-butter vinaigrette, and place in a tight pile right next to the shrimp on the plate.

Butter-Poached Lobster with Yuzu Pesto Tagliatelle, Honshimeji Mushrooms, and Shiso

Erik Battes

Serves 4–6

Lobster

1 half-pound lobster per person, alive
   Salt
   Cayenne
   Butter

Remove the lobster tails, claws, and knuckles while lobsters are still alive. In a large pot, boil water and season with salt until it tastes like the ocean. Add the lobster tails and cook for 2½ minutes and immediately put into ice water to cool. Add the claws and knuckles, cook for 9 minutes, and put into the ice water as well. Once cool, crack open the shells and remove the intact lobster meat. It should be 75 percent cooked. Season with salt and cayenne pepper, and put into a sauté pan with ½" of melted butter. Cook in a 200° oven for 8 minutes or until completely opaque.

Yuzu Pesto

¼   *cup yuzu juice (available in most Asian markets)*
      or lemon juice
½   *cup pine nuts, toasted*
4   *cloves garlic*
¼   *tsp. dry chili flakes*
½   *cup olive oil*
1½   *tsp. salt*

Combine all in a food processor and process until the mixture is mostly smooth but still contains some texture.

Shiso Puree

15   *shiso (Japanese mint) leaves, or mint or basil leaves*
½   *cup olive oil*
1   *tsp. salt*

Cook the shiso, mint, or basil leaves in a pot of rapidly boiling water for 45 seconds. Remove from the pot and immediately put into ice water. Remove from the water and squeeze as much moisture as you can out of the shiso leaves. Combine the shiso with the olive oil and salt and puree in a blender on high until the mixture is smooth. Chill immediately.

Mushrooms

1   *cup honshimeji mushrooms (or other mushrooms such*
      as trumpet, clamshell, oyster, beech, or cremini),
      cleaned and bases trimmed
2   *tbsp. shallots, brunoise (small dice)*

> 2   tbsp. olive oil
> 1   tbsp. water
>   Salt
>   White pepper

Combine all in a small pot and cook covered over medium heat until the mushrooms are tender.

To Serve

> 1–1½ lbs. cooked tagliatelle (or any other long pasta)
>   Grated Parmesan cheese

Toss the pasta with yuzu pesto and the cooked mushrooms, and place in a serving bowl. Top lightly with some shiso puree and Parmesan. Serve the lobster on top of the pasta.

Sautéd Red Snapper with Spanish Lomo, Pickled Baby Bell Peppers, and Fennel

Erik Battes

Serves 4

Snapper

> 4 6-oz. portions of American red snapper, skin on
>   Salt
>   Espelette or cayenne pepper, ground
>   Grapeseed oil

1 tbsp. butter, unsalted
1 sprig of fresh thyme

Season the snapper liberally with salt on both sides. Season with Espelette or cayenne pepper to taste on the flesh side only. Score the skin side three times with a sharp knife. Heat a pan with ⅛" of grapeseed oil over high heat until it has just begun to smoke. Place fish skin side down and press down immediately with a spatula until the skin relaxes and sits completely flat. Turn down the temperature to medium, and cook until the fish is 85 percent done. Add a tablespoon of butter and a sprig of thyme to the pan, and baste the flesh side of the fish with a spoon until done.

Pickled Peppers

1 lb. orange and yellow bell peppers
Olive oil
Salt
White pepper
6 oz. Japanese rice vinegar
6 tbsp. sugar
3 sprigs of fresh thyme

Remove the tops and seeds of the peppers and toss in olive oil and season with salt and white pepper. Roast in a 375° oven until the skin starts to separate from the flesh of the pepper. Do not overcook. Place in a bowl and cover with plastic wrap to steam until cool. Peel the skins off of the peppers and cut into 1" dice.

Combine the vinegar, sugar, and thyme in a small pot and bring to a boil. Pour the vinegar mixture over the peppers and let marinate for at least 2 hours.

Fennel Puree

> 1   *large fennel bulb, top and core removed*
> 2   *tbsp. butter*
> 1   *tsp. salt*

Slice the fennel thinly and cook over low heat with the butter and salt. Once the fennel is completely tender and translucent, puree on high until smooth.

To Serve

> 1   *oz. Spanish lomo (or chorizo), fine julienne*
> 2   *oz. of the pickled peppers*
> ½   *tsp. fresh thyme*
> 1   *tbsp. butter*
>   *Espelette or cayenne pepper, ground*

Sauté the lomo or chorizo in a dry pan until it is completely crispy and rendered. Do not drain the fat. Add the pickled peppers, thyme, and butter, and cook until glazed. Season lightly to taste with Espelette or cayenne.

Place 1½ ounces of hot fennel puree on a plate, place the cooked fish on top, and finish with a spoonful of the glazed pickled peppers.

Crab and Corn Fritters with Lemon-Cilantro Aioli

Chef Bill Park

Manchester, New Hampshire

Makes 12 fritters

Fritters

- ½ tbsp. butter, melted
- 6 ears corn
- ¼ onion
- ½ cup flour
- ½ tsp. baking soda
- ½ tsp. kosher salt
- ¼ tsp. black pepper
- ⅓ cup milk
- 1 egg
- 1 lb. crab claw meat, fresh or canned
  Canola oil for frying

Using a sharp knife, remove kernels from corn. Mix all ingredients together and form into equal-size balls, roughly ¼ cup each. Heat a deep pan with about an inch of oil over medium-high heat. Cook the fritters until browned on all sides. Fry in batches so that you don't overcrowd the pan. Set on paper towels.

Lemon-Cilantro Aioli

- 1 cup mayonnaise

½ tsp. lemon juice

1 tbsp. lemon zest

2 tbsp. cilantro, chopped

¼ tsp. white pepper

¼ tsp. salt

Mix all ingredients together and serve with fritters.

Mascarpone and Limoncello Dessert

Dwayne Minier, Personal Chef
Boston, Massachusetts
www.minierculinary.com

Serves 4

8 ladyfinger cookies

1 cup mascarpone cheese

1 tsp. lemon zest

2 tsp. limoncello (lemon liqueur)

1 tbsp. powdered sugar

2 tbsp. freshly squeezed lemon juice

1 cup raspberries

Roughly crumble 2 ladyfingers into each of 4 martini glasses and set aside. In a bowl, whisk together the mascarpone, lemon zest, limoncello, powdered sugar, and lemon juice until thoroughly combined.

Gently spoon cheese mixture on crumbled cookies and top with fresh raspberries.